P9-DMH-775

Joey's Case

ALSO BY K.C. CONSTANTINE

The Rocksburg Railroad Murders
The Man Who Liked to Look at Himself
The Blank Page
A Fix Like This
The Man Who Liked Slow Tomatoes
Always a Body to Trade
Upon Some Midnights Clear

Joey's Case

K·C·CONSTANTINE

THE MYSTERIOUS PRESS
New York • London • Tokyo

The Mysterious Press, 129 West 56th Street, New York, N.Y. 10019

Printed in the United States of America
First Printing: April 1988
10 9 8 7 6 5 4 3 2 1

Library of Congress Cataloging-in-Publication Data

Constantine, K. C.
Joey's case / K.C. Constantine.
p. cm.
ISBN 0-89296-287-9
I. Title.
PS3553.0524J6 1988 87-20594
813'.54—dc19 CIP

Joey's Case

Balzic had been trying to dodge Albert Castelucci for five months. There were only so many things he could say to a man whose only son had been shot to death, and he had long since said them all. He had apologized, sympathized, commiserated; he had explained again and again that it had not happened in his jurisdiction. It had happened in Westfield Township, only a matter of yards away from the Rocksburg border, it was true, but yards were yards and borders were borders. Balzic knew he was in trouble when he began protesting that he had been in Pittsburgh when it happened, as if that mattered. The more he ducked the old man, the more the old man hounded him; the more he explained, the less the old man heard, or even pretended to hear. In no time, Balzic's sympathy and commiseration had turned to irritation and then to frustration and then to anger; and then, one Sunday after Castelucci had confronted him after Mass in front of St. Malachy's, Balzic heard himself saying,

"Mr. Castelucci, as far as your son was concerned, it was only a matter of time."

Albert Castelucci didn't care about Balzic's sorrow or sympathy; he didn't care where Balzic's jurisdiction ended on a map; he didn't care where Balzic had been when it happened; and he didn't care what Balzic thought of his son in general or of his son's fate in particular. What he cared about was that the Pennsylvania State Police had assigned a *capo tost*, a hard head, to investigate his son's case, and that that *capo tost* had made such a mess no jury would convict the shooter of simple assault or reckless endangerment, never mind first-degree murder.

Balzic had been standing in line at one of the three admissions windows in Conemaugh General Hospital. Time was never slower for him than when he was waiting to learn what was physically wrong with him. This time it was worse: if what was wrong with him was not physical, that meant there had to be another explanation, and every time he had considered that possibility, he'd gotten a cramp in his stomach.

He stiffened the moment he heard the wheezing coming toward him. Albert Castelucci had followed him to the hospital. He came every day to the station, he came to Muscotti's, he'd even started coming regularly to Mass at St. Malachy's, and now, here he was, coughing into the handkerchiefs wadded up in each hand, tracking Balzic down in the hospital.

Balzic stepped out of line and dropped woodenly into one of the molded plastic chairs lined up in a row against the wall opposite the windows, staring at the old man as he approached and stopped.

"What the hell do I have to say to you, huh?" Balzic shook his head and slumped backward.

"You don't have to say nothin' to me. You just gotta listen," Castelucci said, his breathing slurry from a lifetime in the mines.

"Look. I'm not here as a cop. I'm here to get some tests. I'm not on duty here. And this—I'm startin' to get a little mad about this—"

"Good. Then I'm gettin' someplace." Castelucci fell into a chair beside Balzic.

"You're not gettin' anyplace except the hell outta here. I don't know—I don't know what the hell you want—"

"I want you to listen."

"I've listened to you more times than I can count," Balzic

said. "You don't listen to me when I tell you the most important thing. But I'm gonna tell you again. It didn't happen in Rocksburg. It happened—"

"In Westfield Township, yeah, yeah. I know all about where it happened. Thirty feet over the line. One house lot over." Castelucci coughed violently, his spindly body heaving and shuddering as he strove to get air after the coughing passed.

"Then why can't you understand, it's not for—it's for the state police. Them. Not me. They're the ones you talk to—"

"I talked to them until I'm blue in the face. They don't hear nothin'. They don't wanna hear nothin'."

"Just like you, Mr. Castelucci. Just like you."

"Quit tryin' to turn this on me. Talkin' games don't work on me. I never graduated high school and I was a grievance man for twenty years. I argued with the mine lawyers all the time. I know all the crap."

"I've heard all this before too," Balzic said, staring off down the corridor, his gaze falling on an elderly man studying the colored lines on the floor. Balzic snapped himself back and glared at Castelucci. "I want you to quit. I'm gonna be polite. But I'm not gonna put up with you anymore. You been my shadow for five goddamn months now, but comin' up here, this is it. I thought comin' to church was the topper, but this—this is the end right here. Do you understand me?"

"He was my son, Balzic. When he died, my wife—she just sits. She don't even wash herself no more. I shove food in her mouth. She sits in a chair and rocks. She's dyin' right in front of me. She's rockin' herself to death. And I ain't gonna watch that and not do nothin' so I ain't gonna let you alone."

Balzic started to stand up but Castelucci put his hand across Balzic's chest. He didn't have strength enough to restrain Balzic; he just held his hand there. Balzic couldn't bring himself to push against it.

"I don't wanna sound like no movies here, but . . . but what I'm gonna say is the truth. I got nothin' else to lose. And you can't beat me. All you can do is arrest me for harassment. So what? So I'll be even closer to you then. Either you help me or I'll hound you till my lungs give out."

"Oh for crissake," Balzic said, pushing Castelucci's hand away and slumping back in the chair. "Lemme think about it."

"No."

"Whatta you mean, no?"

"You had plenty of time to think already."

"Look, Mr. Castelucci, this is not as simple as you think—"

"I never said it was simple."

"You gonna let me finish?"

Castelucci thrust his palms upward, the hankies slowly expanding. He closed his fingers over them and put them to his mouth as another spasm of coughing shook him.

When the spasm passed, Balzic said, "Police jurisdiction is not something you fool around with, Mr. Castelucci. State cops get very upset when you go trampin' around in their yard—"

"You been friends with Lieutenant Johnson for years. You got friends in the DA's office. You're friends with the coroner. All you gotta do is talk to your friends. Whatta you scared of? You think some of your friends mighta goofed up? Huh? I'm here to tell you they goofed up."

"You still don't understand."

"I understand you can prove they goofed up. Nobody'll listen to me. I can't prove it. You can prove it."

Balzic sighed. "What do you want?"

"I want somebody settin' at the DA's table with all the facts. I want the DA to nail that shiney-ass sonofabitch. I don't want no more goof-ups. I want that shiney-ass where he belongs. That's what I want."

Balzic rubbed his mouth. "You're forgettin' something."

"I ain't forgettin' nothin'."

"You're forgettin' the possibility that there's no case against this guy. Maybe there hasn't been any goof-up. Maybe there's no case. Maybe it happened the way—the way you don't wanna think it happened. Then what? What're you gonna do about me then?"

"Whatta you mean?"

"I mean what I said. What if I find out what you don't wanna hear—then what? You gonna get off my behind? I mean, when do I know that my part of this deal is over?"

"Oh. I see what you're gettin' at. Well. I guess you'll have to take my word on it."

"Well then give me your word. Right now. Promise me that no matter which way it goes, you're finished with me when I finish."

"Okay. You got it."

"No no. Say the whole thing."

"Okay. I give you my word, no matter what you find out, if you did all you can, then I'll be finished with you."

"So help you God?"

"I don't believe in God." Castelucci thought for a moment. "So help me Joey."

"Okay," Balzic said, standing. "Then I don't want you talkin' to me again till I talk to you, is that clear?"

Castelucci nodded.

"Then get outta here. I gotta get some kind of test and I'm nervous as hell already. I don't want you hangin' around."

"I'm goin'," Castelucci said, laboring to stand. "It takes me a while. I don't move fast as I used to."

"Yeah, sure," Balzic said and watched him plod off, his expirations audible with every step.

Balzic shook his head and cursed under his breath. Then he tried to compose himself as he stepped up to the window and put his face near the hole in it. He was sure there was a reason why a window separated these clerks from the people who came to talk to them. It probably had something to do with health precautions. But the hole cut in the glass annoyed him. Its height was designed for average people. Tall people would have to bend to talk through it and short people would have to get up on their toes, Balzic thought sourly, and it must've never occurred to the guy who designed it that some people were going to roll up to it in wheelchairs.

Two women were sitting at the computer terminal on the other side of the glass. One had her hands on the keys and was looking more than a little confused. She had applied lipstick to make her lips seem fuller than they were and her fingernails were bitten down to the flesh. The underarms of her sleeveless blouse were stained with perspiration despite the air conditioning.

The other woman had pulled her chair up close behind the first woman so that they were touching, and she was pointing at the screen. She wore no makeup and had a sweater thrown around her shoulders. She interrupted her instructions to ask Balzic if she could help him.

Balzic slid the prescription for a blood test to determine the levels of prolactin and testosterone into the well under the window.

"Have you been a patient here before?" she asked pleasantly.

Balzic nodded.

"Your last name and phone number please?"

"My name's Balzic but my phone's unlisted."

"Well we have to have it, sir, because that's how all our patients are stored in the computer files. We have two references, cross-indexed, names and phone numbers, because, as I'm sure you can understand, many people have the same last names but you only have one phone number. That's how we make sure we don't get the wrong Smith or Jones." Her tone was even, professionally genial, and she was also good at smiling.

"My name is Balzic, B-A-L-Z-I-C. First name Mario, and if you got names and numbers cross-indexed, then you got to have my file under that name."

"We need your phone—"

"Why don't you just hunt for my name, okay?"

Her smile went first, then her tone. "Type in his name there, where I showed you before," she said to the other woman.

Balzic spelled his name again without being asked.

"Please try to be a little patient, sir. I'm breaking in a new girl here and we all have to be a little patient."

The sweaty woman with the bitten nails said, "I know a Johnny Balzich. You related to him?"

"No 'h' on the end. There are lots of Balziches around here, but there's only one Balzic."

"Oh. Oh. Here it is. Mario?"

"That's me."

"Is your phone number—"

"I'm not tellin' you my phone number, ladies. It's unlisted. You got an address there?"

"Um, 115 Washington Street, Rocksburg?"

"You got it."

"Sir, we have to have your phone number—"

"Lady, I get my phone number changed every three months no matter what, so whatever number's in there is at least three years old and whatever number I give you—which I'm not gonna do—wouldn't be any good three months from now, so can we get on with it? Huh?"

"I'm just trying to do my job, Mr. Balzic, and trying to train this girl at the same time, so it would help—"

"I know, I know. Just try to be a little patient."

"Sir, I will have to leave a memo for my supervisor telling her why I do not have a phone number—"

"Oh, Christ, lady, what do you do with people who don't have phones—don't you let 'em in? They have to go someplace else?"

"Please don't use that kind of language."

Balzic sighed and shrugged.

"We'll just ignore the phone number this time, but you must remember to get it in every other time." She was talking to the trainee.

The trainee nibbled her nails and nodded quickly three times.

"Well, then. What's the purpose of these tests?"

"Whatta you mean—hey, lady, that's between me and my doctor. That's none of your goddamn business."

"Just type in what the tests are, and where it says purpose, just type in 'prescribed by doctor.'" After the trainee typed that, the first woman leaned back and said, "We know what these tests are for."

"If you know what they're for, lady, why'd you ask me?"

"Because it's our job to ask. And you don't have to swear. No one needs to swear."

Balzic understood suddenly why there was glass separating these clerks from the rest of the world. All he could do was glare at the woman. "Anything else you wanna know?"

"Do you still have the same insurance carrier?"

Balzic produced his insurance card and held it up for the women to confirm against the one listed in his file.

The woman put the prescription in the well under the window. "Follow the black line until you come to the—"

"I know where to go, lady."

"Then you should hurry," she said, standing and tugging at the hem of her blouse, "before everything wilts."

"Aw that's good, lady. I guess you zinged me, huh? Before everything wilts. That's real good. Uh, does it say on my file there what my job is? Check that out, lady, and remember how you gave me that little zinger."

Balzic turned and walked quickly away and was amazed to feel that his knees were as rubbery and his hands as cold as if he'd been in a fight. His mouth was dry and his pulses were knocking in his ears and his breath was coming shallow and short. "Fucking, ball-busting, goddamn bitch," he heard himself saying and could not believe that was his voice saying those words. Jesus, he thought. Jesus H. Christ. What the hell is going on here?

By the time he had given up enough blood to fill two syringes, he was soaking with sweat, and if he'd been asked to describe the nurse who had inserted the needle into the vein in his left arm, he could not have done it. He had not seen her. Worse, he would have had to say that he had not even looked at her. Far worse, he would have had to say that he was unable to look at her. Something had been lost between the time he'd first pushed the prescription into the well under the admissions window and the time he'd bent his arm to hold a ball of cotton in place to stop the blood. Something had been lost that he'd never thought about losing, or certainly had never thought about losing in such a public way. Something had been lost that made him feel—and about this Balzic knew there was no other word for it—something that made him feel shame.

He turned left out of the blood lab and crashed chin to forehead with Dr. Wallace Grimes.

Grimes staggered sideways holding his head. Balzic fell against the wall holding his chin. His teeth had snapped shut at impact and he stood there opening his eyes wide and closing them and feeling his lower lip to see if it had been cut.

"Jesus. Hey, Doc. You okay? Huh?"

Grimes took his hand away from his head and looked at it. "God, Mario. Is that you?" He whistled under his breath. "That was some collision. Are you all right? Where'd you hit?"

"My chin must've got your head there. Wow. I guess we both need to slow down, huh, Doc?"

"It would seem so. You sure you're all right? Not cut?"

"No, nah, I'm okay. Let's go in your office, sit down, take a break."

"Good idea." Grimes led the way, walking apparently as briskly as he had when they'd collided.

Balzic hurried to keep up.

"Hey, uh, Doc. I was really coming to see you."

"That so? What about?" Grimes said, leading the way into his office, which was at the end of the hall where the blood labs were. Grimes went to a file cabinet and deposited a folder and motioned for Balzic to sit. Then he sat at his desk and took another swipe across his forehead and glanced at his fingers. "What's on your mind?"

"You remember a guy got shot to death about five months ago, right around Memorial Day? His name was Joseph Castelucci. It happened in Westfield Township."

"I remember it, but let me get the file." Grimes went to another file cabinet and searched the manila folders. "Here it is. . . . Joseph William Castelucci, age 36, male, Caucasian, pronounced dead 4:05 a.m. June 1, by Dr. Rolando Cercone. I did the PM 8 a.m. June 1. Death by gunshot. Five entry wounds, four exit wounds, four non-lethal. The one to the head caused death almost instantaneously. Is this the one you want to know about?"

"That's the one."

"What do you want to know?"

"Tell me about the wounds. Condition of the body, condition of the hands. And please—in words I understand, okay? No latissimus this or centimeters that, okay?"

"Well, first we have an entry wound to the lower right biceps, exit through thc lower right triceps, missing the bone. Then we have entry to the front of the trapezius fractionally above the collarbone and exit through the rear of that muscle in almost a horizontal line, slightly upward from front to back, but very slightly. Then there was entry to the fleshy part of the right palm and exit through the back of the hand; the shaft of the first metacarpal bone, the thumb bone, was shattered."

"That's the base of the thumb right here," Balzic pointed to entry and exit on his own hand.

"Yes. That's close enough. Number four entry was a gutter-like wound running approximately over the tenth rib on the left side. Apparently, I did *not* determine an exit for that. It was the most superficial of the wounds anyway."

"What do you mean you didn't 'determine an exit' for that?"

"Well, it was a gutter-like wound as I said and I did not determine whether entry was made from the front or the back. Since it was clearly not a lethal wound, I didn't even check for the grease mark."

"So it didn't make any difference to you where he took that shot from."

"Well, it made no difference in the sense that he could have taken that shot while he was facing the shooter or perhaps while he was turning. My strongest notion is that he was facing the shooter throughout. All I'm saying is, according to my notes and report here, I did not make a distinction about which end of the wound was entry and which was exit. It would not have made any difference. The last shot entered his face below his left eye, two bullet fragments passed through the medulla oblongata, and I removed three bullet fragments from the mastoid areas of the brain, two on the right, one on the left, and one bullet fragment from between the first and second vertebrae. That latter was the largest fragment of the bullet."

"And that shot killed him?"

"No question. He was dead before his face touched the ground. He fell on his face, all the sinus cavities were filled with congealed blood and his nose cartilage was broken, obviously from the force of the fall when his face struck the ground."

"Okay, now what about his hands?"

"Many abrasions on both sets of knuckles, more severe on the right hand. He had clearly been striking someone or something."

"Anything else?"

"Well, he was in good health, lungs were clear, heart was good, arteries looked fairly clean. He had several previous bone fractures, at least two, perhaps three of the lower jaw. His left arm in three places. Both his legs. Most were fairly old, although one in the jaw looked pretty recent. He also had three instances of scar tissue on his face. One on the left eyebrow, probably caused by a blow, but the two others were definitely old knife wounds, knife or razor. They were both straight, not jagged. That fellow was well acquainted with trauma."

"Oh Christ yes," Balzic said. "'Acquainted' doesn't do the job. 'Close friend' is more like it."

"Uh, what's your interest here, Mario? If it's any of my business."

"His father's convinced the state guys screwed up the case. He's been houndin' me ever since it happened to stick my nose in, and the only way I'm gonna shake the old man is to do what he wants. So I thought you'd be the best start."

"I see. Uh, how's your chin?"

"Okay. How's your head?"

"Sore. Not as sore as it's going to be tomorrow, I guess. Well. Anything else?"

"Nah, that's it. Thanks, Doc. Say, if I need to copy that file—"

"Do it now if you want. There's a copier in the next room."

"No. I won't do it unless I need to. See ya, Doc."

Balzic walked gingerly out of Grimes's office, looking around as though he were a student driver entering city traffic for the first time. He'd taken enough blows today, one to his ego, the other to his chin, and he thought it wouldn't take much of any other kind of blow to play hell with his confidence.

He walked slowly, thinking about himself, his blood tests and the possible results, and about all those fractures in Joey Castelucci's bones. . . . The left arm, he broke falling off a ladder on a roof, I remember that. Yeah, he was puttin' tar on Muscotti's roof. The legs, they happened when his wife chased him over the curb and pinned him against the courthouse—or was that city hall? No. The courthouse before they built the annex. Yeah. Ran her Chevy right into the backs of his legs. Could never figure out how the hell she hit him hard enough to break his legs but didn't hit him hard enough to slam him into the wall there. By all logic, she should've killed him. But all she did was break his legs and his nose. It was like she was just goin' fast enough to pin him there and then goosed it once to break something. A week later she was helping him in and out of Muscotti's, holding the door for him, holding the chair, telling him how his nose was straighter now that she broke it. That really pissed him off when she said that. He was screaming he didn't want it straight and if it was straight it was all her fault—Christ, I remember that like it was yesterday and I know damn well it was five, six years ago at least. . . .

Balzic spotted a pay phone and called his doctor's office. When the secretary answered, he identified himself and said, "Tell the doc I just had the blood taken for those tests he ordered. And tell him when he gets the results to call me at the station, okay? Or you call me there, okay? I don't want that call made to my home, understand?"

"I understand, Chief. Did the doctor tell you when the results would be in?"

"No. Nobody told me."

"Well I wouldn't expect anything before five days at least. More like seven."

Balzic thanked her and hung up. Then he called his station and Sgt. Vic Stramsky answered.

"Anything goin' on?"

"Nothing. Best kind of boredom there is. Only call I got the whole watch is from some old lady wanted to talk to a Mrs. Detore."

"Wrong number?"

"No, it wasn't a wrong number. She had the right number. But she said it wasn't our number, it was this Detore woman's number and if I didn't get out of her house she was gonna call the cops. It was funny as hell to tell you the truth. Best phone call I've had in a long time."

"Wish I'd've been there. I could use a laugh. Listen, I'm goin' to see Walker Johnson. I don't know how long I'm gonna be there. Depends on how much readin' I have to do and whether anybody I want to talk to is there, okay?"

Stramsky acknowledged the information and they hung up, and Balzic went to his car in the lot at the rear of the hospital and drove to the state police barracks. He found Lt. Walker Johnson in his office filling out requisitions.

"Mario! Come on in. Have a seat." He sighed and pushed the papers away. "God, I wish there was some other way to say this, but I'm gettin' so I hate paper."

"That's the job description. Must be all those things Boy Scouts gotta be plus must be able to fill out forms and must be able to convince himself that municipal government will collapse if he forgets one line."

"That's close, that's close. So." Johnson leaned back in his chair and clasped his hands behind his head. "So, you got a problem?"

"Yeah. Before I start, I'm gonna warn you that this one depends on, uh, you and me, and a lotta miles over the road."

"Uh-oh. That bad, huh?"

"Well, I got a guy buggin' me and the only way I'm gonna get him to stop buggin' me is for me to bug you. I mean, the man is seriously on my nerves."

"Uh, let me guess."

"Go right ahead."

"It's Joey Case's old man, right?"

Balzic nodded and threw up his hands.

"Mario, you can sit down, you know."

"Shit, I don't want to sit down. I don't want to be here." Balzic stretched and dropped into a chair beside Johnson's desk. "D'you really assign Walter Helfrick to this?"

"C'mon, Mario. You know better than that. I was asleep when it happened. When the call came in, Helfrick was the nearest body. By the time I heard about it Grimes was already doin' the inventory. There wasn't anything to it. Domestic disturbance, shots fired, and when Helfrick got there, the shooter was waitin' for him with his hands up. Three witnesses standin' around tryin' to out-talk each other, all with the same general story and all confused enough to show they weren't lyin'. Lord knows Helfrick's a fuck-up, but any rookie could've put this one together."

"Got any idea why the old man's so out of joint?"

Johnson shrugged. "Hey, it's his kid. Kid's been fuckin' up all his life, and a lot of that's, uh, probably a lot of that's due to the old man. Hey, you knew 'em both better than I did. You were the one who used to sit around tellin' me Joey Case stories."

"I know, I know."

"Well what's the old man want? I know what he wants from me, he's told me enough times already."

"Which is?"

"Oh shit, life without possibility of parole. I told him, hell, that's fantasy. The reality is one to three and he probably won't do six months. But, according to the old man, that's because we goofed up. If we knew what we were doin', we'd have—"

"Contract murder."

"Yeah. Right. Conspiracy, solicitation to commit murder, aw, he's dreamin'. His heart's full of guilt and his head's full of plots."

"Yeah, you're probably right."

"No probably, Mario. No probably. Okay. So you got to get him off your butt. So what do you want? You want the file?"

Balzic nodded.

"You got it. You want to talk to Helfrick, go right ahead. You want to talk to the witnesses, be my guest. You want me to call them and tell 'em it's okay to talk to you, I'll do that. Far as the shooter goes, hey, that's up to his lawyer."

"Who's that?"

"Oh, I forget his name. He's from Pittsburgh. Helfrick knows."

"What about the shooter?"

"I don't know. Some citizen who got the hots for Joey's wife. No priors. Can't say much for his brains, screwin' around with her, Jesus. Oh shit, I forgot. I got a meeting with the mayor. Look, I gotta go. Helfrick's around here somewhere. I'll send him back. Stay as long as you like. Just one thing."

"What?"

"Take it easy on Helfrick, okay? Three, four months, he's gone. Let him take his pension and go, okay? This, believe it or not, this is the highlight of his career. It's the first time anybody let him do anything besides traffic patrol and give driver exams.

It's the first time in his life he's gonna testify in front of a judge. He's so goddamn nervous he joined a toastmasters club to learn how to talk in front of people. All I'm sayin' is, you could turn his mind to mayonnaise in fifteen minutes. Please don't. Okay?"

Balzic shrugged. "Okay," he said, sighing.

Johnson lurched up from his seat and hustled out of the office.

Balzic stood, paced around the office, sat, stretched, cleaned his fingernails, breathed deeply from his diaphragm, and tried not to think about either his blood tests or about Tpr. Walter Helfrick. It was easier not to think about his blood tests, or rather it was more disconcerting to think about them, so he let his mind wander over recollections of Helfrick.

If it weren't for these circumstances, it would have been fine to think about Helfrick. Helfrick was the best example Balzic could imagine of a man who put a twist in the Peter Principle that every man is promoted to the level of his incompetence—Helfrick was never promoted, he was transferred to get him out of somebody's hair. His nickname—always spoken behind his back—was Headcrabs. He never did anything bad enough to warrant disciplinary action beyond official reprimands; he also never did anything good enough to prompt any of his superiors to try to do anything but dump him on some other unsuspecting sap. He had been in every Troop and in every Barracks and Sub-Station in the state. His performance was always the same, dogged dull mediocrity interrupted by an occasional blunder worthy of spirited retellings wherever cops gathered to exchange stories and nurse their egos or lubricate their boredom or their fear.

Once, Helfrick, responding to an accident that had blocked both lanes of the Parkway East heading to Pittsburgh, got the information wrong, turned off one exit too soon, and by the time he'd made his way to the crash which had prompted the call, traffic was backed up for miles and included three new rear-enders. Because he was single-mindedly searching for the earliest accident, he passed up the later ones without so much as word that he—or someone else—would be back. And then, after he'd finished his work at the first accident, he didn't go back to the more recent ones, and he didn't call them in, and he had no explanation when his watch commander wanted to know why all those citizens were scorching the switchboard. Then the watch commander had no good explanation when the barracks commander was asked by the division commander to explain all those letters delivered to the state Senate, the state House, the state police headquarters about four minor accidents on the Parkway East.

Then there was the time Helfrick was ordered to arrest a prostitute on a bench warrant because she'd failed to appear to testify in the morning session against her pimp who was being tried on various drug charges. Helfrick showed up in the afternoon session with the pros's 80-year-old grandmother, after whom the pros had been named.

Then there was the time Helfrick took his cruiser to an automatic carwash, wandered across the street to a diner to buy lunch, forgot that he'd taken the car to be washed, walked out of the diner, and couldn't find the cruiser, whereupon he immediately called the barracks from inside the diner to announce that the cruiser had been stolen. The part Balzic liked best about that story was that Helfrick, in order to cover himself, also gave a description of the thief and the direction the cruiser was headed, and then, to top it off, when he remembered where the car was, he reported that he had found the car a half-mile from the diner where the imaginary thief had apparently abandoned it. Helfrick would probably have slid clear around that one except that the guy who owned the diner was a volunteer fireman and heard all the reports over his Bearcat police scanner.

While Balzic was enjoying these recollections, he wondered as he had many times, how Helfrick had survived, and then, when Helfrick walked into Johnson's office, Balzic knew why. Helfrick looked like a state cop. If you wanted a model to photograph for a recruiting poster, Helfrick was the cop you'd send for. He was six feet two at least, two hundred pounds, with big shoulders and a square jaw, and how the man believed in spit and polish. His shoes and leatherwork shone, his metal gleamed, and his uniform looked like it had just left a presser. His hair was bristly and his complexion ruddy. If wrong behavior could be put right by a replica of solid authority then the state should have been free of crime wherever Helfrick set his size 13 shoes. Great God Almighty, Balzic thought, it's no wonder old man Castelucci's pissed.

"Aw, hy ya doin', Chief Balzic. Been a while since we had a chance to talk—you think the lieutenant would care if I sat in his chair?" Helfrick had pulled Johnson's chair out and now hovered near it, poised as though he would retreat if Balzic said the lieutenant would care.

Balzic shook his head no.

"Glad you said that. I didn't think he would, but I just wanted to hear you say it." Helfrick eased into the chair and drew it close to Johnson's desk. "Feels pretty good, I'll tell you." He tapped the arms of the chair and then touched the desk respectfully.

"Now. Lieutenant says you want to see me and I have to give you my full cooperation. He also said I was to bring the file on the Castelucci case. I got it right here." He nodded and pointed to the thick manila folder in front of him.

Balzic sighed. "I see you do."

"Well, okay. I'm ready."

"Okay," Balzic said. "So you're on patrol and you get a call that shots were fired, right?"

"No no. First call was a domestic disturbance at—lemme see here." He opened the folder. "Oh, here. It was at zero two thirty-five hours at number fourteen Westfield Drive in Westfield Township. I proceeded to the address. At approximately zero two thirty-nine hours I got the call shots fired. I rogered both calls. Yeah. Then—"

"Well, tell me what you found."

"Well, I was proceeding north on Westfield and I had a little difficulty locating the address because it's not on a mailbox or sign, so I had to turn around—"

"Yeah, yeah, okay. So you find it."

"Correct. I turned right, which was east—no, I mean when I turned around I had to go—I had to do another U-turn."

Balzic inhaled deeply as unobtrusively as he could and exhaled slowly through his nose.

"So I was proceeding east, north I mean, and then I turned right—east—into the driveway."

"Uh-huh."

"And you have to proceed east about fifty feet approximately, and the driveway circles around—oh, the house is on your left, which is north."

"What's the house look like?'

"Huh? Oh. It was brick, two-story—no, three, but the third floor's like an attic. Only there's rooms up there. An apartment. People live up there. A woman does."

"Any other houses visible?"

"Huh? Oh no. It's just—it just sits there by itself."

"Okay, so the driveway is about fifty feet and then it circles around something, you said."

"Yeah. It circles around a tree. Big tree. Huge tree. Trunk's about three feet in diameter."

"And so you circled around the driveway."

"Huh? Oh no. No. I stopped."

"Where and why?"

"I stopped—where? As soon as I got to the—as soon as I got to the end of where the driveway started to bend around."

"Why?"

"Oh. Because the actor put up his hands as soon as he saw me proceeding toward him."

"How did you know it was the actor?"

"Because he had a weapon in his hand."

"So you stopped your cruiser, you got out, and what then?"

"As soon as I halted my vehicle he started hollering out to me. He said, 'I surrender.' He said it two or three times."

"This guy is holding a pistol in his hand and the first words out of his mouth are, 'I surrender'?"

"Yes, sir. As far as I can recollect."

"So what did you do?"

"Well, I approached the actor and I believe I asked him to turn over the weapon, which he did."

"Where was he when you first saw him?"

"He was standing in front of his vehicle, well, I didn't know it was his until later on."

"Where was the vehicle?"

"It was backed up against this tree. I mean, I didn't know that until later on, but it—well, it was backed up against the tree."

"Okay, what else?"

"Well, beside the vehicle—"

"Which side?"

"On the driver's side."

"Go 'head."

"On the driver's side, on the ground approximately ten feet away was the body of a man."

"You saw this around the guy?"

"Yes, but—well, he pointed him out to me."

"And then what?"

"Well approximately at that time the ambulance arrived."

"D'you call the ambulance?"

"No, sir."

"Who did?"

"Uh, I believe—I never ascertained who that was, sir, who called the ambulance."

Balzic sighed again. "Okay, so the ambulance gets there. Two, three paramedics?"

"Three."

"And they go to the body and start to work on it?"

"Yes, sir."

"Was the body alive at that time?"

"No, sir."

"The EMTs tell you this, right? You never went to the body, right?"

"No, sir."

"So how was the body arranged? On its back, front, side, holding weapons, not holding weapons, tell me."

"Well I never really got a good look at it, because the actor was talking, and then, when the EMTs got there, they sort of took over on that."

"Well, later on, did you interview the EMTs about how the body was arranged?"

"Ah, no, sir. Not at that time."

"At what time then? Anytime?"

"Uh, no, sir. I know I should have done that, sir, but I believed that they were trying to revive the man."

"Okay. I'll talk to them about it. You got their names there?"

"Uh, no, sir. I don't believe so."

"Okay. That's all right. I'll check that out. Okay, so when did the photographer get there?"

"Approximately zero three fifteen hours."

"So you called for him when you reported a possible homicide, right?"

"Yes, sir."

"Who else came with him?"

"With the photographer?"

Balzic nodded.

"Uh, nobody, sir."

"Nobody from CID came? Why was that?"

"Well, it was Castelucci. Joey Case."

"So? It was Joey Case. So what?"

"Well, uh, I knew it was—I mean I knew he was dead by then, so . . ."

"So what?"

"Well." Helfrick shrugged nervously. "You know."

"No, I don't know."

"Well, hey, he was—I mean, he was gonna get it sooner or later."

Balzic scowled in spite of himself. "Okay, we'll let that go for now. The photographer showed up and you told him to take pictures of what, exactly?"

"Uh, I ordered photographs to be taken of the vehicle and of the ground around the vehicle and of the back of the house, which is the east side, and also the south side, which is the side fronting the driveway."

"Uh, okay. So now tell me about the vehicle, everything from title to condition."

"It was a 1982 Cadillac Coupe de Ville. White. The windshield had one sunburst in it and the driver's side window was smashed. There was a cinder block laying on the front seat, the driver's seat. Oh, the owner was Francis Paul Collier, 74 Ashland Drive, Westfield Township."

"He's the shooter?"

"Yes, sir."

"Anybody else present?"

"Oh yes, sir. Three or four people. They kept goin' in and out. Of the house, I mean."

"Who were they?"

"Well, there was the deceased's wife and her sister and brother-in-law, and he owned the house. Then, there was a witness named, uh, lemme see here. Ralph Gioia."

"What were the names of the sister and brother-in-law?"

"Uh, that would be Mr. and Mrs. Victor Marcelli. They owned the house."

"You said there was a woman lived on the third floor? What was her name?"

"She wouldn't give her name. She said she didn't see anything so she didn't want to give her name."

"Uh-huh." Balzic had been writing the names in a small notebook. He pushed it aside. "So what did they look like?"

"Oh they were all pretty shook up. Except for Case's wife. She just looked like it was all pretty normal."

Balzic nodded. "So let's get back to the shooter. After you took the weapon away from him—what was it?"

"Uh, the weapon was a thirty-two caliber Colt semi-automatic pistol, chrome plated, with pearl grips."

"Which he was holding when you first saw him and which he turned over to you when you asked him to do that, right?"

"Right. Yes, sir."

"Did he have a permit for it?"

"Yes, sir. Issued in Allegheny County."

"Now, did you give him his rights?"

"Well, I started to, but he never let me finish."

"How so?"

"Well, 'cause he wanted to tell me what happened."

"What'd he say?"

"Well, I gotta refer to my notes here . . . uh, here it is. Actor says he was waiting in the apartment—that's Mrs. Case's apartment—and they walk in, her and Case."

"What time was that, did he say?"

"Uh, why a couple minutes before the thing went down. I mean he didn't know exactly what time that was."

"Okay. Go 'head."

"Okay. So they walk in and Case strikes actor—"

"Just like that? Boom. Case and his wife walk in and no words are spoken and Case hits him?"

"That's what he said, yes, sir."

"Okay. So go 'head."

"So, uh, Case strikes actor repeatedly, throws actor out of apartment, follows him into hall, kicks actor in leg, grabs actor by neck, slams actor's head against wall, knees actor in leg, actor gets away, runs outside to car, Case catches actor, strikes actor in face, throws actor against car, strikes actor with fists in face, actor gets away, gets in car, starts car, backs into tree, car stalls, Case comes out nowhere—out *of* nowhere I guess I meant to write there. Then actor sees Case with block, actor gets weapon from glove compartment, Case throws block through window, actor fires weapon until empty, doesn't see Case anymore."

"Uh-huh. So. D'you check the weapon?"

"No, sir. Not at that time. Later on I did. After I got everything squared away."

"When was that?"

"Oh, probably zero five hundred hours."

"And it was empty?"

"Yes, sir. I checked it before I tagged it and left it right here in this office for the ballistics test. It was empty."

"Okay, we'll come back to that. Now what did this guy look like? Did he look beaten up?"

"Oh yes, sir. He was definitely assaulted."

"Describe him."

"Well, he—his coat was ripped, one sleeve was ripped, his shirt was ripped, there was blood on his face, uh, especially his forehead. There was a lot of blood on his shirt and coat."

"Did you have pictures taken of him?"

"Him? No, sir."

"Why not?"

"Well, I—I didn't think—I mean, I didn't see how that was, how I should've done that."

"Uh-huh. Did he require medical attention?"

"Oh, well, he said he was, uh—Case's wife took him to the emergency room in her car."

"You didn't take him into custody at that time?"

"Uh, no, sir."

"Why not?"

"Well, see, I was the only officer at the scene, and I had a lot of things to do. I had to talk to all the witnesses, and they said where they were goin', so I said I'd be down there and pick him up."

"Is that what you did?"

"Yes, sir. After I finished at the scene, I put the weapon in a bag and locked it in my truck, and then I went to the emergency room and arrested him. Then I took him to the barracks and booked him, and we all went to the duty magistrate's office and I filed the information."

"Who's 'we'?"

"Uh, that would be the actor, his attorney, and me."

"What time was this?"

"When we finished at the magistrate's? That was zero six hundred hours, approximately."

"When'd his attorney show up?"

"When we were at the barracks. He was there when I booked him. No. Wait a minute. He was there in the hospital."

"His attorney was present when you made the arrest in the emergency room?"

"That's correct, sir."

"What's his attorney's name?'

"Uh, that would—I have it here. Oh. Here. Harold Coblentz. You want his phone number and address?"

Balzic nodded and wrote the information in his notebook. "And he was released on recognizance, right?"

"Yes, sir, that's correct."

"Have you interviewed him since then?"

"Uh, no, sir."

"Okay, before we get to the witnesses, what about the evidence. What else did you collect besides the weapon?"

"Well, there was the cement block."

"Regular cinder block, building block?"

"Yes, sir."

"How big?"

"It was eight by eight by sixteen. Actually seven and a half by seven and a half by fifteen and a half."

"Anything unusual about it?"

"Unusual? No, sir. I mean it had a lot of blood on it. But it looked like any old cinder block."

"D'you have the blood tested?"

"I ordered tests, yes, sir."

"And the tests were made?"

"Yes, sir."

"D'you get a blood test from the coroner from the victim?"

"Yes, sir."

"How about for the shooter?"

"The shooter? Well, uh, no. I never thought—"

"Never mind."

"Well why was I supposed to get his blood?"

Balzic rubbed his chin. "Well the way you say the shooter described the sequence, he didn't start shootin' until after the block was thrown through the window. He didn't say anything—or you didn't say he said anything about whether the block hit him, the shooter. And then you said Case was ten feet from the driver's side of the car. Now that's at least three steps from the car. When I asked you before how the body was arranged, you said you weren't sure, or you couldn't remember. But I already heard from the coroner how many times Case was shot and how the only lethal wound had to be the last one, and when that one got him, he dropped face first hard enough to break his nose. In other words, he was probably dead before he left his feet. Now you didn't clarify the exact distance he was from the car—"

"I said he was, uh, approximately ten feet."

"Okay, so Case was about five-eleven, he takes the last one in the face, he goes down on his face, that means he was standing approximately fifteen feet from the car when he took the shot."

"Uh, I don't see what you're getting at here."

"What I'm gettin' at is that you don't know as of this moment whose blood is on the block. Did you have a comparison made of blood from the victim with blood from the block?"

"Uh, no, sir."

"And you didn't have blood tested from the shooter?"

"Uh, no, sir."

Balzic had to chew his lip to contain his frustration, his growing anger. "So I'm repeatin' myself, but as of right now, you don't know whose blood is on the block, right?"

"I—I guess so."

"Now. Did the shooter say the block hit him after it came through the window?"

"No, sir."

"He didn't say or you don't remember?"

"No. I remember. He didn't say anything about it."

"Did he say where he was sitting when the block came in?"

"I don't follow you."

"Well, was he sitting behind the wheel?"

"He didn't say."

"What kind of seats were they?"

"What kind?"

"Yeah. Bucket seats? Or was it one seat flat across? What kind of material? Leather, imitation leather, cloth, velour?"

"What's that have to do with anything?"

"Well, it would have been a lot easier to get out of the way if they were leather or imitation leather and there was just a flat seat, I mean, you could slide on that stuff—never mind. Show me the pictures."

"Of the car?"

"Yes, the car."

"Well, we don't have any of the seats."

Balzic swallowed hard and sighed. "Let me look at the pictures, okay?"

Helfrick handed over a thick stack of eight by tens, and Balzic went through them until he found several of the interior of the Cadillac, views taken from both sides of the car. "We got lots of pictures of the seat. What's that look like to you, leather, right? Or fake leather, right? And a one-piece seat. No bucket seats. So he had no problem movin' his butt."

"Well, see, I thought I told him to take shots of the interior, but I wanted to be sure," Helfrick said.

"Uh-huh. Okay." Balzic thought for a moment. "When you were with the attorney, from the time you first saw him in the emergency room right through the business in front of the magistrate, do you recall seeing a camera?"

"You mean the attorney?"

Balzic nodded.

"Uh, no, sir. I don't recall that."

"Okay. Now when you said before that the shooter's clothes were ripped, were those rips in the seams or were they tears in the cloth? What I'm gettin' at is, did they look like they were caused by somebody pullin' on them or because maybe a corner of the block tore them, do you recall that?"

"Uh, no, sir, I don't."

"Okay, so, uh, d'you recover any bullets or shell casings?"

"Oh, yes, sir, I did. I found four casings inside the car, one on the seat, one on the dashboard, and two on the floor. And then—"

"Which side of the car?"

"Huh? Oh. The two on the floor were on the passenger side. The one on the dash was about in the middle. And the one on the seat was, uh, sort of on the passenger side."

"Okay. Any others?"

"Yes, sir. I found two outside the car on the passenger side. On the ground."

"What's that piece hold, you know?"

"Uh, it's either seven in the magazine and one in the chamber or eight in the magazine and one in the chamber."

"I'll check with the lab on that," Balzic said. "You recover any bullets, anywhere?"

"Uh, no, sir. We got the fragments, uh, three, I think, from the coroner, but he sent them over, I didn't get them myself personally."

"Any bullet holes in the car?"

"Oh. Yes, sir. There was one in the inside of the driver side door."

"Entry and exit both?"

Helfrick shook his head no. "No, there was just an entry hole."

"D'you take the door apart or did you order somebody to take the door apart to try to find it?"

"Uh, no, sir."

Balzic almost threw his pen down. "Uh, was the lab guy who did the ballistics able to confirm from the fragments that they came from the piece you took from the shooter?"

"I—I don't think so, sir."

"They were too mangled, right?"

"Yes, sir. I believe so."

"Where's the car?"

"Uh, I believe Collier has it, but I'm not sure."

"How long did you have it?"

"We had it for about a week I believe."

"And then what—the attorney shows up with a court order sayin' you got no reason to hold it any longer, right?"

"I believe that's what happened, yes, sir."

"So in other words, what you have is a weapon and three fragments of a bullet with no confirmation that the weapon you have fired the bullet that turned into those fragments, right?"

"Well, strictly speaking, yes—"

"Oh strictly speaking my ass. I can hear his lawyer now. 'Your honor, I submit to you that no one has been able to demonstrate conclusively that the weapon confiscated from my client is the weapon that fired the bullet that caused the death of Mr. Castelucci.'"

"But—but hell, he said he shot him."

Balzic leaned forward and growled, "He said he shot him, in your own words, before you ever finished tellin' him his rights. So his statement to you that he shot him doesn't mean shit. And you had his car for a week and you didn't get the bullet out of the door. Well I'll bet you one thing. I'll bet his fuckin' lawyer gave somebody some advice about what to do about that bullet."

"Well, crissake, we got six shells that came out of his piece. The lab guy confirmed that all right."

"Helfrick, you don't understand. Nobody ever died from an empty shell. Juries want to see bullet comparisons, lands and grooves and all that shit. They've seen that on TV and in the movies. When'd you ever see anybody in TV or the movies comparin' firing pin marks on cartridge primers? Lawyers gotta feed juries the bullshit juries know about even if it doesn't have a fuckin' thing to do with anything. Aw never mind."

"Uh, I just don't see what you're tryin' to make out of this. I got six empties and a piece and a dead guy. And I got the piece right out of the shooter's hand and I got three witnesses who heard the shots. What more do you want?" Helfrick sat back in Johnson's chair and looked very proud of himself.

"Helfrick, stop thinkin' like a DA and start thinking like the shooter's lawyer. It's not what you have that makes you a winner, it's what you don't have that makes you a loser. The defense lawyer wants to know that B happened because A happened. He's happy as hell when some cop gets up on the stand and says B happened because he *thinks* A happened. You been a cop a long time, Helfrick. You ever sit through a jury selection in a felony case?"

Helfrick's face flushed. "Uh, I don't believe so, no."

"It's nothing to be embarrassed about. Lots of cops haven't. But you know one of the first questions a lawyer asks a potential juror? He says, 'Do you believe that a police officer's word carries any more weight or is any more truthful than any other citizen's word?' And then he tries to dump all the ones who answer yes to that. That's the kind of shit you got to think about. You think you got a solid smokin' gun case here, and it would've been twenty years ago. But it isn't now. Which brings us to the witnesses."

Helfrick coughed and folded his arms. "I got a good case. I got a righteous case. And no fuckin' Jew lawyer's gonna beat me out of it."

"Uh-huh. Okay. So tell me about the witnesses. Little while ago you said you had three witnesses who 'heard' the shots. Does that mean they didn't *see* the shots?"

"Yeah. They didn't see 'em. But three of 'em heard the fight before the shots, and one of them saw part of the fight. And she got there right after."

"That would be Joey's wife, right?"

"Right."

"Is that what she said? Did she say she saw the fight but she didn't see the shots, she got there right after?"

"Yes, sir."

"What did she do between the time the fight started and the time the shots were fired? Is she tryin' to say that she did *not* follow the fight outside?"

"Yes, sir. That's what she said."

"She's lyin' bigger'n shit."

"I beg your pardon?"

"That woman loves fights more than any woman I've ever

known. No way she stayed behind. She'd've followed that one every step."

"I'm just repeating her statement."

"I'm not complainin' about you here. I just know her, that's all."

"Well, she was there at the beginning," Helfrick said hotly.

"Helfrick, let me tell you what you got here before we go any further, okay? So you know what you're dealing with, okay?"

"I know what I'm dealin' with."

"Okay. Then you tell me. Whatta you got?"

"I got a conviction, a righteous conviction."

"On what?"

"Murder."

Balzic took a deep breath. "Helfrick, you got a very weak voluntary manslaughter is what you got."

"Like hell I do. I've made a case here."

"All right, then tell me about the witnesses. Case's wife's sister and her husband. What'd they tell you?"

"They told me they heard the fight and she came over to get them."

"Where do they live?"

"Next door."

"On the first floor? Adjoining apartments?"

"Yes. Right."

"So, uh, what's the time element here? How long from when they heard the fight to when she came and got them to when they heard the shots to when they got outside—they did go outside?"

"Certainly they were outside. They were outside when I got there."

"Where were they when you got there?"

"They were on a—there's like a little patio. It's a porch but there's no roof."

"And all three of 'em were standin' there?"

"Yes. Correct."

"Not one of them was by the body?"

"No. They were all on the patio."

"And when you interviewed 'em, not one of 'em said they saw the shots fired?"

"Right."

"So how long did it take to get from their apartment to that patio? How far'd they have to travel?"

"Not far. Ten feet maybe. Maybe less."

"How were they dressed? In street clothes or were they in bed?"

"Uh, I don't know. What difference does it make?"

"If they were in bed it would've probably taken 'em longer to get movin', to answer the door, to get outside. If you don't recall how they were dressed, did you ask 'em whether they were in bed or not?"

"I don't recall." Helfrick was beginning to fidget. "I don't see what this has to do with anything."

"Okay. What'd they say?"

"They said they heard a fight, the sister—Case's wife—came to get 'em and they heard shots and they went outside."

"How many shots?"

"A lot. They didn't know how many. One of 'em said six, that was Case's wife. The other two said more, but they weren't sure."

"Any sequence to the shots?"

"Any what?"

"Sequence. Pattern. Was there one or two and then a pause and then some more? Or were they all one right after the other?"

"I didn't ask them that. Why?"

"Maybe he fired a warning shot. Maybe two. Or maybe he just starting pulling the trigger as fast as his finger would move."

"I didn't ask them about that." Helfrick began to rock from side to side in the chair. "I don't see what's so important about it anyway."

"What's important about it is what his lawyer's gonna do with it. And if he's earnin' his money he's gonna do plenty with it, especially if your witnesses can't recall a pattern. Speakin' of witnesses, how many people were in that building. How many cars were there?"

"Six. Six cars."

"Includin' the Cadillac?"

"Including the Cadillac."

"Well now. You got six cars and five bodies. Four alive. Who'd the other cars belong to?"

"Case's wife, her sister, her husband, and the people who lived on the third floor."

"I thought you said it was one person lived on the third floor. Did you say that or do I think you said that?"

"No. I said it. A woman lives up there."

"So one of the other cars is hers. That still leaves another car. D'you take a statement from this woman?"

"She said she didn't hear anything, she didn't see anything. She thought it was firecrackers."

"So she heard something."

"Well she heard it, but she didn't know what it was so she didn't check it out."

"Anybody else interview her, from the DA's office?"

"I don't know."

"Who'd they assign to this?"

"From the DA's office?"

Balzic nodded.

"Yes, sir. Detective Eddy and Assistant DA Machlin."

God, Balzic thought, I'll bet they're having fun. "Listen, I think that's all I need to know. Thanks for your cooperation."

"Uh, you're welcome." Helfrick stood up abruptly. "Would you answer me something?"

"Sure. If I can."

"Why are you askin' me all this? You act—you were soundin' like you were working for the other guy, for the shooter."

"I'm workin'—and that's not the right word but I don't know what the right word is—I'm working for Joey Case's old man. And if it wasn't for Walker Johnson, I wouldn't be askin' you anything. I got no standing in this. Far as this goes, I'm just another civilian."

Balzic gathered his notebook and pen, stood, and left Helfrick looking confused and hurt, standing at Johnson's desk and making odd noises in his throat.

Balzic went looking for the office of the Troop's commanding officer. Before he'd taken more than a few steps, Walker Johnson came into sight and motioned for Balzic to follow him outside. They stopped by Balzic's car.

"You know what dagos call guys like Helfrick?" Balzic said. "They call 'em *capo tost*."

"What's that mean?"

"Well, literally it means hard head. But what it implies is somebody whose head is so hard an idea couldn't break in without somebody usin' a chisel."

"Hey, in two, three months he's gone—"

"Oh bullshit."

"What?" Johnson laughed hard. "What is this bullshit?"

"Two, three months my ass. I know you, Walk. How many days he got left?"

"Well. After today, it'll be fifty-one."

Balzic smiled. "See, now that's the Johnson I know. Fifty-one days. None of this two, three months bullshit."

"Well, see, while you've been talkin' to Headcrabs, I've been talkin' to the mayor. I'm still in my PR voice." Johnson studied Balzic's face. "Was it as bad as you thought?"

"Oh Christ," Balzic said, shaking his head. "I hope to hell the DA's boys come up with something, or this guy Collier's not gonna do a day. And why're you askin' me that? You know that just as sure as you know how many days Helfrick got to do."

Johnson smiled weakly. "It's always nice to have your fears confirmed, Mario. That's how you know you're not paranoid. Listen, you want me to call the witnesses and the DA, tell 'em you're comin'?"

Balzic nodded.

"Okay. Consider it done. I gotta go. Gotta go home and get ready to take my wife to a wedding. God I hate weddings."

"You hate weddings? Why?"

"'Cause my wife always makes me dance. And if there's one thing I hate worse than fillin' out the state's paper, it's dancin'. And then they always do that one that goes, 'Put your right foot in, take your right foot out, da-da-da-da-da-da, then you shake it all about'— chee-sus. If there's anything in the world stupider lookin' than a bunch of human beings doin' that idiotic dance, I don't know what it is. The worst part is, I can't ever get out of it. My wife drags me out there. And all the while I'm puttin' my right hip in and takin' my right hip out, I got this godawful fear that one day I'm gonna turn around and there's gonna be one of my men gawkin' at me with this big shit-eatin' grin on his face. That just eats me up."

"Well, Walk, all I can tell you is if one of your guys did happen to see you, he might be gawkin', but he wouldn't dare grin, shit-eatin' or otherwise. Not even Headcrabs is that dumb. No. I take that back. Headcrabs would grin."

* * *

It was getting close to suppertime, and Balzic knew that he could fiddle around in the station for only so long and that there was no point in trying to interview any of the witnesses. The worst time to interview witnesses was when they were just getting off work and looking forward to getting out of their shoes and thinking about food and refreshment, and that was if they were working. If they weren't working, mealtime was absolutely the last time to try to get them to concentrate on what you wanted to know. Among the employed, only a few people could easily manage to eat and carry on a conversation, mostly salespeople, lawyers, and administrators. Working lunches and dinners were what they did, and so it was easy to interview them; but for most people, empty stomachs and tired legs meant their minds weren't on what you wanted to know and you'd wind up going back to see them at least once more. Over the years, Balzic had learned to spare himself those return visits. All of which meant that Balzic would have to go home, and that was the last place he wanted to go. Ruth would want to know about the tests at the hospital, and his feet hurt and he was hungry.

He found her in the kitchen dicing garlic. He went straight for the refrigerator and reached for the carafe of white wine, and then got a water glass from among the dishes on the rubber drain board. He kissed the back of her head and then poured the glass almost full.

She put the knife down and faced him. "Could I have a hug instead of a kiss on the back of my head? Not that I don't appreciate the kiss, but I really need a hug."

"I could use one myself," he said and put the carafe and glass down beside the garlic and embraced her.

They stood for a long moment, ever so slightly rocking each other, then she pulled her head back from his chest and held her face up, her eyes closed and her lips puckered.

He kissed her, firmly but briefly and then stepped back and reached for the wine. He put the carafe back in the refrigerator and took a long drink from the glass. When he turned around she hadn't moved.

"Look," he said, "I won't know anything for at least a week."

"I didn't ask you anything."

"Yeah but I know what you want to know."

"No you don't know what I want to know. I haven't said what

I want to know. If you want to know, I don't want to know anything. All I want to know is how you are."

"I'm fine, I'm fine. Just thought you wanted to know some other stuff, that's all, and I'm not gonna know anything about that for, for, uh—"

"A week."

"Yeah, right."

"Well . . . in a week, then we'll both know." She turned back to the garlic and resumed dicing it.

"Uh, what we'll know is just the results of this test, that's all. I mean, this is just the first place to start, you know?" Balzic shrugged. "It could be a puzzler . . . that's what the—that's what he said. It could be I'm just gettin' too old—"

"Oh stop it," Ruth said.

"Well . . ."

"Well nothing. Just stop that 'old' business."

"Hey, there's only one way you go, you know? Nobody gets young. Everybody gets old."

"Is that what the doctor said?"

"Yeah . . . among other things." Balzic went to the back door and stared out at some grackles and starlings on the deck. "I know you think I was, uh, I was tryin' to turn this into your fault—"

"You sure as hell were. And I don't deserve that. And I resent it. A lot."

"Well I got—I got a little panicky there—I guess."

"A little!"

"Okay so I got panicked a lot. That—that didn't happen to me—I mean it happened, but not like . . . not like lately."

"It didn't just happen to you. It happened to us. Only you tried to make it into me, my fault, like I forgot how to do what I've done ever since we've been married. No. Like I was purposely not doing what I know how to do. That's the part that gets me about all this. And that's the only part that gets me."

"Look, we all—everybody says things they wish they didn't. Especially when something shakes them up. I got shook. Got rattled. So I said some things. I'm still shook up. I'm—I'm still rattled. I haven't been this rattled in a long time. So—"

Ruth put down the knife and faced him. "Listen, Mario, I'm gonna tell you something. And I don't care whether you get mad or what. But when things go wrong, you start lookin' to accuse somebody. You start pointing fingers, and I don't know whether it's because you're a cop that you do that or whether it's in your nature and that's why you became a cop or what. But it's something you do—but sometimes when you do it to me, it really makes me angry."

"Aw c'mon, Ruth. It's not that simple and I'm not that simple and you know it."

"I know *it's* not that simple. But I also know that the last time we tried and you couldn't, *you* started telling *me* what I was doing wrong. I don't care how complicated you think it is or isn't, but I know that's what happened. Are you gonna say that's not what happened?"

"No." Balzic drank the rest of his wine and went to the refrigerator and poured some more.

"Well, then sometimes you ought to look at where you're pointing your finger, that's all I'm saying."

"I don't want to point it at anybody. I'm not pointing it at anybody. I'm sorry I pointed it at you."

"No you're not. That's another thing you do. You do something wrong and you think if you say you're sorry afterwards that makes it all right."

"Aw Jesus, Ruth."

"No. No aw Jesus Ruth."

"Then what? Whatta you want?"

"All I want right now is to finish gettin' dinner ready. That's all I was trying to do when you walked in."

"Hey," Balzic said, spreading his hands wide. "Then go ahead. I'm not stoppin' you."

"All right. I will."

"Fine." Balzic slouched off toward the living room and dropped into the recliner, where he loosened his tie and sipped his wine in a long, surly silence, punctuated by many long, hurt sighs.

They ate dinner, linguini with scallops, in brittle civility, and Balzic couldn't wait to escape. As soon as he finished one helping, he put his dish in the sink, ran some hot water over it, and announced that he had to leave.

"Uh, you didn't ask so I better tell you," Ruth said as he reached the front door. She was talking to him from the kitchen.

Balzic waited.

"Your mother's not feeling very good."

Oh Christ, Balzic said to himself. He hadn't even noticed that his mother had not eaten with them or that he hadn't seen her since he'd come home.

"What's the matter?"

Ruth shrugged. "I asked her if she wanted to go to the doctor, but she said she just wanted to lay down for a while."

"You think I ought to talk to her about it? I know she never wants to go to the doctor—you think it would help if . . ."

Ruth shook her head no. "Just let her rest. She's just having a bad day, that's all. Go on. Do what you have to. I'll be here."

Balzic nodded and shrugged. "Uh, I can't give you a number where I'm gonna be. I got to talk to some people. I'll try to get back as soon as I can."

"Don't hurry. I'm not going anywhere."

"Yeah. Okay. So . . . I'll see you later."

"All right."

Balzic forced himself to walk out of the house and down to the car, even though every muscle in him was saying, "Run, run, you klutz, before you say something else dumb."

* * *

Balzic drove out Westfield Street to where it became Westfield Drive just over the border, where the city met the township. It was on the crest of a hill and the driveway into the house he was looking for was cut between two rows of hedges that grew so thickly nothing could be seen through them. Once through the hedges, the house was much as Helfrick had described it, three-story, red brick, with a patio at the rear. There was one door in the front of the house, but it struck Balzic that that door was left over from the days when the house was a single residence. Now that it was divided into apartments, it was apparent to Balzic, as soon as he drove far enough along the driveway, that all the tenants used the entrance in the back. That's where all the cars were parked. Straight ahead was the tree Helfrick had described, the one Francis Collier had backed into hard enough to stall his Cadillac. It was a sycamore, its trunk easily three feet in diameter; and even after five months, the wound in the trunk was clearly visible from where a bumper had slammed into it. Well, Balzic thought as he parked his cruiser and got out, at least that part of it's true.

Balzic left his lights on and went and examined the tree, looking at it and rubbing his hand over the indentation, easily three-quarters of an inch deep.

Balzic saw the floodlights come on and heard a door open and then someone approaching him. He started back to his car to turn out his lights.

"Hey," a man called out. "Whatta you doin' there? Whatta you want?"

Balzic shut off the lights and got out his ID case and held it out for the man to see. The man took it. He was short and thick and wore bifocals, and he tilted his head back to read the case and look at the picture and then at Balzic. "Oh oh oh, you're the chief. Hey, I'm Vic Marcelli." He handed the case back and pumped Balzic's hand. "Hy ya doin'. You know, you probably don't remember. We met one time, oh, years ago."

"I remember," Balzic said.

"Yeah, sure, whenever we had to have, uh, when we had to have him committed that time. You remember that, huh?"

Balzic remembered.

Marcelli shook his head. "Cheez, you know, if they'd've done somethin' for him then, who knows, maybe this wouldn't've happened, you know? But they didn't do nothin' for him down in that place. Hey, listen to me. Whatta ya—whatta ya—what's the—" Marcelli held his right hand up expectantly.

"Joey's father asked me to check some things for him."

"Oh oh oh. So that's what you're doin'. Well, hey. Let's go inside. It's gettin' a little nippy out here. You wanna come inside?"

"If you don't mind."

"No, hey, I don't mind. What the hell I mind for?"

"Your wife home?" Balzic asked as he followed Marcelli up onto the concrete patio and then into the small, square vestibule.

"Yeah yeah yeah, she's in here. Sure. Oh oh oh I just remembered. She told me somebody called from the state police says you was gonna come around, but I didn't give it another thought. I didn't know it was gonna be tonight, you know, like right away."

Marcelli unlocked his door and led the way into his apartment. "Hey, Angie, don't come out here without no clothes on, ya hear? We got company." He turned to Balzic. "Just kiddin'.

She don't walk around without her clothes on. I always kid her like that, you know. Uh, so, can I get you somethin'?"

"No, thank you. Just information." Balzic glanced around the apartment. It was furnished in what his wife called "pizza pretentious," based on her observation of what a guy would do to his pizza joint if he suddenly got the idea to call it Giuseppi's Ristorante instead of Joe's Pizza Palace. All the stuffed furniture was covered in a silvery brocade. The table lamps at either end of the couch had aquamarine ceramic bases three feet high and the plum-colored shades had inch-long sparkly fringe. The cream-colored, deep-pile rug was almost hidden by the throw rugs in every color imaginable, from deep purple to blazing orange. There were cut-glass ashtrays on the long, low coffee table that had a top made of ceramic tiles in a geometric pattern resembling a Navajo blanket.

"You sure you don't want nothin'?" Marcelli said. "I got anything you want. Name it. Beer, wine, whiskey, Coke, Pepsi, ginger ale."

"Nothing, thank you."

"Okay. Suit yourself. Sit down, sit down. Hey, Angie, where you at?"

"I'm takin' a bath, okay?" came a distant response.

"Well, she'll be down in a little while. Just takin' a bath there. So." Marcelli dropped onto the couch, motioning for Balzic to sit in a chair that looked like it was supposed to have been made from an old wine barrel. Balzic had seen chairs like it in a cocktail lounge someplace, he couldn't remember where.

"So, is this sorta like unofficial, I mean you said you was workin' for Joey's old man."

"It's unofficial. So you don't have to answer anything."

"Hey, it's no big deal. I'll tell ya whatever. We talked to everybody about this. Cheez, lemme see, there was the state cop, what the hell's his name—"

"Helfrick?"

"Yeah, that's him. He was the first one showed up that time."

"You say he was the first one. Does that mean you talked to other state cops?"

"Oh no no no. He was the only state cop. But then he came back either the next day or maybe the day after and took us up the barracks and he had a secretary there, stenographer, you know, with one of those little machines, and they took our statement there. And then, lemme see, oh, then there was the guys from the DA's office, a detective I think and one, I guess it was an assistant DA, somethin', I forget. Oh, and then his lawyer came out, Collier's, and we spent a long time talkin' with him. And now you. So there you are."

"I see. Well. They're all official, so what you said to them is on the record. What you say to me is not. Is that clear?"

"Well then I don't understand. How can you even do this then?"

"I can do it because I was given permission by the commanding officer of the Criminal Investigation Division of the state police. He did it as a courtesy to me."

"Well, uh, well how come you're doin' it? I mean, what's Joey's old man, I mean, does he have a beef or somethin'?"

"He seems to think so. So, tell me what happened."

"There ain't much to tell. We're gettin' ready to go to sleep, I just came home from the club—"

"What club?"

"Collier's club."

"Collier has a club? What kind? Where?"

"Not anymore he don't. At that time he did, but they got rid of him."

"Who's they?"

"Bunch of doctors from Pittsburgh. They put up this apartment building out here 'bout two miles down the road and they got him to manage it and they also got a club license and he put in a club, private club, after-hours joint, you know, in the basement. So then he hired me to run the kitchen."

"So you worked for Collier at the time?"

"Yeah. Sure."

"Uh, what did you do before that?"

"Before I worked for Collier? I owned my own joint way out on the other end of the township. Bar, restaurant, bowlin' alley. Thirty-five years. Marlanes."

"That was your place? Marlanes. I've been in there, yeah."

"Yeah, I got rid of it. Thirty-five years was plenty. I was all set to go to Florida, then Angie's parents get sick, her mother fell down, broke her hip, broke her leg, then the old man takes a heart attack, and Angie don't wanna go. I said, 'Look, you ain't a nurse. Put 'em in a home.' Christ, she jumped down my throat, so I said then take 'em with us. No, they don't wanna go. They don't wanna get all fussed up with the movin', sellin' their house, and this and that, and I said, Cheez-sus, you know, forget it. So here I am, fifty-five years old, with a pile of money, all dressed up and no place to go."

"So is that when you met Collier, or did you know him from before?"

"Huh? No no no, Angie's sister brought him around. I didn't know him from nowhere."

"So where'd she meet him?"

"Rose? Who knows. Christ only knows where she met him. She's like asphalt. She's everywhere you look."

"But she introduced you, is that it?"

"Yeah. And I told him right away, look, she's my sister-in-law, and don't you ever tell her I said this 'cause it'll get back to my wife and I'll catch holy hell, but, I says, I don't know you and advice is cheap, but, I says to him, do yourself a favor and take a walk and don't look back, 'cause my sister-in-law's a mental case. I told him, squirrels sleep in her head."

"How'd he take that?"

"How d'you think? Walked right in, face first, eyes wide open, didn't see a thing."

"He get upset with you, tell you to mind your own business, go to hell, anything?"

"Him? Nah. Hell no. Couple months later he asked me to go to work for him, run his kitchen."

"Did you ever say anything like that to him again? Did you, for instance, ever tell him about Joey?"

"Hell yes. Half-a-dozen times. I said, look, you don't know these two fruitcakes. I don't know you. You might be goofy as them, I don't know. But I'm tellin' ya, these two are trouble. Let her alone and get out while you can."

"What did he say?"

"Nothin'. He said he was a big boy, he could take care of himself. I said okay, don't say I didn't tell ya. But in the meantime, Angie's gettin' mad at me for stickin' my nose where it don't belong. Angie thinks this guy is gonna straighten Rose out. I said, Angie, ain't nothin' or nobody gonna straighten your sister out 'cause your sister's a macaroni. She got a permanent bend in her. That's the way she was made."

"Well. Okay. So the night it happened, you were workin' in Collier's club?"

"Yeah, but it was Memorial Day weekend. It was dead. There was nothin'. Hell, I closed the kitchen one o'clock. Sat around, I had one drink with Collier, then I come home."

"What time was that?"

"By the time I got home? Quarter after one. I came in, took a shower, had a drink, watched TV for a little while, then I went to bed, watched TV some more."

"Your wife was here?"

"Yeah. Sure."

"Alone?"

"Yeah."

"Did Collier say anything about comin' here, to your sister-in-law's?"

"He came here every night. He didn't say nothin'."

"So it was no surprise to you he was here."

"Hell no. He did everything but move in."

"So he had his own key to her place?"

"I guess. Hell, I don't know. Never came up."

"Did you hear him come in? Did you hear the car?"

"If I did, I didn't pay no attention."

"Did you hear her come in?"

"Nope."

"Okay, so when did you first notice something?"

"When I heard some bumpin' and bangin'."

"What time was that?"

"Oh hell I don't know. I can't say for sure. Must've been around two o'clock. But I can't say for sure 'cause I didn't think to look at the clock. Just heard the noise."

"Where were you?"

"In bed."

"With your wife?"

"Yeah. We was watchin' TV. I took my drink in there, she was doin' a crossword puzzle, I was watchin' a movie, somethin', I don't know what the hell it was."

"Okay. And then what happened?"

"Well, this bumpin' and bangin', you know, then I hear Rose talkin'. Shoutin'."

"Could you hear what she was sayin'?"

"Nah. Just her voice."

"Did you do anything about it?"

"Did I *do* anything? What for?"

"Well did it sound like a fight to you? Did it sound like something you should've checked out? This is your place, right?"

"Oh oh oh I see what you're gettin' at. Hell no, that was just

Rose. That was like that all the time. Hell, once a week, twice a week, sometimes twice a day. See, you gotta understand. Rose should've been a guy. Then she could've been a prize fighter, see, a boxer. 'Cause that's what she wanted to be. Then she would've got paid for it and, who knows, she might've been a champ. But I didn't even think twice about it when I first heard the bumpin' and the bouncin' off the walls."

"You sayin' she fought with Collier too?"

"Oh hell yes. Look. Rose fights with everybody. I told ya, she should've been a guy, then she could've been a boxer instead of a pain in everybody's ass."

"Uh-huh. So when *did* you start to pay attention?"

"When Rose came poundin' on our door. Well I didn't know it was Rose until I went and opened it. But that's the first time I paid any attention."

"So you went to the door and there's Rose. What'd she look like? What'd she say?"

Marcelli shrugged. "Look like? She looked like herself. Whatta ya mean, what'd she look like?"

"Well if what you said about her before is right, if she was fightin' all the time, well, did she ever come over here during any of her other fights?"

"Uhhhhh—no. No, come to think of it, she never did."

"Oh bullcrap," said a short, thin woman in a fuzzy pink robe with a towel wrapped around her hair. She passed by Balzic and said, "Don't believe nothin' he says about my sister. He's prejudiced. He hates her." She disappeared as quickly as she had arrived. In a few moments she was back, holding a glass of milk.

"Uh, Chief, this is my wife, Angie."

"Don't get up, don't get up. I can't stand it when men are courteous to me, I'm so used to my husband."

"Aw, nice, nice, Angie. He don't know you're jokin'."

Angie plopped down beside her husband. "I'm jokin'," she said. "My husband's very courteous to everybody except my sister."

"How do you do," Balzic said.

"Pleased to meet you, I'm sure," Angie said, sipping at her milk. "I know your wife I think. She takes your mother to bingo a lot, doesn't she."

"Yes, she does."

"That's where I know her from. She always looks so good.

She always looks like she just came from, I don't know, you know how people look when they just come from swimmin' or something?"

"What the hell's that supposed to mean?" Vic said.

"She just looks healthy, that's all I'm tryin' to say. Her complexion's so good and she's always tan."

"She lays out on our deck a lot."

"See? I knew it was something'. Me, I lay out in the sun for fifteen minutes I get so dark I could get a job as a token nigger."

Balzic shook his head and laughed.

"C'mon, cut it out, will ya?" Vic said. "You keep talkin' he's gonna think you're nutty as your sister."

"Don't start on her, don't start in on her." Angie leaned forward and said, "You know, if I didn't know better, the way he talks about my sister I'd think he put the make on her one time and she told him to get lost and he's been mad about it ever since."

"Will you listen to yourself? Your sister got a face like a sparrin' partner."

"What difference would that make? You never leave the lights on."

Vic groaned and rolled his eyes upward. "Cheez-sus, Angie, we're talkin' in front of the chief of police here."

Angie grinned mock sweetly and thrust her body back against the couch. She put her arm around her husband's neck. "What do you get for leavin' the lights on, Chief? Thirty days?"

"Angie!"

"He can't stand it when I tease him. Right now I could get anything I want. All I have to do is shut up."

Vic thrust his arms outward and then dropped his hands between his knees and drummed his fingers on the couch. "She never lets up. Rags me to death. Rags me to death. . . ."

"So, uh, where were youse two when I interrupted you?"

"I think we got to where your sister came poundin' on your door and your husband got out of bed and opened it."

"So who do you want to tell you?"

"Either. Both."

"Go 'head, hon. You tell him. I'll just jump in."

Vic stopped drumming his fingers. "Okay. So. I went to the door and there's Rose, lookin' like she always looks."

"No different?" Balzic said. "Even though this is the first time in all her fights she ever came over?"

"She came over lots of times," Angie said.

"What're you talkin' about. She never came over here before that time," Vic said.

"She came over here, hon, lots of times, but you always said you were asleep. I never knew whether you were or not. I think you used to pretend a lot."

Vic made a gurgling sound and wagged his head from side to side. "Pretend. Christ. Well, okay. So I wasn't always asleep. But it was just more of her crap, that's all."

"No no. Don't start."

"Anyway," Vic said, "she come in and says I gotta do somethin'. Joey's beatin' the hell outta Franny, she says. I says so what else is new and she says, no, no, this is different. This time he's beatin' the hell outta him—"

"Wait a second," Balzic said. "Are you sayin' that Joey and Collier fought before?"

"No no no. That's the wrong—that's not what I mean. I didn't mean them two fought before. I meant that, like so what else is new, this is just another fight."

"So as far as you knew Joey and Collier had never fought before, is that right?"

"Yeah. Right. As far as I knew."

"Oh they had words," Angie said. "Coupla times."

"How do you know that? Is that something you saw yourself, or was that something somebody told you?"

"No, I heard them once myself and then Rose told me about another time."

"Did those two times happen here?"

"Well the one time I saw it was here. Out on the patio. And then they almost got into it down Muscotti's. Rose told me about that."

"What were they having words about? Anything specific?"

"Oh yeah. Collier wanted Joey to get off his rear end and take care of the divorce."

"What does that mean exactly?"

"Well, Rose wanted Joey to pay for the divorce so she wanted him to get a lawyer and file all the papers."

"Why didn't she do it?"

"I don't know," Angie said. "She just wanted him to do it. She didn't want to pay for it."

"Didn't she have the money, or was she just trying to make him do it?"

"Oh she had the money. And Collier would've given it to her if she didn't, but she had it. She still had money from the first time they were divorced."

"From the first time who was divorced?"

"Rose and Joey. This was the second time they were married. And they—"

"They were married before?"

"Sure. The first time for almost two years. Then she divorced him and he got stuck with all the bills, which wasn't that much, but I guess it was the principle of the thing with him, he just wasn't gonna go through with it again. He said he didn't care if he never got divorced, that way he'd never be able to get married again, 'cause no matter what else he was, he wasn't no bigamist."

"So your sister was tryin' to make him pay for the divorce and he wasn't goin' for it, is that what you're sayin'?"

"Uh, yeah, more or less."

"No more or less," Vic said. "C'mon, tell the truth. Your sister was tryin' to bust his stones, that's what she was tryin' to do, and you know it. She had the money to take care of the whole thing."

"Vic-tor, don't get start-ed on my sis-ter," Angie sang.

"Could she've paid for the whole thing or not?"

"I just said she could, didn't I?"

"Well if she could pay for it, then what'd she want from him? Huh? She wanted to crush his onions a little bit, that's all." He turned to Balzic. "See, my wife don't wanna believe what a royal pain in the ass her sister is. She don't wanna believe anybody in the whole world is as petty as she is. Her sister I mean."

"Victor, why do you do this about her? Jesus Christ, you'd think she didn't have enough problems."

"Is she screwed up or what, tell the truth. And don't defend her. Just tell the truth."

Angie appealed to Balzic. "My husband cannot understand that I am never gonna say nothing bad about my sister, I don't care what my sister does to anybody. She could murder half the world, I wouldn't care. She's still my sister. I don't have no brothers, and she's the only sister I got."

Vic threw up his hands and let them drop. "How you gonna talk to somebody like this?"

"Victor, you're just jealous 'cause you don't have no brothers or sisters who would do for you what I would do for my sister or what she would do for me."

"What would you do for her that you wouldn't do for me, huh? Or what would she do for you that I wouldn't do for you? C'mon. What what what?"

"You wanna know? Huh? You wanna know one thing?"

"Yeah. Yeah, tell me, c'mon."

"Okay, okay. I'll just tell you one thing. You know when I used to get cramps so bad before I had my hysterectomy? Remember?"

"How can I forget, cheez-sus."

"See? See? That's what she didn't do. She *didn't* roll her eyes and say, 'How can I forget, Jesus'— that is exactly what she did not do."

"So what's she do that was so great?"

"She came over, she talked to me, she'd get the heating pad, she told me put my feet up, she got cold rags for my head, she rubbed my feet with ice cubes, she'd—"

"She rubbed your feet with what?"

"Ice cubes."

"What the hell she do that for?"

"It would just feel different, you know? It would make me think about something beside the roller coaster in my insides, you know? What am I talkin' about, you don't know. Soon as you seen me gettin' out a pad, you'd run for the car, you gotta go to work, you gotta go play golf, you gotta go to the club, you gotta go bowlin', you gotta get a new muffler." She turned to Balzic. "Do you do that to your wife?"

Balzic shrugged. "I probably needed a new muffler once or twice."

"But not every month, right?"

"What can I tell you," Balzic said, shrugging.

"And that's what she did that was so great, rub your feet with ice cubes?"

"What I just say?"

"Well you don't have no periods no more, so what? So what's she do for you since you quit havin' periods?"

"She talks to me, Victor. We talk, you know?"

"Oh, yeah, right, you talk. Big deal. We don't talk?"

"Uh, could we get back to what happened after you let your sister-in-law in?"

"Huh? Oh. Well she came in, all outta joint, and then—"

"Then I got outta bed and came out here and I told him to, Vic I mean, to go stop it—"

"And no way I was goin' out there and stop nothin'. I wasn't gettin' in between that goofy Joey and nobody."

"Yeah. Right. So we got into it—"

"And we're all hollerin' at each other and all I wanna do is go back to bed."

"So how long were you squabblin' in here?"

"Huh? Couple minutes. Five maybe," Vic said.

"Oh it wasn't that long. Two minutes maybe. It wasn't no five minutes."

"And then what?"

"Then boom! We hear a shot."

"One? Just one shot?"

"Yeah."

"Then what?"

"Then I said I'm callin' the cops and she said no you're not and we started in on each other all over again—am I gonna call the cops or ain't I, and round and round, back and forth, Jesus Christ, so I said bullshit, I'm callin' the cops. So I went to the phone and dialed nine-one-one."

"And then what?"

"Then boom boom boom boom boom, one right after the other."

"Five shots?"

"More than that. Six or seven," Angie said.

"I don't know how many it was, five, six, seven. A bunch."

"One right after the other?"

"Yeah. All in a row."

"First you hear one, then you argue whether you're gonna call the cops, then while you're dialin' nine-one-one, you hear a series of shots, is that it? Both of you agree on that?"

Angie nodded several times, and Vic said, "Yeah."

"How much time would you guess passed between the first shot and the rest?"

Vic shrugged. "Thirty seconds maybe. I don't know."

"It was longer than that. A minute at least."

"No it wasn't. What the hell you talkin' about. Jesus. A minute's a long time."

"It was a minute," Angie said. "At least."

"Either one of you hear a car start while this was goin' on?"

"A car? I didn't hear no car."

Angie shook her head.

"Didn't hear a car start or didn't hear it bang into that tree?"

Both shook their heads no.

"Okay, so then what?"

"I went outside," Vic said.

"Yeah, listen to him. We had to practically push you out the door."

"Hey, I didn't wanna go out there. What the hell I wanna go out there for? I ain't no hero. I didn't know who was shootin' or what they was shootin' at."

"But you went out. How long after you heard the shots did you go out?"

Vic shrugged. "Five seconds maybe. Ten the most."

"Is that right, Angie?"

"Yeah, that's about right. We had to push him, but he went finally."

"Did you and your sister go out then?"

"No. Not then. After Vic came back inside we went out."

"Okay, so when you got outside, Vic, what did you see?"

"Uh, I saw the car backed into the tree and Franny standin' by the car."

"Where exactly?"

"He was, like uh, beside the passenger side. Yeah. He was standin' there, the door was open—"

"The passenger door?"

"Yeah."

"Where was he standin' in relation to the door?"

"He was like—it was like he just got outta the car."

"Okay. And then what?"

"Well, I looked at him. He was, uh, he was all bloody."

"Bloody from where, could you tell?"

"Well, he was bleedin' from the top of his head, his forehead, and he had blood all over his face and it was all over his shirt. I couldn't tell if he had any on his coat, he had a dark coat on, but his shirt was white, so the blood was real plain."

"You see anybody else?"

"No. Not right then."

"Okay, go on."

"So I said what's goin' on or somethin'. And he just had this real blank look on his face, like he was lookin' at me but like he didn't even know I was there."

"Was he holdin' a gun?"

"Oh yeah. In his right hand. I seen that right away. That stopped me right in my tracks."

"Did he say anything?"

"Not right away. I asked him again what's goin' on and I think maybe the third time I asked him, he said, 'He's over there.'"

"Did he point or make any move to show where 'over there' was?"

"No, uh-uh. But I couldn't see nothin' so I figured he was over on the other side of the car."

"So then what?"

"So I told him take it easy, take it easy, you know. Then I sorta walked real slow around the car and there he was, face down and he wasn't movin' and I said, 'Oh shit.' Then I came back around the car and I'm sayin', 'Take it easy, take it easy,' 'cause he was lookin' like somethin' outta the twilight zone."

"So then what?"

"Then I come back in here and called nine-one-one and told 'em to get an ambulance up here, a guy was shot."

"And then what? D'you go back outside?"

"Yeah."

"Just you or all three of you?"

"All of us. Well, they went out while I was still callin' the ambulance, then I went out."

"Then what?"

Vic thrust his thumbs upward. "Then? Pretty much nothin'. We just sorta stood around lookin' like a bunch of idiots. Nobody knew what to do."

"Anybody go over to Joey?"

"Rose did," Angie said.

"Nobody else?"

"Well I started to, but Vic grabbed me, told me to stay out of it."

"So you two were standin' on the porch, is that it?"

Both nodded.

"What did Rose do?"

"She just went around the car and I guess she bent down 'cause I couldn't see her for a little while. Then she came back around the car and went up to Franny."

"He hadn't moved? He was still standin' where he was when you came out?"

"I think maybe he shut the door—"

"Nah, he didn't shut the door," Vic said. "He didn't shut the door till the state cop showed up."

"Oh he was here real fast. Four, five minutes."

"And while you were standin' on the porch, Rose was talking to Collier?"

"She wasn't just talkin'. She was tryin' to wipe his face. He kept pullin' his head back. Then she came away from him and come up on the porch, and I asked her if she was all right."

"What did she say?"

"Nothing. She never said a word."

"How did she look to you?"

"Numb. She just looked numb."

"And then the state cop got here, right?"

"Right," Vic said.

"Did you hear any conversation between Collier and the cop?"

"All I heard him say was, 'I surrender.' He said it a couple times. And then the cop came over to him and took the pistol offa him."

"And then the ambulance got there?"

"Yeah, right."

"And in all that time Rose didn't say nothing to either one of you?"

"Not a word."

"First time in her life she ever been speechless," Vic said.

"Then what happened?"

"Rose went inside. And then after the ambulance left, the cop started—no, wait. Then Rose came back out and she took our car, yeah, she asked Angie for the keys and said she was gonna take Franny to the emergency room."

"Did she do that?"

"Far as I know," Angie said.

"And then you talked to the cop?"

"Right. He asked us some questions and then he told us we had to go to the barracks the next day, ten o'clock I think it was, and had to give statements in front of a secretary. And we had to sign 'em."

"So, uh, what about this fellow, Ralph Gioia? Where was he during all this?"

"Upstairs. In his apartment I guess."

"You never saw him?"

"Not until we got through talkin' to the cop. We were gettin' ready to go inside, that's when he showed up."

"He lives on the second floor?"

"Yeah. He's got the apartment above Rose."

"Anybody in the apartment above you?"

"Us. That's our second floor. We don't rent that out."

"So who's on the third floor?"

"That's the teacher. What the heck's her name?"

"Cooper. Joellen Fitzgerald Cooper. That's what's printed on her checks."

"And she lives up there by herself?"

"Yeah."

"She had company that night?"

"Hell I don't know," Vic said.

"The state cop said there was a car here he couldn't account for."

"There's a guy comes around," Angie said. "I've seen him a bunch of times, but I never paid any attention to him. It's her boyfriend probably."

"Did you see him that night?"

"No. But if the cop said there was another car here, it was probably his. But don't ask what kind it is 'cause I don't know."

"It's a Chevy," Vic said. "She got one of those little Jap cars and he got a little Chevy. Not the real little one, not that there Chevette. A Citation I think it is."

"Uh, does she have a window that looks out on the parking lot?"

"Two of 'em."

"Okay. Listen, I don't wanna keep you any longer. I want to thank you both. I appreciate your takin' the time to talk to me. You've been very helpful."

"Hey, no problem. You want anything else, just come on up, give us a call."

"Is your sister at home now?"

"Nah. She's workin'."

"Where?"

"She's waitin' tables for Collier."

"I thought you said he didn't run that club anymore."

"Nah, this is another joint. Roadhouse on the way to Pittsburgh."

"She work every night?"

"Except Mondays and Tuesdays."

"Uh-huh. D'you know if Gioia's home now?"

"He's probably out cattin' around. You could check."

"I'll do that. Thanks again."

Vic Marcelli let Balzic out and they said good night, but just as Marcelli started to step back into his apartment, Balzic called him back.

"Uh, what about this Collier?"

"What about him?"

"What kind of guy is he?"

Marcelli shrugged and frowned. "I don't know what to tell ya. I worked for the guy, but I don't know that much about him. We were never what you'd call buddies. Don't ask me why. He run the club and I run the kitchen. I'd have a drink with him when we'd be closin' up, but I never spent a whole lot of time with him."

"Well, what did he do, when he wasn't workin'?"

"Oh, you mean like that? He was always in court."

"He was what?"

"In court."

"You mean he had legal problems?"

"No no no. No, he used to watch the trials all the time. You know how some people do. Some people go to the trials instead of goin' to the movies."

"He do that all the time?"

"Yeah. I mean, I don't know what else he did. He never talked about nothin' else. He never talked much about that either, but if he talked about anything, that was what he talked about. And, wait. Come to think of it, he belonged to a couple cop organizations. You know, like the sheriff's auxiliary and the FOP. Like that?"

Balzic nodded and grunted and said good night, and then he went up one flight of stairs that obviously was part of the original house before it was partitioned into apartments. Though the partitioning had been neatly done, all the materials were of recent manufacture, making the stairs look out of place, older and more decrepit than they were. There was a narrow hallway leading back to the only door on that floor, and Balzic went to it and knocked. He could hear music from a stereo, rock and roll, and he had to knock several times before the door was jerked open.

A muscular man in his early thirties, wearing only a pair of slacks and carrying a bottle of shaving lotion, eyed Balzic warily. "Yeah?"

Balzic held up his ID case.

The man squinted at it, and said, "What's the problem?"

"You Ralph Gioia?"

"Yeah. What's the problem?"

"No problem. I'd like to talk to you about a shooting that happened in the parking lot on June—"

"Hey, I told everybody in the world about that already."

"I'm sure you have, but I'd like you to tell me. Okay if I come in?"

"Listen, I got a date, I should've been on the road five minutes ago. Do I have to talk to you?"

"No. You don't *have* to talk to me. I'd just appreciate it very much if you would."

"Well if I can get dressed while we talk, okay. C'mon in." That said, Gioia rushed away to turn off the stereo on his way into another room. In a moment he was back, carrying shoes, socks, a shirt, and sport coat. "Whatta you wanna know?"

"Anything you can tell me."

"Hey, it was a fight between two guys, one of 'em had a gun, end of fight."

"I'd like you to be a little more specific than that."

"What for? Joey Case was an asshole. He was born an asshole and he died an asshole. In between he lived like an asshole. If it wasn't this guy it would've been some other guy." He continued to dress as he spoke.

"That may be true, but I'd still like something more specific about the way he died."

"Look, I told everything I know to a state cop, a county detective, an assistant DA, and some lawyer, at least twice to every one of those people. Is this official business or what? 'Cause if is isn't, I got a date with this chick I been tryin' to scheme on for about a month and I really don't wanna appear too anxious, you know, but in the meantime I don't wanna be too cool either, so, uh, is this official, did you say or what?"

"No, it's not official, but—"

"Well, then I got to tell you. I already did my bit as a citizen and I'm gonna have to testify and all that number, so I'm gonna pass on this. All I'm gonna say is this. Joey Case was three years ahead of me in school, and as long as I can remember he was forever lookin' to get his ass kicked, and he finally got it kicked all the way, and from where I stand, that means there's just one less asshole in the world, you know? And that's all it means to me, 'cept I got to do my duty because he got his lunch where I live. So, uh, maybe some other time, okay?" Gioia went to the door and held it open for Balzic.

"When?"

"Aw come on, man, I gotta go, I can't make appointments."

"Okay, okay. I'll catch you some other time."

"Fine, right." Gioia waited for Balzic to leave, then made sure his door would lock behind him, and hustled past Balzic and down the steps.

Balzic watched with a mixture of irritation and envy as he left. He was upset that he'd gotten so little out of Gioia—he hadn't even looked through Gioia's windows to see how the parking lot looked from there—and he was more than a little envious to see a young man so eager to be off to meet a woman. The envy surprised him. He smelled the aftershave that hung in the narrow hallway and he suddenly wondered why he had never worn aftershave lotion for more than a day or two after he'd received some as a gift. And he thought about Gioia wearing a gold chain around his neck and not wearing a tie. Balzic had worn a tie every day of his working life for so long he couldn't say, but seeing Gioia without a tie and with a necklace disturbed Balzic for reasons he could not decipher. This was all nonsense, Balzic thought; some men had been wearing what had seemed to be feminine jewelry for years. There was a college student who worked last summer in city hall who had three earrings in his right ear and two in his left. They weren't rings exactly; they were small jewels, fakes probably, on posts pierced through his lobes. He was a nice enough kid, polite, conscientious, nothing remotely effeminate about him, and the sight of him had not disturbed Balzic in the least. Yet here Balzic was, standing in this dimly lit hallway, trying to explain to himself why the sight and smell of Gioia had evoked this anger and envy.

"This is crap," he said aloud and forced himself up the steps to the door on the third floor.

He had to knock only once. The door was pulled open quickly and then came a muffled gasp from a woman who immediately shut the door and fixed a chainlock to it. After a moment, the door opened as far as the chain stretched.

Balzic held up his ID case and said, "I'd like to talk to you about a man who was shot to death. In the parking lot? About five months ago?"

"I've already talked to the police about that. Some attorneys, several people. . . ."

Balzic waited. He thought it might work to force her to speak by saying nothing. Some people became unnerved when they had to look at a person who stared at them without speaking.

"I don't know what I can tell you that I haven't already told them. . . ."

Balzic could see from the narrow rectangle of her face that her makeup was fresh. Because of the way she threw open the door at Balzic's knock, she was clearly expecting someone.

"I didn't tell them anything because I don't know anything. . . . Are you just going to stand there and stare at me?"

"I'd like to come in and see what you can see from your windows."

"I just told you. I told everybody I didn't see anything. Are you sure—how do I know your identification is real?"

Balzic pushed his ID case through the opening. "Look at the picture. If that doesn't satisfy you, you can call my station and ask them what I look like."

She took the case and studied the picture and then Balzic's face. After a moment, she closed the door, undid the chainlock, and held the door open. "I guess it's all right." She handed the ID case back.

Balzic stepped into a very neat, modestly furnished living room. Along the walls were many bookcases, filled mostly with paperbacks. There were stacks of papers on a low coffee table, and Balzic could see an open grade book. The woman, thirtyish, wearing a full skirt, a high-necked long-sleeved blouse, and low-heeled shoes, backed into the center of the room and folded her arms. Her straight hair was cut short, and except for her makeup which seemed excessive—she wore heavy blue shading on her upper eyelids and bright red lipstick—she looked like many teachers Balzic had seen. She wore no jewelry, only a wristwatch.

"May I see the windows, please?"

"There's one there," she said, nodding to one on Balzic's right, "and there's another in the bedroom. Through the door."

Balzic went to both and saw that the parking lot below was plainly visible through both of them. In the bedroom he noticed the position of the double bed: a person would have had to take no more than two steps after getting out of bed to see through the window. With the floodlights on at the corners of the house, all the cars were easily seen and so was the tree into which Collier had backed his car. Near the bed, a small table was stacked high with magazines.

Balzic went back into the living room where the woman was still standing, her feet together, her arms locked across her chest.

"You're Miss, uh, did you say your name?"

"No. I didn't say. It's Cooper."

"Uh, Miss Cooper, what do you do?"

"Why?" She shifted her weight onto the heel of her left foot and raised the toe of her right.

"Just curious."

"I don't think it's any of your business what I do. Am I being investigated for something?"

"No. What would make you think that?"

"Well if I'm not being investigated, why do you care what I do?"

"I told you. Just curiosity."

"Well I don't see that I have to satisfy your curiosity."

"You, uh, don't mind if I make some guesses?"

"About what?"

"About what you do."

She closed her eyes and bit her lower lip and then raised her brows and opened her eyes and began to rock on her left heel and right toe. "Is this official police business, what you're doing?"

"In a way."

"What way? Specifically, if you don't mind."

"I've been asked by the father of the victim to confirm the investigation made by the state police. I've gotten authorization from the commanding officer of the state police Criminal Investigation Division to do that. His name is Lieutenant Johnson. You're free to call him to verify that if you want. I'll give you his number."

She thought that over for a moment, still rocking on her heel and toe. "Why does the—why do the state police need to have their investigation confirmed? Are they incompetent?"

"Father of the victim thinks so."

"I would imagine that the parents of many victims think the

police are incompetent. Some parents think anybody who deals with their children is incompetent."

"Like teachers maybe?"

"What's that supposed to mean?"

"Just means you're probably a teacher."

She turned quickly and sat on the front half of an overstuffed rocking chair. "How long do I have to listen to you speculate about who I am and what I do—do I have any recourse?"

"You could just tell me. Then I wouldn't have to guess."

"What purpose would be served? I did not witness the—I did not see it, I did not hear it, I don't know anything about it, and I have repeated that many times to various policemen and lawyers. What possible difference could it make to you to know anything at all about me personally?"

"You didn't hear it?"

"Please don't try to change the subject."

"I can understand if you say you didn't see it, but you didn't hear it? Why would you say that? The guy got shot with a thirty-two caliber handgun. That makes some noise. That's not like a BB gun goin' off. Up here on the third floor, you're no more than thirty-five, forty feet from where it happened. You had to hear it. Why would you say you didn't?"

She took a moment to respond. "I'm sure that in your line of work persistence is a—a necessary thing, but I find it offensive, and unless you can give me a very good reason why I should even be talking to you, I'm—"

"You want a reason, I'll give you a reason. I'll give you a damn good reason, lady. There was somebody here with you that night. Right here. And that—"

"That's preposterous. That's absurd."

"Oh yeah?" Balzic had been standing in the center of the room. Now he went over until he was a step away from her. He bent from the waist and put his hands on his knees and stared coolly at her. "Preposterous, huh? Absurd, huh? You know what I say to that, lady? I say bullshit."

She jumped up and quickly put some distance between them. "I beg your pardon! You have no right to use that kind of language with me! You think that because you're a chief of police in this provincial little . . ."

Balzic straightened himself and closed the distance between them. "You know what, lady? You dress like a teacher, you talk like a teacher, you get indignant like a teacher. You're a teacher. Am I right or not?"

"What is this idiotic game you're playing?" She backed away.

"You a teacher or not? Yes or no?"

"Yes. I'm a teacher. So what!"

Balzic shrugged and walked to the center of the room. "Hey, I'm just checkin' myself out, that's all. Some people guess what other people weigh. I guess what people do."

"I do not understand this conversation. What is going on here?"

"You had somebody with you that night, Miss Cooper. And you're defensive as hell about it. And I don't know why. If you got nothin' to hide, why're you actin' like you do? Or do you want me to keep on guessin'?"

"Listen, you. You just listen. If I've done something illegal, then I want you to say what it is, right now. This minute. And if you can't say that, then you leave. This instant! I will not be badgered like this."

"Something illegal, huh? How about withholding evidence? How about obstructing justice? In plain language, how about tryin' to say there was nobody here who saw what happened—how about that, when both of us know there was somebody here. Know how I know? His car was here. At least two people observed that little fact. Wanna tell me who was here?"

She stomped past him to the door and pulled it open. "You are no longer welcome in my residence. Please leave. Now."

Balzic threw up his hands and let them fall against his thighs. "Miss Cooper, a very sick old man had his only son shot to death practically under your nose. This old man's wife, the victim's mother, is in pretty bad shape over all this. The state cop who investigated and who is the prosecuting officer has made a couple of serious mistakes. What I'm tryin' to tell you is, right now, the case is pretty much a dog. Weak, in other words. And what I think is, the case could use a good eyewitness. Now, I don't wanna mislead you into thinkin' that eyewitness testimony is very good. It isn't. Truth is, eyewitness testimony is very unreliable. Truth is, the more cops and judges learn about eyewitness testimony, the less they tend to rely on it. But in this particular shooting, there's a time element that needs to be straightened out. Why don't you close the door and I'll try to explain it to you."

"I don't want you to explain it to me. I want you to leave. I don't believe you when you say I have done something illegal. I want you to get out of here now!"

Balzic approached her slowly. "Miss Cooper, it will take me about an hour to find out where you work. Now I know that there are only two reasons why a teacher can be fired in this state. One's incompetence, which is practically impossible to prove, and the other one's moral turpitude. The reason I know this is I've had to prosecute a couple teachers. So, what I'm tryin' to tell you is, you better think about what you're tryin' to hide. And I think you better talk it over with the person who was here that night. And I want you to know that if you two don't talk to me voluntarily, I'm gonna find out where you work and I'm gonna go there and I'm gonna ask a whole lot of very insinuating questions about your moral behavior."

"You—you scum!"

"Scum? Hey, not quite, you know? I'm not, uh—sometimes I don't feel real, real good about what I have to do, but that doesn't usually stop me from doin' it. And if I don't hear from you in a couple of days, I'm gonna do what I said. Give it some thought. Talk to your friend. Good night."

Balzic hurried out and down the stairs before she could say anything else. By the time he got to the second-floor landing he'd convinced himself that she was by that time on the phone complaining to the state police about him. By the time he got to the first floor, he was positive she was phoning the mayor to complain. Out in the parking lot, he was sure she was searching for the home numbers for the district attorney and the president judge, and if she was, he growled mentally, she had every right. That was the meanest, most miserably inept interview of a witness he'd ever heard—and he'd been listening to himself. If somebody needed a textbook case of how to turn a witness into an enemy all they needed to do was write a transcript of what he'd just done. Threatening a woman teacher, for crissake. . . . He fell into his cruiser and took his glasses off and rubbed his closed eyes until he started to see colors.

"Threaten a goddamn teacher about her job," he said under his breath. "What in the fuck are you thinkin' about?" You need a witness, he thought, and what do you do? You get pissed off—jealous—because a guy won't talk to you because he has a date. You browbeat a woman, threaten her, because she won't admit she was with a man. She doesn't understand the conversation, and you're telling her you guess what people do. As an interview, that belonged in a carnival. . . .

Balzic started the engine, put it in gear, and drove around the tree and backed out toward Westfield Drive. He had to jam the brakes to avoid colliding with a car that was turning into the drive. The other car skidded to a halt, its front bumper inches from Balzic's cruiser. Balzic put it in reverse and back up far enough for the other car to get around him. The other car eased forward around him; the driver, a man, waved sheepishly as he passed, and disappeared around the back of the building.

Balzic thought for a moment, climbed out, and hustled back to the rear of the house in time to see a man in a dark suit going inside. Balzic looked at the car in the floodlights. It was a gray Chevrolet Citation. He walked behind it, took out his notebook, and copied the license number. He glanced up to the third floor window in time to see Joellen Cooper step back quickly out of sight.

He went back to his cruiser and called his station and told Desk Sergeant Joe Royer to run the license through the state motor vehicles computer to get a name and address for the owner.

About a minute later, Royer called back.

"Mario, that's a Chevrolet Citation, 1982, four-door sedan, gray, owner John Paul Itri, as in ivy, tiger, roger, ivy. Date of birth June 1, 1945. Address box six, five, zero, Millerdale-Knox Road, Rocksburg, RD 10. No priors, no warrants."

"Okay, Joe, thank you. Out."

Okay, Balzic said to himself, now we're getting somewhere. Millerdale-Knox Road, if he remembered it correctly, was about six miles out into Westfield Township, very near the borough of Knox. He took a county map out of the case attached to the sun visor and found the road. Fifteen minutes later, he was driving on it, aiming his spotlight at mailboxes on posts at roadside. He found box 650 and turned into the driveway of a split-level brick and wood house with a two-car garage on the lowest level.

He bounded up the steps and rang the bell. Moments later, the red steel door was opened by a woman with dyed blonde hair—her roots were showing—wearing a black, pin-striped suit, coat and slacks, with a white blouse, under the collar of which hung the ends of a burgundy bow tie. The woman peered intently at Balzic with eyes the color of robins' eggs and her gaze was so direct that Balzic had to look away for a second to collect himself.

"Well," she said, "are you going to say something?"

"Oh. Yes. Uh, I'm here to see—is this the Itri residence?"

"Yes."

"Mr. Frank Itri?"

"No."

"I don't understand," Balzic said.

"I don't either."

"Uh, you said this was the Itri residence."

"It is. But there's no Frank Itri here. Never was. Not as long as I've been here. And I've been here as long as Mr. Itri's been here, and unless he's not telling me something, his name's not Frank."

"Well, uh, this is box 650, Millerdale-Knox Road, right?"

"That's right," she said, smiling quizzically.

"Rocksburg, RD 10?"

"Right again."

"Uh, does your husband—it is your husband, the Mr. Itri you're talkin' about?"

"He's my husband, right again."

"Uh, does he sell fleet insurance for trucks, buses?"

"No, he does not. That's one wrong. Got any more?"

"He got a brother named Frank?"

"Two wrong. You were doing very well there for a while. Got any more?"

"I'm confused," Balzic said. "Why would a guy give me an address with the same last name and, I don't understand this at all. You sure your husband doesn't sell insurance."

"Dear man, you don't know how I wish he did. But he doesn't. No, sir. My husband's a soldier in the war against ignorance."

"Uh, I beg your pardon?"

"My husband's a school teacher. And before you ask, because I don't want you to get anything else wrong—you look like you might take it too hard—my husband's name is John. John Paul Itri. Not a 'Frank' in the bunch."

"Uh, no brothers named Frank either I guess, huh?"

"We've already been over that one."

"Oh. Well. I guess somebody's tryin' to pull my leg. But why would anybody do that?"

"I'm sure I don't know."

"You don't sell insurance, by any chance?" Balzic said, grinning broadly.

"Now do I look like an insurance salesman?"

"Matter of fact, uh, no."

"I should hope not."

"Uh, if you did, I'll bet you'd be a good one."

"Uh-huh. I think—I think the game's over now."

"What game?"

"Whatever one you're playing. Good night." She shut the door quickly and, just as quickly, opened it again. "Just so we're both clear about this, if I don't hear your car leave in about ten seconds, I'm going to call the police." She shut the door.

Okay, Balzic thought. Okay. So now we have a little bit more here. He hurried down to his cruiser and drove off with two seconds to spare, thinking that sometimes he could still do it, sometimes he could still ask the right questions the right way and even, in praise of St. Holy Patrolman, plant a good crop of doubt. All was not lost just yet.

He drove back to Rocksburg wondering why he was thinking lately so much of winning and losing. He thought he'd left that behind long ago. All that adolescent crap about winners and losers had annoyed him even when he was an adolescent. And any residue of it that might have survived otherwise, had been destroyed forever the moment on Iwo Jima when he saw a Marine younger than himself blown apart by a howitzer shell, his head and torso alive down to his pelvis, his eyelids fluttering, his mouth and jaws working to form sounds that did not come, his life bubbling and spurting out onto the black ash from where his legs had been. . . . What the hell was all this stuff about winning and losing, this scorekeeping?

He drove around Rocksburg until he could no longer deny it: he was afraid to go home.

He went to Muscotti's.

The bar was empty except for a lone figure at the end and for Fat Bobby, the bartender Dom Muscotti hired when he was too irritable to work at night himself. Six or seven students from the county community college sat around two tables they had pushed together.

Balzic walked to the end of the bar and took the stool next to Mo Valcanas, who was staring somberly at a double-shot glass full of clear liquid, probably gin. Valcanas acknowledged his presence with a glance and a feeble wave.

Fat Bobby followed Balzic down the bar and asked what he wanted. Fat Bobby once weighed two hundred and fifty pounds. He weighed a hundred pounds less now and had for five years, ever since he was told by a doctor that he was going to die if he didn't lose weight. The fat was gone but the nickname stayed.

"Did Dom open any good wine or do you just have that bar shit?"

"Dom's sick," Fat Bobby said. "He didn't open nothin' today."

"What's wrong with him?"

"Cold, flu, somethin', I don't know."

"Gimme a draft." He nudged Valcanas with his elbow. "You want something?"

"Huh? Oh. Yes. A woman who doesn't want to get even and a man whose car was rear-ended by a Brinks truck, whose driver was drunk, and whose license had been suspended."

"I mean a drink."

"I just got one."

Fat Bobby put a glass of beer in front of Balzic. "You still runnin' a tab here?"

"No, I'll pay for this." Balzic put some bills on the bar. "Dom's gettin' too much noise from the state."

Fat Bobby took a dollar, rang it up, and brought Balzic the change. He went to the other end of the bar and looked out the window at the street.

"Uh, so how's it goin', Mo?"

"Don't call me that," Valcanas said evenly.

"Sorry. Panagios," Balzic shrugged. "So how *is* it goin'?"

"Well, I sincerely would like to have a guy in a wheelchair get pushed into my office who said he was just sitting at this intersection when a Brinks truck plowed into him . . . that's an old lawyer's fantasy. I mean it's an old fantasy of mine. I think I could negotiate a reasonable retirement for myself out of that one."

"What was this other thing you said—a woman who doesn't want to get even?"

"Amen. With the settlement from the Brinks company I could pursue my search for the perfect woman—and I don't give a fuck what she looks like—all I ask is that she doesn't want to get even."

"Seems reasonable."

"Most reasonable thing there is. Old Ziggy Freud said that he didn't know what women wanted. He should've asked me. I could've told him. Women want to get even."

"Okay. I'll bite. For what. With who?"

"With *whom*. With *whom*."

"Uh-huh. Okay. With whom?"

"With men. Who else?"

"For what?"

"For what? For all the bullshit they've put up with. For all the bullshit up with which they have put."

"Uh, correct me if I'm wrong, but, uh, you've been doin' divorces, right?"

"Oh Christ, I can't believe that is what I was put here for. Listen to this one. This woman, she's thirty-nine years old, five feet three, a hundred and sixty pounds, married to the same guy since she was eighteen, and what the hell do you think? Huh?"

Balzic shrugged. "So?"

"So she's been readin' all these feminist books and magazines. All of a sudden, she believes she should be having multiple orgasms. I said to her, 'Madam, is your husband a good provider?' She nods her head yes. I ask her all the standard stuff, does he beat you, does he take care of the children, blah blah blah, and then I ask her, straight out, if, since her desire is to divorce her husband and to pursue this dream of multiple orgasms, whether she had, in fact, ever had any orgasms. The answer, of course, is no. She has not. So I look her in the eye, I fix her with my most professional stare, and I say to her, 'Madam, why do you think God gave you hands?' She was, of course, nonplussed."

"She was what?"

"Speechless. She looked at me as though I were fucking demented. So I asked her, 'Madam, have you ever heard people say that half the world goes to sleep hungry?' And she said that she had heard that. And then I said, 'Do you know what the other half goes to bed doin'?' And she shook her head no. So I told her, 'Madam, the other half goes to bed masturbatin'.' And she looks at me like I'm three-headed, with four eyes in each head. The woman is thirty-nine years old and I say to her, 'In all these books you're reading, does it ever tell you in any one of them how to make love alone?' The woman doesn't know what the hell I'm talkin' about."

Balzic took a sip of beer and scratched his head. "Uh, d'you really tell all this to this woman or you makin' this up?"

"Makin' it up? Of course I'm makin' it up. That's just what I wanted to say to her, but, Christ, I didn't say it. I'm not that drunk."

"Well Jesus, you had me goin' there for a second, but I figured that was pretty goddamn bizarre even for you."

"What the hell's bizarre about it? Somebody ought to say that to her. If she doesn't know how to get herself off, how's she supposed to show her husband how to do it? And if she can't show him, then what the hell's the point of divorcin' him? All she's gonna do is tie herself up with another belly-banger—if she can find one—and then she's back where she started, except her ex-husband's got a pile of new debts. And what happens to the kids in the meantime? Christ, if all I wanted to do was split people up and collect the fee, I'd go someplace where the husbands had money and the wives knew how to use a camera."

"I didn't know you had this thing about savin' the family."

"Oh savin' the family my ass." Valcanas drank half the clear liquid in front of him. "You know, until a couple of years ago, before the county got the two new judgeships, I spend a lot of time as a master in divorce and custody suits. Christ, that was the most depressing thing I've ever done. All those goddamn three-piece brief-casers marchin' in there, and I'd take 'em aside and tell 'em, 'Look, who the hell's gonna pay for this? How's the man supposed to afford a separate residence and still support the kids on his wages?' And they'd give me this crap about mental cruelty and abuse and whatever, and I'd say, 'Just how much abuse d'you think there's gonna be when he finds out he's broke all the time, when he's workin' full time and can't even afford a few beers now and then?' I'd tell 'em, 'Jesus Christ, sometimes you have to consider the social scheme of things here, you can't see every goddamn thing in terms of your won and lost record.' Hell, it was nothin' but wasted words. . . ."

"Jesus," Balzic said, shaking his head, "all this because of one overweight lady who doesn't know how to satisfy herself?"

Valcanas scratched the end of his nose and said nothing.

"Say, listen, uh, didn't you do some work for Joey Case?"

Valcanas nodded. "Several times too many."

"How well'd you know him?"

Valcanas shrugged. "How well does anybody know anybody in this world?"

"Yeah, but I mean, was he pretty straight with you?"

"Nah. Christ, he was never straight with anybody. He had a lot of problems, that boy. He did a lot of weird things. You know what he did one time—and I know this is true because I talked to the doctor who had to straighten it out. That crazy bastard, he had hemorrhoids, and I guess they were givin' him a lot of pain. So he heard somewhere that they were varicose veins, so he thought all that meant was that there was too much blood in 'em, that all the blood was backed up or pooled up or something. Hell only knows what he thought. But anyway, he thought all he had to do was let the blood out and everything would be fine."

"Oh no," Balzic groaned.

"Oh yes. He got a mirror and a razor blade and opened 'em up."

Balzic shuddered convulsively.

"Yeah. And then the sonofabitch put on a sanitary napkin and tried to walk around like that. He was tellin' me about it right in here. Dom and Vinnie were behind the bar and I was sittin' right where I am now, and he was standin' there at the end of the bar. He told us and then he said, 'Hey, I got the rag on, just like a broad. I'm finally havin' a period.' He said, 'I always wondered what a period felt like.' He said, 'It ain't so bad.' Christ, you should've seen the look on Vinnie's face. Dom's standin' there, you know, he's just starin' at him. But Vinnie, Christ, I thought Vinnie was gonna faint."

"D'you believe him?"

"Hell no, I just thought it was one of his stories. But about three days later he called me from the hospital to bring some money and pay his bill, or they weren't gonna let him out. They'd chased him too many times before."

"You paid his bill?"

"No, no, I didn't pay it. It was *his* money. Everytime he got a couple hundred ahead he'd ask me to put it in my safe. He didn't trust banks and he didn't want his wife to know he had it so I'd hold it for him, 'cause if somebody didn't hold it for him, he'd go through it in one day instead of one week."

"So the hospital confirmed it?"

"Yeah. After he left here, he went to the Sons of Italy and he just keeled over, and somebody called an ambulance and, hell, the blood was just pourin' out of him. He had to have three units of blood. Imagine. Oh yeah, I stopped in the emergency room before I paid his bill, all these nurses kept walkin' in and lookin' at me, you know, like, this man is *your* friend?"

"Christ, you mean he lost three pints of blood?"

Valcanas nodded. "You know when I got in his room, the first thing he said to me? Honest to Christ, these were the exact words. He said, 'Well, it almost worked.' Yeah. 'It *almost* worked.' Jesus, what a piece of work he was."

"Oh God," Balzic said, "d'you hear about the time he was in the Columbus Club—I heard this from Harry Lynch. Lynch was in there off duty, and he hears this argument and looks over just in time to see this guy pop Joey in the jaw. Hit him so hard he lifted him off his feet. Lynch said Joey was airborne for about two feet backwards, and then he went down on his can and slid another couple of feet right under a pinball machine. Lynch goes over and identifies himself to the puncher and here comes Joey staggerin' up to this guy and he says, 'Shit, if that's all the harder you can hit, you don't wanna fight me.' Meanwhile, Lynch says Joey's lower jaw's moved over about an inch. His jaw was broken on both sides. And here's the topper. Lynch said he and the puncher was standin' there and Joey takes both hands and tries to shove his bones together. Hospital had to fix that one, too."

Valcanas kept nodding his head. "Yeah. That's him. That's him." Valcanas squinted as though trying to recall something. "You know, I've dealt with so many screwy people that very little surprises me, but none of them was as screwy as he was. I could just never make any real sense with him, either to him or in my own mind about him. I worked everything from divorce to incorporation to burglary, theft, embezzlement, God knows how many D and D's, bankruptcy, Jesus. As far as I know he was never indicted for murder, arson, or molesting children, but otherwise, you name it, I worked it for him. And the toughest one was gettin' him out of Mamont after his old lady had him committed there, before the Mental Health Act in '74?"

Balzic nodded.

"I had to prove that he was sane. To that goddamn funeral director—what was his name?"

"Moseby—was that the one?"

"Yeah, that fat ass. His name was Moskowicz. Stupid Polock tried to tell everybody he was English. He had a face like a ham and an IQ to match. Can you imagine tryin' to explain to that pile of protoplasm that Joey wasn't nuts? Purely in terms of argument that was the hardest I ever worked in my life."

"I thought there were three people on that board," Balzic said.

"There were supposed to be three. One of 'em was laid out in Moseby's funeral home at the time. I don't remember where the other one was. Probably drunk."

"So what'd you say?"

"Hell, what I said didn't matter. That fat ass didn't understand anything I said. I finally got him to agree to go to my brother's house and showed him all the work Joey'd done. He'd just put in all new duct work, rebuilt the kitchen, built a porch and a patio, and I said a crazy man could not build all that. A man could not do all those calculations, buy the material, do all the labor, and still be considered such a danger that he needed to be locked up. That, he understood. Christ, imagine having to convince a shit like Moseby that you're not nuts. And all the while I'm thinking, if there's anybody in this world who's nuts it's Joey. I mean, the one thing didn't have a goddamn thing to do with the other. I'm trying to persuade Moseby to turn Joey loose and I'm trying to convince myself that Joey ought to be turned loose. And the only thing I had goin' for me was that I knew nobody down at Mamont was doin' a damn thing for him except makin' sure he didn't escape. 'Course, that was the system we had then."

"It isn't much better now," Balzic said.

"Oh I know, I know. Theoretically it is—"

"Not in practice. The only way you get somebody committed now is if he's a danger to himself or to others," Balzic said, mimicking the speech he'd been hearing at the Conemaugh Mental Health Clinic since 1974. "Naturally, they don't take your word for that at four o'clock in the morning. You gotta bring the crazy back when there's a psychiatrist there who can evaluate him. Take him up there the next day, and the shrink's secretary says maybe he can evaluate your guy in five or six weeks—if they get some cancellations. So what the hell."

"It's still better than it used to be." Valcanas motioned for Fat Bobby to refill their drinks. After Fat Bobby had done so, Valcanas said, "You know, I used to think about insanity and the law a lot. When I was young. I used to fantasize about writing a brief, or arguing a case that would drain that swamp. You know, one blinding burst of legal insight that would put my name up there, Christ I don't know, the Valcanas Rule instead of the M'Naghten Rule." Valcanas snorted and shook his head. "I actually used to think about bullshit like that."

"Hey, who knows? Maybe you will," Balzic said, smiling.

"Get serious for crissake. Talk about the law and you're already half-bagged on rollerskates. Throw psychiatry into it and you're half-bagged on rollerskates on a frozen pond in the springtime and the ice is startin' to crack. Right now in this state, if you're charged with murder and you can prove you were under the influence of alcohol, it has to be considered a mitigating factor. Right now in this state, you get stopped because you're driving erratically and you're so drunk you don't understand the question when the cop asks if you're willing to submit to a breath test and you tell him to go to hell, you lose your license for a year. Why is alcohol a mitigating factor if you shoot somebody and an aggravating factor if you're too drunk to know whether you should submit to a breath test? And then you wanna throw in the psychological questions about why these people are drinkin' in the first place? Shit.

"A part of me says, 'You can never know enough.' Another part of me says, 'No matter how much you know, you'll never understand.' And another part says, 'Fuck it. Who cares. My name's never gonna be on any rule.' And another part says, 'Only an arrogant sonofabitch would even worry whether his name was gonna be on a rule.' And another part of me says, 'There's no pity like self-pity.' And another part says, 'The M'Naghten Rule, right or wrong, that's the question.' And another—"

"A part of me is saying, 'Take a walk, Balzic, the Greek's losin' it.' "

"I'm not losin' anything I haven't lost a thousand times before," Valcanas said, snorting. He turned obliquely on his stool and leaned toward Balzic. "What would *you* tell this woman?"

"Jesus, this is really eatin' you."

"Of course it is. Five, six centuries ago, this woman wouldn't have any problem. She wouldn't expect any goddamn sexual fireworks out of her marriage. People didn't get married for fucking love. It was strictly an economic arrangement. And that's what this woman has. Only for her, all of a sudden, she reads a couple of books, and she decides she's supposed to have the whole party right at home, or else she's gonna tear the rest of it up."

Balzic shrugged. "Send her to a marriage counselor."

"That's out. I suggested that, and she said forget it."

"Then it sounds to me like she doesn't want anything except what she wants, which is out. So give it to her."

"It's not that simple. The woman has no marketable skills, she has three minor children, and her husband is a bricklayer. He's averaged thirty weeks of work a year the last six years. They split and what we got—you and me—is more numbers for the welfare department. This woman's decision to split affects not only her husband and her kids, it affects us all. Her only dissatisfaction in the marriage is sexual. Why can't she bring herself to go outside the marriage to find that? Or why can't she get herself off?"

"How the hell should I know?"

Valcanas propped himself against the bar and smiled perversely. "As the ranking authority figure in this town, you're supposed to know about stuff like this."

"Oh fuck you."

"As the ranking, paternalistic authority figure, you're supposed to have a handle on this stuff. If you don't know what to do about this shit, it's welfare chaos for us all. Innkeeper!" Valcanas slapped the bar and pointed to their empty glasses.

"I swear to Christ, Mo, sometimes you're comin' from so high off the wall I don't know what the hell you're talkin' about."

"Don't call me that."

"Okay. Panagios. Okay. . . ."

* * *

Balzic drove around Rocksburg until he felt certain everybody would be asleep when he got home. He'd tried to con himself that he was thinking about Joseph Castelucci, about Joey Case's death and how it happened, but every time he tried to think about Ralph Gioia or Joellen Cooper, he was led back to his reactions to them rather than to what they told him or didn't tell him about Joey Case, and the next side step led him to what was really boiling in his mind. He'd had two tests made on his blood: one was to determine the level of testosterone; the other was to determine the level of prolactin. When the doctor had prescribed the tests, he'd told Balzic not to fume and fuss about what these tests meant or might not mean, and Balzic had shrugged it all off as though to say that he understood what the tests were about and that, of course, he wouldn't give them another thought. He was good about faking understanding. He'd purse his lips and nod once or twice and then look as though he was ready for the next step in the process—whatever it was—and he'd calculate how long it would take for the next step to be explained. Then he'd back up and fill in the gap. But this was different.

The "lactin" part of prolactin sounded like it had to do with milk. And milk had everything to do with mothers. And mothers were women. And by the time he got to a dictionary after he'd left the doctor's office, he was struggling to stay calm. Prolactin, he learned from the dictionary, had a one-word definition: *luteotropin.* And that word meant "an anterior pituitary hormone that, in mammals, regulates the production of pregesterone and stimulates lactation of the mammary glands." That was the biochemical definition. There was another definition, for pharmaceutical use, that he did not copy into his notebook. Then he looked up "progesterone" and found to his bewilderment that it was "a hormone that prepares the uterus for the fertilized ovum and maintains pregnancy." When he looked at the pharmaceutical definition of that, his eyes glazed over, and all he saw were black marks on the page. He hurriedly turned to "testosterone." That was the "sex hormone secreted by the testes, that stimulates the development of masculine characteristics."

Jesus Christ, he'd thought, I'm gettin' tested to see whether I can give milk and have a baby and whether I got anything that might develop masculinity. That was the most optimistic he'd been that day. Everything after that sort of reminded him of why he'd finally called his doctor. . . .

Now here he was, slinking into his house after midnight with his greatest hope being that he could make it to bed without having to talk to his wife.

When he tiptoed into the kitchen to get a glass of water he nearly tripped over his mother's feet.

"Ma! What the hell're you doin' sittin' in the dark?"

"I'm waitin' for you."

"You okay? You sick?"

"I said I'm waitin' for you. I didn't say nothin' about sick."

"Okay if I turn on a light?"

"It'sa your house."

Balzic turned on the dimmest light in the kitchen, the one over the sink. "It's my house, huh? Every time you start out talkin' about whose house this is, I'm . . ."

"You what?"

"Nothin'. Never mind." He filled a glass with water and drank most of it. He leaned against the sink and looked at her and shrugged. "So?"

"Okay. So. I live in your house, but I stay outta your life, is that right?"

Uh-oh, he thought, here it comes.

"Yes or no?"

"That's right, yeah."

"Well, I gotta say somethin'. Since you beena chief, my daughter-in-law is more daughter to me than you been a son."

"You get no argument from me on that one."

"Me and Ruthie, we almost more than a daughter and mother. She's like, uh, she's my best friend."

Balzic sighed and stifled a yawn. He was thinking about how close he'd almost come to making it to bed. "I know that, Ma."

"You know that, huh?"

"I just said I did."

"Well, I'ma glad you know it. Because you make me so mad sometimes."

"Hey, Ma, I'm really tired, you know, so—"

"You're not that tired. Now you listen to me."

Balzic shifted from one foot to the other and drank the rest of the water noisily.

"You listenin'?"

"I'm listenin', Ma, I'm listenin'."

"You listen to what you wanna hear most of the time, but you listen better to this, okay?"

"Okay, okay. Tell me."

"I don't like what's goin' on here. Two, three months now, you two been walkin' 'round here like you botha sick and you don't neither one wanna catch what the other one's got."

"Is that what it looks like, huh?"

She leaned forward and glared at him. "Hey. You stopa bein' such a wise guy with me. I don't care how you talk to all thosea bums, but I'm still your mother and I can still box you one."

"I'm, uh, I'm sorry, Ma."

"Don't give me that sorry business either. That'sa what you do to Ruthie. I don't like that either."

"What—what, uh, do you want?"

"I want you start actin' like a man. I don'ta know why you stop. I don't wanna know. But your wife don't deserve you behave like a pouty-puss kid. You don't walk around here with your face hangin' down, seein' all the time, hurry up, hurry up, how fasta can you get outta the house. What the heck you call this, huh?"

Start acting like a man? Jesus, he thought, I got people checkin' my blood to find out whether my uterus is ready for the ovum and yesterday the one thing in this world I would've bet on was that I didn't have one of those.

"Answer me," his mother said. "Say somethin'!"

"I don't know what you want me to say, Ma."

"Don't give me that—that's what you used to say when you was in high school. You in high school?"

"C'mon, Ma."

"You in high school? Or you a man?"

"I'm not in high school," he said, sighing with great frustration, "so I guess that means I'm a man, if those are my only two choices."

"Oh you! What do I have to do? Shake you?"

"C'mon, Ma. I know there's a little bit of tension around here lately—"

"Little bit!" Her mouth fell open. "You lose your glasses?"

"There's some tension around here lately, and I know you're tryin' to—I know you think you're doin' the right thing right now, but, uh, but you're really not—you're really not doin' the right thing."

"Oh? Oh. Oh. Not the right thing, huh? So what is the right thing I should do, huh? Stay shut up, huh?"

"No. I'm not talkin'—hey, that's the last thing I'm gonna say to you is shut up. Just, uh, just keep on bein' friends with Ruth. Just keep on doin' that, and, uh, and just please get off my case. Just for a little while, okay?"

She fell back against the chair, sat there for a moment, then leaned forward again. "No! I'm not get offa your case. You actin' like a kid. Grow up. Talk to your wife. Straighten this business out. And do it tomorrow! You hear? Tomorrow. The more time pass, the worse it gets. Some things don't go away. You have to make 'em go way. The Pope ain't gonna come, make everything nice. You have to do. You!" She stood and shook her index finger up at his face. "You!" She turned and padded wearily out of sight.

Balzic looked at his shoes. God, he thought, I'd rather serve a warrant in a bar full of drunked up bikers than see that woman's finger in my face.

* * *

Balzic slept on the couch after he'd crept into the bedroom and lifted the alarm clock off the table on his side of the bed. When Ruth stirred he mumbled something about having to get up much earlier than usual and turned and made his getaway with less sound and more speed than a burglar.

He woke at seven and was out of the house fifteen minutes later, wearing the same clothes he'd worn the day before. He showered and shaved in the basement locker room in city hall, and fled his station with as much stealth as he'd fled his home. He got a cup of coffee and some orange juice from a fast-food restaurant along the highway leading north out of Rocksburg and then looped back through town just in time to finish the coffee and fall into morning traffic behind Joellen Cooper as she left the driveway at 14 Westfield Drive on her way to work.

He kept two cars between her Datsun and his cruiser and had no trouble following her as she drove over two-lane asphalt roads and turned off into a vast parking lot in front of Westfield Area Senior High School. He parked in the first available space he came to and waited, sipping orange juice as bus after bus roared in, dropped its passengers at one of three sets of doors into the sprawling, yellow-brick building, and then left.

Among the buses came a fleet of cars. Every time Balzic had to visit a high school, he was awed by the numbers and kinds of cars driven by students. He could never comprehend where these kids got the money to buy all these cars. There was no explaining it. Thousands of people in Rocksburg were living on unemployment insurance or welfare; thousands more in the townships surrounding the city were in the same fix, yet all Balzic had to do to get thoroughly confused about the economic health of the place was to drive into the high school parking lot and observe the rows upon rows of cars owned and maintained by teenaged kids, all of whom paid the highest rates charged by insurance companies. It defied all logic.

When no more buses arrived, Balzic put his cruiser in gear and crawled forward, looking for the parking area reserved for the faculty. In no time he found Joellen Cooper's Datsun and John Itri's Chevrolet. He parked near the center of the three doors in a no-parking zone and went inside in search of the administrative offices. A stout woman with a practiced scowl interrupted him as he made his way toward the principal's office.

"Just a minute, sir. You can't go in there without an appointment."

Balzic produced his ID case.

She put on and adjusted glasses that hung from a black ribbon around her neck. She inspected the ID and said, "If you'll just have a seat I'll see if Doctor Wilmoth can see you." She walked to a phone on a long counter, turning Balzic's ID case end over end as she pressed three buttons. "What is the nature of your business, sir?"

"Personal," Balzic said. "And private."

"My, my. Aren't we—yes. Doctor Wilmoth? There's a policeman here to see you. He has no appointment and he says his business is, and I quote, 'Personal and private' . . . uh-huh. Yes, sir." She hung up and returned Balzic's ID. "He says you're to come right in."

I'll just bet he did, Balzic thought. Probably dustin' off his bolt cutters right now. Can't wait to dump the contents of a couple dozen lockers in search of a garbage bag full of pot, street value ten or twelve thousand as the papers would say. The man should've been a narc. . . .

"Chief Balzic," the principal said, having flung the door open just as Balzic reached for the knob. "Come in, come in. What's the problem? Sit down, sit down."

"That's all right, I'll stand."

Wilmoth shut the door with a bang and hustled to get behind his desk. "This can't be about dope because we've been staying right on top of that. Yes, sir. Suspended two sophomores last week. Put the fear of God into the rest of them. But that's what has to be done, otherwise things just get out of control. No control, no teaching. No teaching, no learning. Even in the best of times, we're always on the edge—"

"Of losing control," Balzic interrupted him. He'd heard it before.

"Right!"

"And with drugs and rock and roll and, now, this rise in X-rated movies . . ."

"Yes! Of course." Wilmoth glowed with an unjustified and unjustifiable belief that he was in the presence of a man who shared his most confirmed hatreds.

"Well, Doctor Wilmoth, you can stand easy. This has nothing to do with drugs or rock and roll. I just wanted to have a talk with one of your teachers and I didn't want to do it without clearing it with you."

The principal sagged noticeably, despite his best effort to maintain a military bearing. He had served as an officer in the Marine Corps in Korea after the truce had been signed, and he had, during his first meeting with Balzic, learned to his delight that Balzic had "seen action" as a Marine during World War II. Balzic winced every time he recalled their first conversation. Wilmoth had belabored Balzic with their *esprit de corps* despite their separation of times of service, and Wilmoth had "confessed"—he had used that word—that one of his deepest regrets was that he had not been permitted to "see action."

"One of our, uh, teachers? Hm. Well. What's the difficulty?"

"No difficulty. I just want to talk to him about something he might have witnessed."

"Oh. Oh! Well, of course. Who?"

"Itri. John Paul."

"Ah. I see. Well. Let me just page him, and we'll see whether he can be of any assistance."

"Uh, no sir. I'll have to see him alone. This is a private matter."

"Aha! Yes. Well." Wilmoth picked up his phone, jabbed at three buttons and said, "Mr. Itri, please report to the principal's office at once. Mr. Itri please report to Dr. Wilmoth." He replaced the phone and looked wistfully at Balzic. "You know, the older I get and the more I think about it, sometimes when I've, you know, I've given some thought to what I've done with my life, why, more and more I wonder whether I made the right move getting out of the Corps."

"Really?" Balzic canted his head as though to fake interest in what was sure to come.

"Yes. I've often wondered what sort of turn my life would've taken if I'd stayed in. I got out in June of '58. Two more years and we had advisers going into Vietnam. I would have had my own company by then. Before long I would've been battalion exec. And that war, God, what opportunities there were there." Wilmoth thrust his right index finger upward and stabbed the air twice. "Do you know that two men I went through OCS with came out of there with birds on their collars? Full colonels by 1967 and 1968. Many engagements. Covered themselves with glory. Rose like mortar rounds. Yes, sir. I seriously question whether I made the right choice—"

The knocking interrupted him, and Balzic blew out a long sigh of gratitude. Wilmoth was just warming up.

"Come!"

Jesus, Balzic thought, he's still telling people to enter his office the way he did as a Marine officer. That one-word command let people know that the speaker didn't waste time saying "in."

"Ah yes," Wilmoth sang out as Itri, looking winded and flustered, came in. "There you are, Chief. There's your man. Mr. Itri, this is Chief Balzic of the Rocksburg Police Department, as fine a police officer as I've ever had the pleasure to work with. The chief and I have been involved in several . . ."

Balzic tuned him out and shook hands with John Paul Itri. Balzic was always curious to see how reality coincided with his expectations and presumptions, and ever since his conversations with Joellen Cooper and with Itri's wife, he'd been busy in his spare moments drawing Itri's profile. Itri, tall, slender, boyish, with pale skin and a bluish cast to cheeks and jaw, and wearing carefully tailored clothes, greeted Balzic with a clammy handshake and wary eyes. He forced a smile and had to clear his throat three times before he could speak, and when he did it was with a formal, "How do you do."

Balzic interrupted Wilmoth who was still rumbling on. "If you don't mind, I'm going to take Mr. Itri outside. I don't want any interruptions."

"Interruptions? Why don't you stay right here? I'll have my secretary hold the calls, and this office is totally secure."

"I'm sure it is, but I think outside is better. I won't keep him long."

"That's—that's okay," Itri said. "I don't have a class until second period. And, uh, activities period hasn't even started. There's an hour at least."

"That's fine. Let's go outside." Balzic had to keep protesting to Wilmoth that it would be better to go outside and finally took

Itri by the elbow and steered him through the door and out into the hall.

"Uh, what's—what's this about?" Itri said as soon as they'd cleared the administrative office.

Balzic held up his finger and said, "Outside," as they slipped and sidestepped through the halls jammed with students rushing to and from their lockers. Once outside, Balzic set off briskly toward his car, forcing Itri to hustle to keep up. At the car, Balzic opened the passenger side door and motioned for Itri to get in, then he got behind the wheel and drove to the end of the parking lot near its entrance and parked in a zone covered with diagonal yellow stripes. He turned the engine off and then switched off the radio.

He twisted obliquely to face Itri and said, "Tell me about yourself."

"What?"

"Tell me about yourself."

"I don't understand. What for? What's this about?"

"I'll tell you that in due time. And you don't have to understand. Just tell me."

"What—what am I supposed to say? I don't know—"

"Okay, we'll do it a different way. You don't want to do it that way, we'll do it another way. How old are you?"

"Thirty-three. Am I—"

"What do you teach?"

"Social studies."

"Social studies? What's that? I don't think they had that when I was in school."

"It's—it's a bit of several different things. It's, uh, it's sociology, a little anthropology, a little cultural history, a little social psychology, a little bit of government—"

"It's a lot of little things, huh?"

"No. I mean it is and it isn't. I don't see—"

"Married?"

"Yes. Yes, I'm married."

"How long you been teachin'?"

"Ten years."

"That all you've done?"

"Done? You mean work? No. First year—my first year out of college I worked in a bank."

"Didn't like it, huh? Why was that?"

"I didn't say I didn't like it."

"That's right, you didn't. But if you liked it you wouldn't've quit, right?"

"Well I suppose you could say that, but—"

"You got married about the same time you started teachin', right?"

"Yes. What does this—what are you asking—"

"Meet your wife in the bank?"

"Yes. No. We were in college together. Then she started in the bank and—and, uh—"

"She's still with the bank, right?"

"Yes. Yes, she is. Listen, it sounds to me as though you know these things you're asking me—"

"Some of them I do, yes. That's absolutely right. A lot of these things I know." Balzic stopped talking and looked away from Itri. It was the first time he'd taken his eyes off Itri's face. Balzic counted out seconds to himself, one-thousand-one, one-thousand-two, one-thousand-three, the while staring out the windshield as though absorbed by something across the road. He could sense Itri trying to see what he was staring at. He was up to one-thousand-twelve before Itri sputtered, "What is going on here?"

"What's fourteen Westfield Drive? What's it mean to you? Mean anything to you?"

"I—I don't know what you want me to say."

Balzic laughed softly. "What *I* want you to say. John, all I want you to say is what that address means to you. It does have some meaning to you, doesn't it? now if I'd said to you, for example, *two hundred* Westfield Drive, why we'd both know that that wouldn't have any meaning to you. Or if I'd said *number six* Westfield Drive, that wouldn't have any meaning for you either. But *number fourteen* Westfield Drive, now we both know that means something to you. I mean, it has a meaning for you that it wouldn't have for lots of other people. For example, uh, that address wouldn't have any meaning for your wife, now would it?"

Itri's glance darted around the dashboard, the windshield, to Balzic, and to the slim notebook he'd been clutching in his left hand since he walked into Wilmoth's office.

"You're, you're a police officer, you're not—you can't be involved with—what are you—why are you talking to me like this?"

"The name Cooper mean anything to you, John?"

"What? What's she—are you accusing me of doing something wrong? If you don't tell me—am I allowed to go? Can I just get out of this car and go?" His voice was cracking and he had to stop frequently to clear his throat.

"You know," Balzic said softly, "when I saw Miss Cooper and I thought about you, I thought, you know, you'd probably look pretty much like what she looked like. Not quite mousy, but no traffic-stopper, that's for sure. And then I talked to your wife, and I said, wow, wait a minute. Call the photographer, this is a stunner, this one. I mean when she opened the door, I had to stop and regroup, if you know what I'm sayin'. And so naturally, I had to ask myself what kind of guy is this, he cuts out on a wife that looks like she does to spend time at fourteen Westfield Drive. Now that's a real puzzle, John. That baffles me. That really does."

Itri's mouth had slowly opened as he stared at Balzic. After another long silence from Balzic, Itri shook his head several times, but he could not bring himself to speak.

"See," Balzic went on as softly as before, "when I look at you after seein' your wife, I say, yeah, those two go together. In his way, he's as good-lookin' as she is. But then I look at you and I think of Miss Cooper, and I say, something's wrong here. They don't fit. They don't fit at all. So what's goin' on here."

Itri shook his head again, hard this time, as though trying to clear away the effects of being struck. "I'm—I'm going now. I'm going to open this door and I'm going to go. I haven't done anything and you're talking about me as though I was fooling around—as though what I've done is some kind of crime." He had to stop to even out his breathing, which had become so rapid he was on the verge of hyperventilating.

He reached for the door and tried to open it. Balzic reached across him in a blur and pulled it shut.

"Hey, John," Balzic said, "I don't give a rat's ass who you're screwin'. You can screw dogs for all I care. You can take a broom handle and poke a hole in a pile of mud and try to fuck that for all I care. You listenin' to me?" Balzic pushed his index finger into the middle of Itri's chin. "What I care about is this, John. And pay attention here. What I care about is how come it is, five months after it happened, five months after a man got shot to death, John, you have not come forward to tell anybody what you know about that—*that's* what I care about."

Balzic withdrew his finger and relaxed backward against the

door. "See, John," he said softly, "when I was asking you what fourteen Westfield Drive meant to you, I was thinkin' about what it means to an old man and an old lady whose only son it was, yeah, the only kid they ever had, the guy that died there that night you were in Cooper's apartment."

Itri leaned backward as far as he could get from Balzic. He closed his eyes and swallowed hard and struggled to take deep breaths.

"Now I don't wanna mislead you, John. But I do want you to know some things. The guy who died there that night was not your all-American citizen. He had been convicted of many misdemeanors and at least one felony. Probably more. I'm just talkin' about the things I know about. And he was probably nuts. I don't mean a little bit weird. I mean there were times when he was about three feet off the ground. But to his parents, no matter how goofy he was or how much trouble he caused, he was still their kid. And his parents are takin' it about as hard as you can take somethin' like this. And his parents are—"

"*His* parents! *His* parents!" Itri shouted, tears welling up in his eyes. "For God's sake, man, what about my parents? I am a Catholic. I am a de-devout Catholic. My broth—my brother's a priest. My sister is a—is a nurse in a Catholic mission in Mexico . . . my mother goes to church . . . every day of her life . . . I am co—I am committing a—adul—adultery . . . I am co—I am committing a mortal sin . . . oh, God . . . my father is the janitor at St. Mary's . . . I went to college to be a priest . . . I never kissed a woman . . . never until I kissed my wife. . . ."

Itri flung open the door and bolted away from the car, retching and heaving.

Oh shit, Balzic thought. He lurched out of the car and went after Itri, putting his hand on Itri's back and patting him as Itri emptied himself of his breakfast.

Itri straightened up after a moment and leaned away from Balzic's hand. Then he took a full step away and fumbled to get a handkerchief out of his pants pocket. He wiped his mouth and then looked down at his shoes and squatted down and cleaned the toe of his right shoe. He stood and, with his back to Balzic, said, "I'm sorry."

Balzic shrugged. "Hey, it happens to everybody. Nothin' to be sorry about."

"I'm not sorry about that. I couldn't—couldn't help that. I'm sorry that I—you have to understand—I can't help you. I know what you want me to do, but I'm sorry. I can't do that." His voice was full of phlegm and he was close to sobbing.

"Look, John, if anybody ought to be apologizin' here, it ought to be me. I did a really shitty thing to you here. But I did it 'cause I misread you. I saw you walk into that office all cleaned and pressed, and I thought you were, uh, a smooth dago boy on the make. I should've known from lookin' at Miss Cooper, uh, that wasn't it."

"She's a good person."

"I'm sure she is."

"I'm—I'm a good person." Itri's shoulder shook.

"I'm sure you are."

"I've done—I've done a bad thing . . . I'm paying for it. That's painful enough . . . I can't make . . . I can't make my family pay for it . . . my parents have been married—they just celebrated their fiftieth anniversary . . . I cannot even think of divorcing my wife as long as my parents are alive . . . you said the man who was killed was not a good man . . . there are all kinds of goodness, all kinds of rightness that I cannot explain to my parents. What you want from me . . . is a kind of goodness they would never understand . . . I don't have—I am not a—I don't even know how to say this . . . I am a very timid person. People—not just you, believe me—people look at me and assume I'm some kind of ladies' man. That's been happening to me for years . . . I really wanted to enter the priesthood . . . I thought I was good enough, I thought I had courage enough, but I watched a priest try to console a man who had cancer . . . his nose was just eaten away by the cancer and part of his jaw and he was in the bed next to my uncle and I saw the priest praying and afterward he was joking with the man and I knew I could not do that . . . I knew there was nothing I could ever learn that would give me the courage to do that . . . I know that I did not have the kind of courage you need to do God's work . . . I cannot explain the disappointment I saw in my parents' eyes when I told them I could not go into the seminary . . . do you think I could make them understand why it was right and good for me to tell . . . in court . . . what I saw . . . and where I was when I saw it?"

Itri's whole body was trembling.

"Uh, we better get in the car, John. It's gettin' cold out here. C'mon. I'll drive you back up."

Balzic waited until Itri turned and then he held him by the elbow and led him gently to the car. When he'd stopped the car by the school doors, he said, "Look, I'm not apologizing now, I'm just tryin' to explain. My wife tells me it's a weak spot in my character. I do something wrong and then I apologize and I think that makes everything okay. I don't agree with her necessarily, but what I'm . . . oh shit. Listen, I read your advertisin' and I got fooled. I thought I had to put some heat on you. So anyway that's enough of that. But, uh, I do have a problem and if you can think of any way I could take care of it, I'd really appreciate your help."

Itri stared at Balzic. "My God, you're—you're relentless."

Balzic sighed and chewed his lower lip. "Hey, man. Some people die of cancer. That's for doctors and priests. Some people die 'cause other people shoot 'em. That's for guys like me. You think it takes courage to make jokes with a guy with cancer? How much courage you think it takes to deal with a man whose son got shot? I ran from this guy for five months, that's how much courage I got. I won't tell you about the other things in my life I don't have the guts to face right now. What I will tell you is I finally did face this guy. And I gave him my word I'd try to do something for him. So your story—sad as it is, your problems—hey, it doesn't mean anything to me right now except how do I get around it. And you can call me relentless or any other name you want to call me. You better go inside now, John, before I say somethin' you really don't wanna hear."

Itri struggled to speak. "I can't help you." He threw open the door and ran toward the school doors and disappeared into the building.

Balzic stared after him, shaking his head and trying to make sense of what Itri looked like and what he was, what he did and why, and what he couldn't do and why. Itri was tall, handsome, graceful, meticulous about his clothes, married to a woman equally attractive, apparently equally concerned about her appearance, and, yet, she'd managed to brush Balzic off in minutes. Itri had practically turned into a puddle. The question to Balzic then, wasn't what Itri was doing with Joellen Cooper; the question was, what was Itri doing with his wife. The next question, far more important, was how could Balzic turn that question to his advantage. He stewed about that all the while he drove back into Rocksburg and parked in the garage under the Conemaugh County Courthouse.

* * *

Balzic had to use the stairs because, as usual, the elevator in the courthouse was operating at less than peak performance. He loosened his tie, undid his collar button, and shed both coats before he walked into the District Attorney's office on the fourth floor.

There was a new receptionist in the outer office. She was on the phone, taking messages, generally directing phone traffic, and glancing at Balzic between calls.

"May I help you?" she said during a lull.

"I hope so. I'm Mario Balzic, chief of Rocksburg PD. I want to see Assistant DA Machlin. I don't have an appointment."

"Uh-ha. Go right through that door and turn right. He should be in the first cubicle on the right."

"You mean I can go right in now?"

"He just went in before you came in. He said he didn't have a thing to do until after lunch. He said he had two postponements before he ever got inside the door."

"Uh, what's his first name?"

"Horace. He's black." She covered her mouth and smiled. "I hope he never has to prosecute me. He's scarey."

Balzic nodded. "Okay. Nice talkin' to you. What's your name?"

"Terry." She beamed. "Terry Jones. I'm so glad. Before I was married it used to be Colieczny." She spelled it, smiling radiantly the while.

"Good for you, Missus Jones."

Balzic ducked inside and waved and exchanged greetings with the assistant DA's and county detectives he knew. He glanced around, trying to spot Detective Ted Eddy, but couldn't find him. He looked around for a black guy, but he didn't see any, so he turned toward the first cubicle on the right and knocked on the frosted plastic partition.

"Yo. Come on in," said a bass voice.

Balzic stepped into the cubicle and saw a man so black his skin glinted blues and purples. He was starting to bald in two places behind a thick tuft of hair at his widow's peak. He wore a pearl gray suit with a pastel blue shirt and a polka-dotted blue tie, and his aviator glasses had silver rims. He was rolling a pencil between his palms and his skin was taut over his bones. He was probably no more than twenty-five, but there was something about him that seemed older.

"You Horace Machlin?"

"I am," Machlin said, standing and thrusting out his hand. "And you are?"

"Mario Balzic. I'm chief of the Rocksburg PD."

"Ohhhhh, say. I am glad to meet you, sir. I have heard of you. My pleasure. Please, have a seat. You want some coffee?"

"No. No, thanks." Balzic sat.

"So," Machlin said, resuming his seat, "what can I do for you?"

Balzic related as quickly as he could his interest in the shooting death of Joseph Castelucci.

Machlin listened, his fingers pyramided against his chin and lips, and then turned and reached into the drawer of a file cabinet behind his desk to collect a manila folder. He laid it on his desk and said, "Okay. So what's your interest here?"

"I want to know what you got out of the witnesses, especially Ralph Gioia and Joellen Cooper."

Machlin opened the folder and flipped through the unattached pages, pausing now and again and then quickly moving on. "So the old man thinks we're a bunch of clowns, huh?"

"More or less."

"Well, that remains to be seen. But I have to tell you that, as far as I am concerned, I sincerely hope my momma didn't raise no clown. . . . Well, here's Gioia's statement if you want to read it."

"No. Just tell me about him. Did you interview him?"

"I did."

"What'd he see, what'd he hear—and did you believe him?"

"Did I believe him?"

"Yeah."

Machlin laughed.

"What's so funny?"

"There's nothing funny. That is the nicest thing anybody has said to me this week." Machlin laughed again. "Yeah, I believed him. And before you ask, I have to tell you, I look a lot older than I am, and so when a white chief of police, who got a rep like you do, asks me if I believe somebody, I take that as a compliment."

"Hey, be my guest. So, uh, what'd he say?"

"Well, according to his statement here, he said he heard what sounded like a fight—"

"Verbal or physical?"

"Physical. But he said he heard that plenty of times before so he didn't pay any attention to it. Before I continue I think I ought to tell you that he said he'd been partyin' all that weekend and he'd put away a lot of beer. You want me to continue?"

"Is there any point?"

"Well, if you're asking me whether I'm going to use him, the answer is a very hesitant maybe."

"Just because of the alcohol?"

"Well, that, yes, but the time it happened, the available light, and plus his window is partly screened by a branch from that tree. There were leaves all over that tree when it happened. Even in the daytime when I interviewed him I couldn't see much. But my problem with him, he gave us a very tricky piece of sound evidence. It's what he heard that I'd like to use him for, but I know if I use him for that the other guy's gonna try to discredit him because he couldn't see anything. Some people tend to get confused about the word 'witness.' They think it means seein' something, and if the defense gets to pickin' nits over whether he could or couldn't see, I worry that they're gonna razzle-dazzle the jury into thinking he couldn't *see* the stuff he claims he heard."

"So what exactly did he hear?"

"Well, you got to promise you won't fall out laughin', but what he heard is the only reason I made a case to prosecute. I got to tell you, Chief, this one came very close to bein' walked."

"Well now that you have my attention, what'd he hear?"

"Okay. In this order. He heard the scufflin'. He heard the door bangin'. He heard more scufflin'. Then he heard somebody runnin'. Then he heard a shot. Then he heard car doors. Then he heard a car startin' and throwin' gravel and then a big bang. Then he got up and went to the window and the next thing he heard—maybe fifteen seconds later—is the sound of glass breakin' and a whole series of shots."

"He heard a shot before he heard the car doors?"

Machlin nodded many times slowly. "That's what kept buggin' me. You asked about the Cooper woman. That woman absolutely refuses to talk about it. And the other witnesses, Victor and Angeline Marcelli, they didn't get outside 'til after it was over. And then there is the victim's wife, and she was apparently with her sister-in-law."

"Sister."

"Huh? Sister and brother-in-law. What'd I say?"

"Sister-in-law."

"Okay. I got 'em backwards. So the important thing to me was the sequence of that shot and *then* the car doors. So it bugged me so much I interviewed this guy four times myself and I sent Detective Eddy to interview him twice. And the guy won't wobble. Comes out the same every time. So I got this guy with a weekend's worth of beer in his body sayin' something six times. And all the while he's sayin' that, he's also sayin' that the victim is an all-pro asshole and got exactly what he deserved."

"You check out the victim's rap sheet?"

Machlin smiled. "Not your, uh, first choice for man of the year. You know that was a large part of the problem in me sellin' this case? I mean large, as in wide-body big? Lots of white folks around this office just ready to throw a party over the boy's departure. Finally I said, hey, seems to me like there's a weird kind of see-lectivity goin' on. You know, since when does the shootee have to be a Noble Prize winner before we prosecute the shooter? And then there's that state cop, speakin' of all-pro assholes. I know the first rule of this office is never bad-mouth a cop, but do you know that man?"

"I know him."

"Now you know that some people are behind the door when they pass out the smarts but that boy was not even in line. That boy got there a day late."

"I know, I know."

"Oh but you don't know," Machlin said, leaning forward, his chin rising. "That man has misplaced—I don't want to use the word that's the truth because I'm hopin' he's going to prove me wrong—that man has misplaced all the empty cartridge cases he collected."

"Oh no."

"Oh yes. We have not one—I repeat—not one piece of physical evidence to connect that gun to that body. And you say you talked to him so you know that even though he had that car impounded for a week, seven days and nights, it never once occurred to him to try to recover the bullet that had to be in that door." Machlin leaned back and closed his eyes. "I have not told the main man about this latest, ahhhh, misplacement, because I know if I did he would tell me to walk it."

"Why don't you?"

"Why don't I?" Machlin squinted hesitantly at Balzic. "You know, I have heard a lot about you, and I have to tell you that if somebody else asked me that question I would tell them something that wasn't the truth. But it's you that's askin'. So I'm goin' to tell you. First time I took the bar exam I was so scared I couldn't remember a got-damn thing. Don't ask me how I passed it the second time, I don't know. But I did. 'Cause the simple fact is, the only kind of law I'm interested in is criminal law. Corporate law, torts, municipal law—man, if I had to wake up tomorrow knowin' that all I was gonna do was search somebody's title or unscramble somebody's warranty, man, I wouldn't get out of bed. But this? This tryin' to make a case when everybody in this office said there ain't one? This is my cocaine, man. This is what gets me up in the mornin' and this is what keeps me up all day. My girl told me last week I'm the only guy she ever heard of gets ready for sex readin' the Crimes Code."

In another time, Balzic would have probably roared with laughter about that, but because of the kind of test results he was waiting for, he could only manage a weak smile.

"C'mon, Chief. That was supposed to be funny."

"Oh it was, it was. I'm just a little preoccupied with, uh, how you're gonna make a case on what you've got."

"Hey, that's easy. Gettin' ready is almost as much of a kick as doin' it. And I really don't plan to make a fool out of myself. I'll just lay a preponderance of circumstantial evidence on 'em."

"Hell, you don't have any."

"Not yet. But I got time. And I never get tired of askin' questions. Pretty soon I'm gonna find somebody with the answers I need. And then I'm goin' take Mr. Francis Collier's justifiable force defense and break it off in his ass."

"Uh, does the name Itri mean anything to you?"

Machlin smiled meanly. "You found him, huh? Yeah. I found him, no thanks to the jive-ass Helfrick. Had to park Eddy outside that building for two weeks. The boss gave me two weeks of overtime for Eddy to find him and that was it. Itri showed up the last night. But he's deaf, dumb, and blind.

Finally I just told him, either you talk to me or I'm goin' talk to your wife."

"When did you tell him that?"

"Yesterday. Told him I'd call him today. And I will, soon as he gets home from school."

"You're wastin' your time, I think."

"What? Why?"

"'Cause he's not gonna tell you anything."

"The hell he won't."

Balzic shook his head no. "I had him so rattled a little while ago he was cryin' and throwin' up. His wife's not who he's worried about. Your threat there isn't gonna work."

"Hm. Really. Who *is* he worried about?"

"I don't know," Balzic said, unsure whether he was telling the truth or not.

"Listen, uh, if you know something, I need all the help I can get."

Balzic laughed. "That's what I told him. That's exactly what I said. No. He's got a—his problem is a little bit more complicated than just his wife. Some people—well, let's just say the usual threats ain't gonna work with this guy."

"Okay, then what kind will? There got to be one."

"I honestly don't know." Balzic stood up to leave. "You were straight with me a little while ago, so I'm gonna be straight with you. I also don't honestly know if I'd tell you if I did know." He started for the door.

Machlin called him back. "Uh, Chief, I don't like the sound of that. I mean I don't know what's on your mind, but that just doesn't sound right to me."

"I'm sure it doesn't. But right now that's the way it is. Thanks for your time. I'll let you know what's happening."

"Yeah. Okay. You do that. I'll do the same."

Balzic extended his hand, they shook hands tentatively, and Balzic left.

* * *

It took Balzic nearly fifteen minutes to get out of the courthouse; on every floor somebody he knew stopped him to chat. He'd left the DA's office just when all the courtrooms were emptying for the morning recess, and he couldn't go more than a dozen steps without another cop or deputy sheriff or bailiff or tipstaff calling out to him and stopping him to exchange some bit of gossip.

He walked out into rain so fine it felt like steam on his face, and he walked quickly, covering the block to Muscotti's in a few minutes. Once inside he stopped near the front door and motioned for Vinnie the bartender to come and talk.

"So," Vinnie said, "is this for free or is this a full consultation? My fee's goin' up you know."

"Yeah, yeah. You know Francis Collier?"

"The guy that shot Joey Case? Sure I know him. I mean I don't *know* him, know him, but I know who he is."

"He come in here?"

"Uh, maybe five, six times. Maybe more."

"He ever get into a thing with Joey in here?"

"Depends how far you mean. They started to, couple times. But it never come to too much. I stopped 'em once and Dom stopped 'em once."

"D'you have to get between 'em?"

"Nah nah no, nothin' like that. Nah, I stayed on this side of the bar. Nah, they was just mouthin' off, you know."

"What about?"

"What the fuck you think? Her."

"Yeah, but what specifically, you remember?"

"Hey, you know how she is. She come in with Collier and they'd sit up this end for a while, then Joey'd be down there, then pretty soon she's down there, pattin' Joey on the face and pushin' her belly into him, and then here comes Collier sayin', 'Hey, it's time to go,' and then Joey's sayin', 'She's a big girl, she'll go when she wants,' and they're all a bunch of jagoffs anyway, so what?"

"Never anything more specific than that?"

Vinnie frowned and shook his head no emphatically. "Not the time I had to tell 'em to take a walk. Just her typical bullshit. Hey, you know her, what the fuck you askin' me for? Besides, whatta you askin' me all this for? Dom's the guy you wanna talk to. They was in here the night it happened. Right before it happened, this was the last place they were in."

"I talked to Dom about this plenty of times already. What I wanna know now is whether you ever heard Collier say anything specifically to Joey about say, uh, gettin' a divorce."

"Nah, you kiddin'? Who said that? Is that what somebody said they was arguin' about?"

Balzic nodded. "Rose's sister."

"Angie? She never come in here. Oh oh oh, wait a minute. That time that happened, yeah, she was in here with them. Yeah, I remember now." Vinnie spread his hands wide and scowled. "Hey, maybe that's what it was about, if she says it was, I didn't hear it, but what the fuck, I'm not really listenin' to 'em. They're all jagoffs."

"Everybody's a jagoff to you."

"That's it. You got it. Same thing I tell everybody I'm talkin' to. The whole world's a jagoff, except you and me. And when you leave I say the same thing to the next dummy."

"That include Collier?"

"Hey, how smart could he be, he get tied up with Rose, huh? He gotta be as stupid as Joey, right? Listen, Mario, I don't know about this Collier—but more than one time, I gotta tell ya, Joey was okay as long as he wasn't juicin'. He could even be a pretty good guy. But when he started to fuckin' drink, look out. More than once I come close myself, you understand? More than one time he got me so pissed off I couldn't see what I'm thinkin'. So I'm not sayin' nothin' about this Collier, whether he was right or what—I mean how the fuck do I know what happened. But I'm tellin' you straight, I could see where Joey'd get you goin', man, so you'd be thinkin' about tryin' to take him out. Hey, what am I tellin' you for. You knew him."

"Yeah, yeah, I knew him."

"Hey, you know one time in here, reporter from the *Gazette* walked in, he's gonna have a beer, mind his own business, and here comes Joey with a paper. And he sticks it under the guy's face and he starts in on the guy. 'What's clockwise mean?' And before the guy can say anything, Joey's screamin' at him. 'Didn't you ever see a clock you can see through? Made out of plastic? And if you stand behind the clock and look at it, clockwise don't make no sense. Clockwise only makes sense if you're facin' the clock and it's the kind you can't see through.' Jesus Christ, he was speechin' at this guy for five minutes. Now who the fuck thinks like that? Just Joey, that's all. Dom threw him out finally.

"'Course, Dom was always throwin' him out. Then when somethin' broke he had to let him back in to fix it. Put a toolbox beside him, he was a fuckin' magician. Then, when the job's finished, you look at him he got blood all over himself. You ask him what happened, he says, 'Ah, I nicked myself a little bit.' I never saw it fail. He'd do the job perfect, you couldn't ask for better work. Next time you look at him, he's bleedin'. Fixed our fuckin' roof, he's comin' down the ladder with the tools, boom, two fuckin' stories he falls. Busted his arm, fuckin' bone stickin' outta his arm, made me fuck-ing sick, Jesus."

Balzic stared at the bar and blew out a sigh until his cheeks puffed. "I'll see ya," he said.

"Hey. Come up with somethin', will ya?"

Balzic rooted in his pockets and found two quarters. He put them on the bar and started to leave.

"Whoa. Wait a second," Vinnie said, his left hand up and his fingers dancing back and forth. "One more quarter for crissake. I'm not drinkin' a draft on this."

Balzic found another quarter and put it down. "What's that worth?"

Vinnie shrugged. "That gets me cheap vodka and orange juice."

Balzic shook his head.

"Hey, all the information you get from me, you ought to be one of them doctor of psychology or whatever they call 'em."

"Doctor of psychology," Balzic muttered, heading for the door. "Jesus Christ. . . ."

* * *

Balzic pushed the doorbell outside Rose Castelucci's apartment. He drummed his fingers on the doorjamb below the button, trying to tell himself that he was doing what had to be done. He knew he couldn't avoid trying to talk to her at the same time he knew that he might wind up having to defend himself. He could count on one hand the number of women who'd attacked him in all his years as a cop; he could count on the other hand all the times he'd been attacked by Rose. And when he was being as objective as he could be, the best he could say for himself was that he and Rose were fairly well-matched, even though with her heaviest jewelry on she didn't weigh a hundred and fifteen pounds.

The door jerked open and Rose peered up at him, her head canted to the right, her feet planted wide, her muscular body evident under a black T-shirt and black satin shorts. Her toenails and fingernails were painted a shade of purple so dark it was almost black. She had cotton balls stuck between her toes of her right foot. The nail on her smallest toe was clear. Her coarse black hair was cut close to her skull and was beginning to show gray strands here and there. Her skin was darker than women who spent hours daily in the sun, her pupils as blackish as her nail polish, and her nose cartilage had been broken so badly once that her right nostril was noticeably flatter than her left. Her lower lip was twice as thick as her upper and her squarish jaw, combined with everything else, gave her the appearance of a toy bulldog. Every time Balzic saw her he was relieved to know that she never carried weapons, a relief tempered with the dismal awareness that she didn't need to.

"I was wonderin' when you was gonna get around to me," she said. "I guess you wanna come in, too."

"Unless you wanna carry on the whole conversation where everybody can hear it."

"You think I have something to hide?" she sang unpleasantly.

"Why don't we go inside so you can finish your little toe there."

"So you can finish your little toe there," she mimicked him. But she stepped aside and swept her arm ahead of him, a gesture so large she temporarily lost her balance.

Balzic stood in the middle of the living room, which was furnished much like her sister's place, the furniture heavily brocaded, the colors mostly blues, greens, turquoises, and aquamarines.

Rose settled on the floor on a large towel and went to work on her little toe. "I'm not gonna ask you to have a seat, Balzic, so if you're gonna sit you're gonna do it uninvited, so do it. I don't wanna get a crick in my neck lookin' at you."

"Look, uh, just so we know where we are here, this is unofficial—"

"I already heard that already. Angie told me. So ask me what you're gonna ask me. So Joey's dad thinks I what? He thinks I set him up or something? He thinks we planned it or something?"

"No, that's not what this is about."

"Oh will you stop that bullshit right now. You know goddamn well that's what this is about. Joey's dad thought I was tryin' to kill him for years. Everytime I smacked Joey I was tryin' to kill him. Everytime Joey smacked me around, that was just a lovers' quarrel according to his old man. And his mo-ther! She used to go to church every day, every day she used to walk past our apartment when we was livin' up on Walnut Street. She used to go three blocks out of her way every day so I'd see her, she'd be carryin' her rosary with her and she'd be peekin' over at our windows and she knew I was watchin' her. And what d'you think she was prayin' for, Balzic, huh? Can't you guess?"

"You tell me."

"Oh come on. She was the happiest woman on this planet when we got divorced. Jesus, she had a party! She invited all the ladies from the Rosary Altar Society and all her choochamolies from the Monte Grappa League. For crissake, she borrowed a hundred dollars from the credit union down the Sons of Italy, she threw the biggest party those old bags ever went to in their lives. She hired a band for crissake! When we got married she didn't show up. When we got divorced she threw a wedding. And you know what I did?"

"You probably went to it."

"Probably nothin'! Absolutely! And I walked right up to her and I said, 'Mrs. Castelucci, he's all yours.' And I bought her a drink. And she threw it on the floor. Threw it all over my shoes. And I just laughed. So you can give me whatever bullshit you wanna give me, but I know what this is about, Balzic. They think I killed him. And they're fulla shit, both of 'em."

"Am I gonna get to say anything?"

"Talk fast, maybe you will." She finished painting her little toenail, gathered up the polish and a bottle of polish remover and a bag of cotton balls and hobbled into another room. In a minute she was back, carrying cigarettes and an ash tray. She dropped into a chair and put her feet on an ottoman.

"You gotta talk faster than that, Balzic. I'm gettin' bored."

"Okay. So tell me how Joey got here that night."

"How he got here? I brought him."

"You brought him? Knowin' Collier was here?"

"Sure. I used Franny's car."

"Uh, why'd you do that?"

"'Cause I wanted him to get off his dead ass about the divorce." She took a cigarette out of the pack, tapped the loose tobacco down on her thumbnail, and lit it.

"Did you tell Joey Collier was gonna be here?"

"Sure I told him. Why wouldn't I?"

"Did you tell Collier you were goin' to get Joey? And you were gonna bring him back? Here?"

"Certainly. Why you lookin' at me like that, Balzic? Franny and me been talkin' about it for a long time. And before you say anything, I already know Angie told you either she or Vic told you I had the money to pay for the divorce or Franny would've given me the money. So what's the look you're givin' me?"

"Forget about my looks. What'd Joey say when you told him Collier was gonna be here and what you wanted to talk about?"

"Probably he said the same thing he always said, which was, 'Go to hell,' or something like that."

"No probablies, what did he say?"

"How the hell am I supposed to remember that? You remember what somebody said to you six months ago? How about last week? I bet you can't even remember what—"

"I wasn't involved in a shooting six months ago. Five months ago."

"Oh sure. But if you were you'd remember every goddamn word I guess."

"What I remember is not the point. Which is, what do you remember?"

"Jesus, Balzic, I don't remember what he said exactly. All I can tell is what he probably said, 'cause it was the same thing he was always sayin'."

"Which was?"

"Okay, it probably went something like this: I'd say something about what was he gonna do. And he'd say he wasn't gonna do anything. He'd say probably he already paid for one divorce and he wasn't gonna pay for another one. And I'd tell him about how much of my money he spent all the time we was married and the least he could do was come up with the money for the lawyers, and that's when he'd usually tell me to go to hell or kiss his ass or whatever."

"And that's how the conversation went when you got him in the car, right?"

"Pretty much, yeah."

"Where'd you pick him up?"

"Muscotti's."

"Was he drunk?"

"No. He had one beer. He said he'd been asleep all night, like from ten o'clock in the morning on. Said he was shootin' crap all night the night before. So he just woke up about midnight. Then he got cleaned up and came down Muscotti's."

"D'you know he was gonna be there?"

"Oh quit tryin' to turn this into a goddamn setup, Balzic. I went lookin' for him. I went down the Merchants Hotel and he wasn't there, and then I went to Bruno Fiola's joint and then I went to Muscotti's."

"What time was that?"

"I got there about one-thirty, quarter to two, I forget exactly."

"Was he there when you got there?"

"He must've just walked in ahead of me because he had a glass of beer in front of him and there was still some in the bottle. I remember that 'cause I tried to buy him a beer and he said he just bought one."

"Who else was there?"

"Dom. Just Dom. No. There was a guy Dom was talkin' to. And before you ask me I don't know the guy. Never saw him before or since."

"Okay, so how'd you get him to go with you?"

"Whatta you mean?"

"How'd you get him to get in Collier's car and come up here with you? What'd you say to him?"

"I just told him we had to have a talk. All of us. Me, him, and Franny. I told him we had to get this thing straightened out—the divorce—'cause I was seriously thinkin' about gettin' married to Franny."

"Just like that. And just like that he went outside, left Muscotti's, and got in the car with you."

"I told him he could drive. He always wanted a Cadillac."

"So he drove up here?"

"Yes. Didn't I just say so? Balzic, what's the big deal? No matter how you try to twist this around, it's all gonna come out the same way. He came up here, he drove the car, he parked the car, he walked in here, Franny opens the door, and, wham, he climbs all over Franny."

"And you had no idea, not a hint, not a clue he was gonna do that?"

"Joey?"

"Yes Joey, who the hell we talkin' about?"

"No. I did not."

"Rose, you knew Joey better than anybody. You were married to him twice for crissake, and you gonna sit there and tell me you didn't have a clue, not one, what Joey was gonna do?"

"Look, Balzic, when Joey started in on people, he started in hollerin' at 'em first. All his fights started out—with me, with whoever—they all started out arguments. I mean in all the time I knew Joey I never saw him just start beatin' up on somebody without runnin' his mouth first. So when he jumped Franny like that, without yellin' at him, without a word, it surprised me more than anybody."

"Uh, you sure Collier didn't say something to him?"

"If he did I didn't hear it."

"Where were you, exactly?"

"Whatta you mean 'exactly'? I was right behind him."

"How big's Collier?"

"Franny? How big? He's about five foot seven. He ain't too big. He wears a thirty-eight regular coat. I just bought him one for his birthday."

"Does he think he's short?"

"Does he think he's short? What the hell kind of question is that?"

"Hey, some guys are real conscious of how tall they are, you know? Some guys wear boots with high heels, or they put lifts in their shoes. He do that?"

"Hell no. That's stupid. Franny's a lot of things, but stupid ain't one of 'em." She butted out her cigarette and put the ash tray on the floor. "He's not one of those guys with one of those complexes or whatever."

"Okay, so if Collier's five-seven and Joey's five-eleven, almost six feet, and you're behind Joey—what are you, five-three?"

"Five-three and a half," she said disgustedly.

"So you were directly behind Joey, is that what you're sayin'?"

"That's what I said. So what?"

"We both know Collier had a gun that night. Did you know Collier had a gun before then?"

"Certainly I knew. He's got a whole cabinet full of 'em."

"A whole cabinet full, huh? How many did he carry? One on him, one in the car, like that?"

"He always had one on him, in a little hickey, oh whatta you call them things—"

"A holster?"

"Yeah. One of those. On his belt in the back." She leaned forward and motioned toward the small of her back.

"Why'd he carry a gun, he ever tell you?"

"He carried a lot of money, especially when he closed up the club."

"Did he have some reason to think he needed to carry a gun? Lots of people who carry money around don't carry guns."

"Oh come on, Balzic, Jesus. Look. I been waitin' tables since I was fifteen years old. I worked in twenty different joints in my life. More like thirty. I never seen a guy that owned a saloon that didn't think he was Humphrey Bogart. You ask any one of them guys what their favorite movie is, it's *Casablanca.* They all think they're Rick, I don't care if they never get laid, if you get 'em drunk enough, sooner or later they're all gonna come on like they're this guy in a white dinner jacket and any goddamn minute now some gorgeous chick is gonna walk in and lay down on the floor in front of 'em and spread her legs, just because he's him and just because he owns a saloon. *And they all carry guns.*"

"Uh-ha. I see. So what you're sayin' is, Collier just left the club that night, took the money to a night deposit, and came up here. Then you took his car and went and got Joey, right?"

"Right."

"So what you're sayin', if I follow you right, is Collier had the gun on him. He didn't have to go out to the car to get it, right?"

"Right."

"So if he opened the door, for all you know he could've had the gun in his hand, right? I mean, with Joey between you and him, you couldn't see his hands, right?"

"Oh Balzic, you are such a pain in the ass. No, I couldn't see his hands. He could've been holdin' a goddamn salami in his hands, I wouldn't've seen that either. Just because I didn't see his hands doesn't mean he had a gun in 'em."

"Yeah. Uh-ha. But see, the thing that bothers me is, a little while ago you said if Collier said something you didn't hear it. And then you said that all Joey's fights started with him runnin' his mouth. And then you said you were as surprised as anybody when Joey jumped him. And I gotta ask you again. Were you really surprised?"

"I told you I was."

"I'm askin' you again."

"Yes. I was surprised. Surprised as hell."

"'Cause this wasn't Joey's style, right?"

"Right. It wasn't." She screwed up her face and canted her head. "What the hell you tryin' to make me say?"

"I'm not tryin' to make you say anything. I'm tryin' to get you to remember what happened and to tell it as clearly as you can, that's all. For instance, just so we're both real sure about this, I understand you to mean that you left the club with Collier in his car, and after you went to the night deposit to drop the money, where *he* dropped the money, and then you came up here and you both came inside, was he in your sight all the time?"

"Where else was he supposed to be?"

"Yes or no, was he in your sight all the time, from the club to the car to the bank to here and inside to this apartment, yes or no?"

"Yes."

"So in all that time, if Collier would've taken the gun out of his holster and put it in the glove compartment, say, or under the seat, or on the dashboard, you would've seen that?"

"He never did that. None of those. The only time I seen the gun was when I went outside, when it was over."

Balzic wiped the corners of his mouth. "Okay if I get a glass of water?"

"Kitchen's in there," Rose said, pointing over her shoulder. "Glasses are in the cabinet over the sink, on the right a little bit."

Balzic found a glass, filled it and drank, then refilled it and drank most of that. He went back into the living room and sat opposite Rose. "Now what I want you to do is describe the fight. Everything. Blow by blow. What they did and what you did and when."

"You gotta be kiddin'."

Balzic stared at her.

"Balzic, I don't make my livin' announcin' fights on TV."

He continued to stare at her.

She threw up her hands and groaned. "Balzic, it happened so goddamn fast I don't know what happened, Franny opened the door and the next thing I know Joey was all over him. I tried to get him off, I tried to tell him to knock it off, they were wreckin' my place, I can't give no blow by blow. All I know for sure was I had Joey by the hair and he let me have it in the—he came back around with his elbow and the next thing I knew I was on my ass out in the vestibule. And when my head stopped ringin' I saw him, he had Franny bent backwards over a chair and was just poundin' the hell outta him, blood was flyin', Jesus, and then the chair broke and I just finished payin' off that chair and the legs just went pop, like that, and I thought, Jesus Christ, if I don't get somebody in here he was not only gonna kill Franny, he was gonna ruin my furniture, so that's when I went and got Angie and Vic."

"How long before anybody answered the door over there?"

"Now how the hell would I know that? You think I was lookin' at my watch?"

"Well was it a minute, a couple minutes, five minutes, what?"

Rose shook her head and breathed noisily through her mouth. "I just told you, you dumb sonofabitch, I wasn't lookin' at my watch. Whatta you want from me?"

"I just want you to remember how long it took, that's all."

"Oh God, you're such a pain in the ass. I told you, I don't know. All I knew was Joey was beatin' the hell outta Franny, they were breakin' my furniture and—and the thing that scared me was Joey wasn't sayin' a word. He was just gruntin'. And I could hear my furniture breakin'. And I could hear his fist smackin' Franny. Jesus Christ, they broke a lamp, that lamp cost me fifty-nine dollars. And that chair, and I had this beautiful end table and that table cost two hundred and forty-nine ninety-five and I got it on sale half off! And it was just splinters! And you're askin' me how long it took?"

"Well, you know how much everything cost—"

"Of course I know how much everything cost. When you wait on six dinners and they leave you a goddamn fifty cent tip, you know exactly how much everything cost. And you also know how long it took you to pay it off and you also know you don't have no insurance and you also know you gotta get somebody to help you otherwise everything you worked your ass off for is gonna get thrown in the garbage. That's what I was thinkin' about, Balzic, you dumb ass. I wasn't thinkin' about how long it was takin'. If they wasn't breakin' anything it could've took forever for all I cared. But the more stuff that broke, the longer it took. All I can tell you is it felt like I was standin' there for a goddamn hour tryin' to get somebody to answer the door at Angie's."

"Okay, you made your point. You gonna give me another speech if I ask you how long you were in Angie's before you heard the shootin' start? Or you gonna just try to make a guess."

"Balzic, sometimes you make me so mad I could just smack you one, honest to God." She leaned forward suddenly and took the balls of cotton from between her toes and flung them at Balzic.

He put up his arm instinctively and drew back. "That's enough of that, Rose."

She jumped up and glared at him, her hands doubling into

fists. "Yeah. You're goddamn right, that's enough. You say this ain't official, then you just—I don't have to talk to you. I don't have to say a goddamn word to you. So you get lost. I got a headache."

Balzic stood up and started for the door. "So's your friend Collier."

"What? What headache? He got no—that was self-defense. What the hell you talkin' about? Joey would've killed him."

"Maybe he would've, maybe not. But according to the law, your friend's in a lot more trouble than he thinks."

"Oh you're so fulla shit. What trouble? Huh?"

"You'll see," Balzic said, reaching for the doorknob.

Rose darted around him and threw her weight against the door. Balzic took two full steps backward.

"Don't fool around, Rose. Get out of the way and let me out."

"Not until you tell me what you're talkin' about. I'm stayin' right here."

"Look, all you got to do is read the Crimes Code. It's very specific about the use of force defendin' yourself."

"Oh yeah? Well Franny knows the Crimes Code backwards and forwards, how do you like that, smart ass?"

"He does, huh?" Balzic's eyebrows shot up. "That's interesting. That's interesting as hell."

"Yeah. He knows 'em probably better'n you. And if he says he ain't in any trouble, he ain't in any trouble, I don't care what you say."

Balzic nodded several times. "Good for him. Uh, does that mean I can leave now? You gonna step aside and open the door?"

She pulled the door open with a flourish, cocked one knee forward, and fluttered her eyelids. "Be my guest. Don't let the door hit you in the ass on your way out, okay?"

Balzic sidestepped around her, fully prepared to throw his shoulder into the door if she got it into her head to slam it on him.

She waited until he was almost to the outside door before she slammed her own door, and then he heard her growl, "Asshole!"

* * *

Balzic sat in his cruiser for a long moment, trying to put his thoughts in some order and to gain some control over his emotions. What Rose Castelucci had said unsettled him and her twisted energy just plain scared him. It was while he was trying to collect himself that the memory of his first encounter with Joey Case popped into mind. He wasn't sure when it was, twenty years before, maybe twenty-five. It happened at the firemen's carnival, the one all the hose companies sponsored on the old Rocksburg High School football field, the one they used to raise money to replace worn-out equipment or to retire their debts. Until the firemen went for bingo and door-to-door solicitation to raise money, the carnival was the highlight of Rocksburg's Labor Day celebration; it lasted for a week, ending Labor Day night at nine or ten o'clock with an hour's worth of fireworks. Every year a traveling carnival would come in and set up every conceivable scam and hustle to separate people from their money, and the carny folks would split fifty-fifty with the firemen.

The year Balzic was thinking of was the year the carny folks advertised a wrestling gorilla and fifty dollars to any man who could last three minutes in the ring with him and a hundred dollars to any man who could put the gorilla on its back. All it took was the guts to try, the ads said, and ten dollars for the opportunity.

When the wrestling gorilla made its entrance into the boxing ring that had been set up on the fifty-yard line in the middle of the midway, its trainer was almost laughed out of town. His "wrestling gorilla," wearing heavy leather muzzle and a red satin cape, turned out to be a chimpanzee.

Balzic remembered the laughter fading fast, as night after night, a succession of steelworkers, coal miners, hod carriers, bricklayers, firemen, current and former football players, and even a few cops, struggled mightily only to discover that it would have been simpler and less embarrassing to have just handed their ten bucks to the chimp's trainer and moved on to try to beat the Chuk-A-Luck wheel. Though it weighed barely eighty pounds, the chimp could not be put off its feet. Most men tried to bowl it over or tackle it, but the chimp was too quick. When they gave up trying to tackle it, they tried to ease up on it, which the chimp would allow, but the moment they tried to lift it up, the chimp would dart up their backs, throw his arms around their necks and his legs around their middles and hang on until the three minutes were up. What fascinated Balzic, as he'd watched the whole week, was that nobody could understand that the chimp had been trained to do exactly that, and that once the chimp got arms and legs around a man, only the trainer could get him off. Still they kept coming, many of them three and four times, and the crowd that had laughed so hard at the first sight of the chimp, had now become its fans and began to bet—heavily—on how soon each challenger would become helpless in its grasp.

Then Joey Case showed up. When Joey stepped into the ring he wanted it made clear that all he was required to do was put the chimp on its back in order to collect the hundred bucks. The chimp's trainer played the crowd with Joey's request for a long time. The crowd was hooting and hollering at Joey and betting that the chimp would be on Joey's back in no more than thirty seconds. Some of the betting went for ten seconds. When the bell rang, Joey walked to the center of the ring and waited for the chimp to meet him. When it did, Joey planted his feet and slugged the chimp flush on its muzzled jaw, knocking it flat on its back. The crowd fell dead silent. Then Joey held out his left hand triumphantly and said in a loud voice, "Pay me, sucker." To which the chimp's trainer shrieked, "You weren't s'posed to box him, you dumb bastard, you were s'posed to rassle him!"

That conversation began to be repeated among the spectators, especially among the bettors, and each repetition ended with a push, a shove, some curses, and, in no time at all, a punch. What followed was the worst riot among people of the same race that Balzic had ever seen. When it was over, more than forty of them had been treated in Conemaugh General's Emergency Room, including every cop in Rocksburg that night, and it took until four o'clock the next day to process all those who'd been arrested.

Balzic could see Joey in the ring as plainly as if he were standing on the hood of the cruiser. His expression had said, "There, you assholes, that's how you do it," just as his extended palm had said, "Give me what's mine." And when the chimp's fans and backers surged upward into the ring after him, his expression never changed; it just grew more intense, even as he was beaten down under their rage. A couple of days later, when Balzic had visited him in the hospital, all Joey wanted to know was not who had managed to get him out of the ring but why.

"What were we supposed to do," Balzic had replied, "just stand there and watch 'em kill you?" Joey's response to that had mystified Balzic for years. "Shit," Joey had snorted, "you ever hear people say, your face is your fortune? Well, I knew I was busted the minute I found out I was born beautiful."

At the time, Balzic attributed Joey's response to the effects of the beating, but over the years as he encountered Joey after one and then another in a long succession of fights in which Joey seemed to take at least two blows for every one he delivered, Balzic always returned to the words that had come out of a face swollen and discolored so badly that Balzic didn't recognize it as the one he had seen in the ring, and always Balzic felt incapable of understanding those words.

Balzic started the engine and another recollection formed. He was sitting in Muscotti's early one afternoon, perhaps ten years before. No one had seen Joey for months—not that anybody in Muscotti's was doing anything more than gossiping about what might have happened to him—when he walked in wearing a tuxedo but with no shirt, shoes, or socks. Vinnie had laughed at the sight of him and said, "Where the hell you been?" And Joey had replied, "Where the fuck you think? I been in Hollywood posin' for holy pictures. Some Jews out there thought I was better lookin' than Jesus." An hour later he was so drunk he was on the floor wedged into a corner between the jukebox and the stairs leading to the side door. . . .

Balzic shut the engine off and called his station and told Desk Sergeant Vic Stramsky to patch a call through to Assistant DA Horace Machlin.

"Chief Balzic, I'm glad you caught me. I had some questions I thought of after you left."

"Well, before you ask me anything, there are some things I have to say."

"Okay, fire away."

"Uh, I don't know if I'm doin' the right thing here, but—hell I don't know if it's even worth pursuing, but you do need some help. If you want to get to John Itri, you're gonna have to threaten to go to his family, and my advice to you is to think long and hard about whether you wanna do that, because if you do it, you're lettin' yourself wide open for a charge of official oppression, so for crissake, make sure you don't do it in front of a witness."

"I think official oppression is a bit heavy, don't you? How about highly unethical behavior."

"Hey, Machlin, this is no joke. I pull shit like this all the time, but that's because everybody knows cops are rotten. You do this and you handle it wrong, you're settin' yourself up for real problems."

"Okay, okay, I'll think on it. Just give me a reason why this boy is vulnerable. What's his family holdin'?"

"They wanted him to be a priest. And he wanted to be a priest."

"That skin hound wanted to be a priest? You jivin' me?"

"Yeah, I know. If it walks like one and talks like one and dresses like one it gotta be one, but not with this guy. He's scared to death how he's gonna explain to his parents where he was and why he was there. And hell, for all we know, maybe the sonofabitch didn't see anything anyway."

There was no response.

"You still there?"

"I'm here, I'm here. I'm just thinking."

"Well, while you're thinkin', think about this. Rose Castelucci just told me without hesitation that the shooter always carried a gun in a holster in the small of his back. He did not, as Helfrick said he said, get that piece out of his glove compartment."

"I am amazed," Machlin said. "I am—how did you get that woman to talk to you?"

"That would take too long to explain. And I probably couldn't even if we both had the time. But that's not the point. The point is, either Helfrick got the story wrong—which is probably what happened—or else Collier danced him around."

"Suppose Helfrick got the story wrong?" Machlin hooted with laughter. "That boy hasn't got anything right yet."

"Agreed, agreed," Balzic said, rubbing the end of his nose. "But what if he got it right?"

"Okay. What if?"

"Well, hell, man. If Helfrick got the story right, if Collier said he got the piece out of the glove compartment, then he's lyin'."

"Wait a minute, wait a minute. This is a man talkin' in the heat of the moment. I mean, I got to give him his due."

Balzic chewed the inside of his lower lip. "You talked to his lawyer?"

"Several times. He's one shrewd mother. I was a fan of his before I ever knew I wanted to be a lawyer."

"Huh? What? What'd you say?"

"I said I was a fan—"

"Yeah yeah. Where'd you watch him? In court, right? I mean, where else would you watch him."

"Of course I watched him in court, where—"

"You go to court a lot?"

"Sure. I just said so."

"No. What you said was you were a fan."

"Yeah I was a fan. I was a fan of a lotta lawyers. Judges, too. Juries. I watched 'em all."

"Why?"

"Why? Whatta you mean, why? 'Cause I was fascinated. It was better than movies, TV—it was great stuff. Where exactly is this conversation goin'?"

"I don't know," Balzic said. "You know what Collier does in his free time—when he's not runnin' saloons or clubs?"

"No."

"He does what you used to do. He's a trial freak."

There was a long silence, almost twenty seconds.

"You still there?"

"I'm here, I'm here."

"Well? Whatta you think?"

"I think that's interesting as hell, that's what I think."

"Uh, you got a number for Collier's lawyer?"

Machlin snorted. "Wait a minute now. You might know how to talk to Rose what'sherface. But Old Harold Coblentz, now that's a different matter. That man never said a word—you hear what I'm sayin'?—that man never speaks without a purpose."

"Just give me his number," Balzic said. "Let me find out how good he is all by myself."

* * *

Balzic plodded through the next six days in a damp funk. Every time he phoned Harold Coblentz he heard some variation of the same message from Coblentz's secretary: Mr. Coblentz was either in court or in conference with a client and not taking calls and his home phone was unlisted and she was absolutely forbidden to divulge his number. Balzic tried to turn his attention to Joellen Cooper, but every time he phoned her she hung up as soon as he identified himself, and both times he went to her apartment she refused to let him in. As for John

Itri, the school switchboard operator said he'd called off sick every day since Balzic had talked to him in the school parking lot, and nobody was even answering the phone at his home.

At home, Balzic was leaving in the mornings before Ruth or his mother were awake, and he wasn't going home until he was sure they were both asleep. He was eating all his meals out and enjoying none of them. To deepen his funk, four of his men had come down with the flu and he'd been forced to take over the desk on the three-to-eleven watch.

And then there was the rain.

It had started with a fine mist as soon as he'd left Machlin's office and hours later became a downpour, and in the six days since, the rain had not stopped for more than two or three hours at a stretch. It seemed that every basement and cellar in the Flats was flooded. Volunteer firemen and crews from the county water and sewerage authorities had been working around the clock pumping out cellars and clearing debris out of the storm sewers; and when his men weren't helping out there, Balzic was dispatching them to direct traffic through or around the Flats, or to one or another accident. Most of the accidents were fender-benders, except for one that happened during a blinding downpour on the third night, involving an elderly couple and seven cars, six of them parked. The couple had been shopping when, three blocks from their house, the old man apparently had a stroke. Nobody could say for certain what happened, but the speculation was that the stroke caused him to tromp down on the accelerator instead of the brake, sending his car careening off three cars on one side of the street and then three on the other side before sheering off a wooden utility pole. It took firemen nearly an hour to get the hot wires under control and to cut enough of the metal away to free the couple. The woman died in the emergency room and the man flickered in and out of consciousness for three days before he died.

That's when their children—two daughters and a son—and their spouses descended on Balzic and accused his men of every bad decision and every wrong act imaginable, insisting that police blunders had directly caused their mother's death. The elder daughter was hysterical, and when Balzic tried to explain that his men had never touched the woman, that firemen had cut away the wreckage, and that Mutual Aid Ambulance paramedics had removed her from the wreck and had transported her to the hospital with speed and great care, she spit on him.

Balzic wiped his face and shirt with a paper towel and calmly retrieved the file on the accident and offered it to the woman to read for herself that his men had never touched her mother. She snatched the file out of his hand and ripped the reports to pieces.

Balzic sank into his chair and said evenly, "My men did not cause your mother's death. Your father did. And now he's dead and you're looking for somebody to blame. I can understand that—"

"You can't understand nothin'!"

"I can understand that you want to find a reason why this terrible thing happened to your parents—and to you. But you're gonna have to look someplace else—"

"You cops are a bunch of clowns! You don't know what the hell you're doin'!" The woman was sobbing and shrieking and her eyes burned with a rage so bright that Balzic had to turn away. It was like looking at the sun.

"We don't always know what we're doin', that's true. I won't argue that. But we were not at fault here, and my best advice to you is to talk to a lawyer."

Later on, Balzic could not recall how much longer they had stayed or when they left or what prompted them finally to see the futility of staying. All he could recall was that he could not look at the woman's furious grief. There had been a time when he would have dismissed her by thinking that she had probably harbored some long unresolved conflict with her mother and that she was merely projecting her guilt over this onto Balzic and his men. But that was when he had been reading all the psychology he could lay hands on; now, he could no longer allow himself an easy explanation, even if it was more or less true. Reading about the sun under artificial light was one thing; nothing you'd read could keep you from turning away if you were suddenly caught in its glare. . . .

Every day, just when he was telling himself to pay attention to duty, when he was rehashing all the facts about Joey Case, when he was telling himself that he was not thinking about those tests that had been made on his blood, that's exactly what he would find himself thinking about. Prolactin and testosterone. His funk settled in and hunkered down, spreading outward and downward from his neck and onto his shoulders and into his lower back so that he couldn't sit still for more than five minutes at a time. He kept jumping up and stretching, twisting this way and that to try to untie the knots in his back muscles.

Also, he reminded himself morosely, he had not tasted alcohol in six days. Jesus, Mary, and Joseph, he was willing to try anything, even that. Tomorrow was the day, he kept thinking, tomorrow the results would be in. Tomorrow. . . .

Spliced into these nagging, nibbling debates about his manhood and about what manhood meant or didn't mean or could mean or couldn't came the phone calls from the old woman demanding to speak to Mrs. Detore.

"Hello. Mrs. Detore? Hy you doin'?"

"No, ma'am. This is the Rocksburg Police Department. May I help you?"

"I no want your help. I want speak Mrs. Detore."

"You have the wrong number, ma'am."

"I have right number. Where's Mrs. Detore? Who is this?"

"This is Mario Balzic. I'm the chief of police."

That brought a disgusted sigh, and then she hung up.

The next night at about the same time, she called again.

"Rocksburg PD. Chief Balzic speaking."

"Where's Mrs. Detore?"

"I told you last night, ma'am, you have the wrong number."

"I call this number every day. Whatta you doin' there?"

"Ma'am, there is nobody by that name here. You're dialing the wrong number. You need—"

"I'm dial the right number! You the wrong person. Go away."

The third night, when Balzic identified himself, she said, "Mrs. Detore, where are you?"

"Ma'am, if you tell me Mrs. Detore's first name and address, I'll get her number for you—"

"I got her number! This her number!"

The fourth night, after Balzic answered, she said, "What's this number?"

Balzic told her.

"That not Mrs. Detore's number."

"That's what I've been trying to tell you for three nights, lady."

"If this not her number, then whatta you answer the phone for?"

The fifth night, after Balzic answered, she shrieked, "You do not answer the telephone when I call! This is Mrs. Detore's number. You stop answer this phone!"

"Lady, when the phone rings, I answer it. That's the way it works. Oh, lady, sweet Jesus, you're losin' your mind. If you give me your friend's name and address, I'll be happy to get her—"

"You shuddup. I'm not losin' you mind. Goo-bye!"

After the last call, Balzic called every Detore in the Rocksburg phone book, trying to find a woman who might have a friend she hadn't heard from in a week or so. None of them did.

He was thinking about the woman, shaking his head about the wild things the woman had said, when Patrolman Harry Lynch came and placed a computer printout sheet in front of him.

"What's this?"

"It's that report from the ER you asked me to get."

Balzic stared blankly at Lynch.

"You know. About that Collier that shot Joey Case?"

"Oh, Christ, my mind's not workin' right, Harry. Okay," Balzic said, sighing. He read the report quickly and let it fall to the desktop. "Hell, this is just bare bones stuff here. Christ, I can't even make out the attending physician's name."

"Oh that's what'shisface. Cercone. The one, uh, he got his nickname on his name tag. Beans. He said you got any problem, call him up. You want anything else? I gotta go."

"Nah, go 'head." Balzic spun the Rolodex file until he found the emergency room number. The receptionist connected him with Cercone.

Balzic identified himself and said, "This Beans?"

"You got me. The one and only. Garbanzo, kidney, and Mexican jumpin'. Whatta you need?"

"Well I'm tryin' to figure out this report on Francis Collier and I can't even read the damn thing, the type's so light. And what I can read I don't understand."

"Hey, that's computers for you. Whatta you expect? So what do you wanna know?"

"You treat Collier that night?"

"Just so we're talkin' about the same thing, is this the guy that shot the guy, they brought him right after the body came in?"

"Yeah. The victim was—the shooting victim was one Joseph

Castelucci, age 35, 36, shot once in the face, four or five other places—you got him now?"

"Yeah I remember that. But you wanna know about the other guy, right?"

"Right. So tell me what you did, what he looked like, and so on."

"Well, as I recall, he was pretty beat up. Lotta cuts on the face, one bad one on the top of his forehead. I put a lotta thread in him."

"Did you talk to him about it?"

"You mean did I ask how he got like that?"

"Yeah."

"He wasn't doin' a whole lotta talkin' as I remember it. Matter of fact, he didn't do much talkin' at all until his lawyer got there."

"Uh-huh. You recall any of their conversation?"

"Not really. Mostly his lawyer was just tellin' him to keep quiet and let him do the talkin'—the lawyer. Besides, the lawyer was too busy takin' pictures. I had to tell him to knock it off 'cause the flash was botherin' me."

"He take a lot of pictures?"

"Dozens. Dozens and dozens. He took shots of that guy from angles I didn't know existed. Hell, he took a bunch of the guy's clothes. Laid 'em out on the floor and took pictures from the coat to the shoes, then he turned 'em over and did it again."

"Uh-huh. You take any glass out of him?"

"Glass? Broken glass you mean? No. No, I didn't take any glass out."

"Not even out of that bad cut you said was on the top of his forehead?"

"Nah. No glass. I'd remember that. Nah, that's a bitch to clean out."

"You smell any alcohol on him?"

"No."

"You sure?"

"Hey, how sure can you be about somethin' that happened that long ago. I clean up a lotta people, you know?"

"So, in your judgment, how do you think these wounds happened?"

"Oh no question. He'd been punched and kicked."

"Did he need any blood?"

"Oh he hadn't lost that much blood."

"So you didn't take any of his blood for a sample to match, right?"

"No. No need for that. I never even thought about it."

"Okay. So, uh, anything unusual, anything that didn't fit, anything at all, anything that aroused your curiosity?"

"Nah. Somebody put a thumpin' on him, but there was nothin' out of the ordinary about it. Hell, he walked in, he walked out. I never even thought about takin' pictures of his head. His eyes were bloodshot, but, no, he reacted normally to light. I mean the guy was beat up, but some people can take a hellofa poundin' and never even get woozy, and some people take one shot in the chops and never wake up. This guy could obviously take a ton of punishment and still motor. It's hard to explain these things sometimes, Chief. Hell, I saw guys in Nam, they had holes you could put your fist into, I mean they were not supposed to be alive, but they were. And I saw other guys, one second you were sayin', you know, 'Hey, what the hell's wrong with you?' and the next second you couldn't get a pulse, and you'd peel their clothes off, man, and just start turnin' 'em over and over and you'd find this little hole and just a trickle of blood and they'd be gone, man. Just gone. And there's no explainin' it . . . no explainin' it. I quit tryin' a long time ago."

"Okay, Beans. Thank you. If I think of anything, I'll give you a call."

"You do that, Chief. I'm here every night except Mondays and Tuesdays. Hey—customers. I gotta go. Bye."

Balzic dropped the phone into its cradle and tossed the ER report on Collier into the In basket on the desk in his office. He came back to the desk in the duty room and dropped morosely into the chair, propped his cheek on his left hand, and stared up at the clock. It was 10:30, which meant he still had a half-hour to go before the watch changed.

The front door opened and Louie Woolmer came lumbering in, every step a test for the floor. Louie was a guard at Southern Regional Correctional Facility, originally from Pittsburgh, who'd moved to Rocksburg because he'd heard about the weight room the Rocksburg PD had in the basement of city hall and wanted to be within walking distance of it. He worked out there six days a week, Mondays, Wednesdays, and Fridays on his upper body, and the other days on his legs. Louie had played football well enough to be drafted by the Cleveland Browns, but he'd never made it past the exhibition season. He was big enough, strong enough, and smart enough, but his feet didn't move fast enough for that level of competition. Then he took the job as a guard, moved to Rocksburg, and there continued lifting weights as though the strength he gained could somehow take the place of the speed he never had.

Balzic was puzzled now because Woolmer looked a bit tipsy.

"Hey, Chief, hy ya doin'?"

"I'm doin' okay, how you doin'?"

"Good, good. Nah. Not so good. Okay if I sit down?"

Balzic shrugged and nodded to a chair.

"You mind if I talk to you?"

"Depends what it's about," Balzic said. "You want to borrow money or you want to confess to a bunch of crimes you didn't do, no, I don't wanna hear it."

Woolmer giggled nervously. "No, nah, nothin' like that."

"Hey, don't be coy. In about twenty minutes I'm gone, so you got something on your mind, say it."

"I-I saw some scrawny guy in the Regional benchin' three seventy-five today." Woolmer looked at the floor and his right heel started bouncing up and down.

"So? That's it? That's what you wanna talk about?"

Woolmer grinned sheepishly and shrugged. "Yeah."

Balzic waited, but Woolmer was lost in thought. "So is there more than that or what?"

"No, that—that's it."

"Uh-huh. So the sight of this guy doin' whatever, this caused you to go out and, uh, get a little swacked and then come and tell me about it, right?"

"Yeah, I guess." Woolmer giggled under his breath.

"Well I'm sure there's a point to this, Woolmer, but I haven't got it yet, so you're gonna have to give me some clues."

"The point? The point is, this guy didn't weigh a hundred and sixty pounds and he was benchin' three seventy-five, man, that's the point. Three seventy-five."

"Still cold, Woolmer, still cold. I don't know what the fuck you're talkin' about."

Woolmer squared his shoulders. "Look at me, Chief. I weighed, as of this morning, two-seventy-one. The best day of my life I can't bench four-fifteen. I outweigh this con by a hundred and ten pounds easy, and this guy was pushin' up thirty-five pounds less than I can do. Now you understand?"

"And this disturbs you, is that it?"

"Dis-turbs me! This has been drivin' me wild all day."

"Uh, how old are you, Woolmer?"

"Me? Twenty-three."

"Twenty-three, huh. So what is it that disturbs you? Is it that the guy's scrawny or that he's a con?"

"Huh? Both—I guess. I don't know."

"So just to narrow it down, you never been around anybody who picks up more weight than you before this guy?"

"Oh no. Lots of guys do that. But they were bigger than me or they were only a little bit smaller and they were football players. And they weren't cons."

"They weren't cons, huh? So one scrawny con comes into your life and you get loaded. You think maybe you got this a little out of perspective?"

"Hey, Chief, I walk around those guys eight hours every day. What protects me is them knowin' I can pick 'em up and throw 'em against the ceiling if I have to. I don't carry a weapon down there. They see me as a no-bullshit horse, that's my weapon."

Balzic shook his head wearily. "So you see one guy that doesn't fit into your scheme and what—your weapon empty now, is that it? Or you shootin' blanks or what?"

Woolmer stood and sighed disgustedly. "I thought I could talk to you. I guess I made a mistake."

Balzic shrugged. "You didn't make any mistake with me. But you're sure makin' one with yourself. I mean, you keep seein' things down there in terms of one-on-one, you're makin' a serious mistake. If nobody told you better than that, then you need to talk to somebody else down there."

Woolmer stood and began to pace, his arms folded across his chest. "Well, see, I was tryin' to talk to you."

"About what? Wait a minute. You come in here talkin' about this con, and now where you comin' from? I lost you somewhere."

Woolmer put his hands on his hips and his head started bobbing quickly from side to side. "Look," he said after nearly ten seconds of this bobbing, "I can't talk to anybody down there. The thing is, all they talk to me about is football. My watch commander, the assistant wardens, the other guards, the cons—that's all they wanna talk about. I tell 'em, I say, I got a degree in criminal justice, you know? And they look at me like, who do you like in the Steeler game? Am I takin' the points or not? So I come up here to talk to you, 'cause I heard you're straight. I heard you don't like football."

Balzic bit his lower lip and squinted at Woolmer. "So what is your problem? The joint's not like your teachers said it was?"

Woolmer's head stopped bobbing, and he quit pacing. "Something like that—I think."

"And every time you try to get real information out of the other guards, all they wanna talk about is somethin' you don't do anymore?"

Woolmer nodded, hesitantly at first, and then several times rapidly.

"And you thought all you had to do was show the cons the muscles and they'd never give you a problem, right? I mean, in lieu of information, uh, muscle would have to do, is that it?"

Woolmer continued to nod, and he faced Balzic.

"And then you see this con pick up almost as much as you do, and suddenly, what? The panic light goes on? The anxiety alarm goes off?"

Woolmer blushed and closed his eyes, nodding vigorously.

"So, uh, what'd you learn from this?"

"I learned that muscles aren't enough, that's one thing."

"Nah, you didn't learn that. You already knew that. That isn't what sent you to the sauce, kid."

"Yes, it was. But it was a lot more. What scared me wasn't him. It was lookin' at the cons around him and lookin' at them lookin' at me while I was lookin' at him. I had to talk to myself to get my legs to move. I've never been that scared in my life. And I knew it didn't matter what I felt. 'Cause it hit me like nothin' ever hit me. I was in a room with seventy cons and the only reason I was walkin' around was 'cause they were lettin' me. I was bigger than every guy in that room and I never felt so small in my life. I mean it just—boom—I said to myself, if these guys want to take me out, it's their choice, not mine. I'm a guard and they're the cons because those are the rules, but they run this place, not me. Up until that second, I actually thought I could take care of myself. . . ."

Balzic yawned, stretched, and looked at the clock. It was ten to eleven. He could see headlights in the parking lot. The next watch was coming on.

"Hey, Louie, in a couple minutes it's gonna get crowded in here. Why don't you call it a night?"

"Call it a night? Are you—how'm I supposed to go back there tomorrow?" Woolmer threw out his hands helplessly.

"You won't have any trouble goin' back. You already learned the lesson. You *already knew* the lesson. They want you, they take you, that's the lesson. Your ass is grass. You just didn't understand until today. Today? Today you made the physical and psychological connection with the words. Tomorrow? Tomorrow, when you go back, you'll find out what kind of guard you're gonna be."

"What kind I'm *going to be*! Christ, that isn't what I want to know. I want to know what kind I ought to be—or whether I even ought to be."

"You want *me* to tell *you*? C'mon kid. Forget it. I got enough problems. When I leave here, I'm goin' straight to a priest."

Balzic didn't wait for Woolmer to respond. As soon as he saw Sergeant Joe Royer step through the door to take command of the next watch, Balzic jumped up and headed for the door. All he said to Royer in passing was, "It's all yours, Joe. Good night and good luck." It was about as unprofessional a change of watches as Balzic had ever seen, never mind been a part of, but he figured that six days of sixteen hours a day on the job entitled him to it.

In his cruiser, backing out of his slot and turning toward Main Street, he caught a glimpse of Woolmer coming down the steps out of the duty room, his shoulders hunched, his hands deep in his pockets, his chin sinking. He seemed to have lost two coat sizes. He looked like a man getting ready to get the flu, like a man getting ready to take his year's worth of sick days all in a row.

* * *

Balzic drove to the rectory of St. Malachy's hoping to see some lights on. With any luck he'd catch Father Marrazo still awake. There were lights around the side between the rectory and the church; Balzic could see that at once. But just as he parked and turned off the ignition, the lights on the front porch and in the vestibule went out.

Balzic hustled up on the porch and rang the bell. He had to ring it again before the lights came back on. A great hulk of a woman, her hair dyed an awful auburn color and her eyebrows penciled in the same color, frowned at Balzic.

"What do you want?" she said.

"I want to see Father Marrazo."

"It's time for Father to go to sleep. Come back tomorrow." She started to shut the door but Balzic stopped it with his hand.

"Get your hand off the door. What do you think you're doin'?"

"I want to talk to—"

"I heard you before. But you didn't hear me. I said come back tomorrow durin' the daytime like a normal person."

"Oh for crissake." Balzic leaned his shoulder against the door just as she got the same idea. In no time at all Balzic recognized that he was going to come in second in this match, so he jerked out his ID case and held it up for the woman to see. That effort cost him his balance and the door banged shut.

"Hey," Balzic said. "I'm the chief of police. Hey!"

The lights went out. The woman started to walk away.

Balzic rang the bell and pounded on the door and shouted, "Hey!" several times.

No response.

"I'll be a sonofabitch," he growled and started off the porch. Then he heard someone talking, then two people, then the lights came back on, and then the door opened.

"Mario! How long have you been standing there, come in, come in."

"Father, the Bishop said I was to see that you get your sleep and that's—"

"It's all right, Mrs. Dombisky—"

"Dombrisky, Father."

"Yes, Mrs. Dombrisky, I'm sorry. But this is the chief of police and also a good friend and I'll get my sleep when I get tired, if it's all right with you.

"Mario, come in, come in. It's all right, Mrs. Dombrisky, you can go to sleep now."

"I'll stay up till he's gone."

"You don't have to stay up. I'll let him out or he can let himself out. He's done it many times."

"If I go to sleep you'll stay up way past when you should."

Marrazo made a clucking sound and threw up his hands. Then he took Balzic by the elbow and started to lead him back to his office.

"If he was your friend he'd know not to come around this late. Normal people are in bed this time of night."

"Mrs. Dombrisky," the priest said, "will you please go to your room? I assure you I will not need another thing tonight. Whatever I need I will get myself."

"I'll be up anyway until he's gone."

"Mario, come along, come along, come along." He led Balzic quickly back to his office and shut the door and locked it.

"You have to lock it?" Balzic said incredulously.

The priest waved at a chair and went to a cabinet and got a bottle of wine and two glasses.

"Uh, I don't want any," Balzic said.

"Well, you know what the drunk said. I either drink alone or with somebody, makes no difference to me."

"Help yourself. Don't hold back on my account."

The priest removed the cork on a bottle of Valpolicella. He filled his glass to the brim and drank two long swallows before he bothered to sit down. He let out a long sigh and stared woodenly at Balzic. "That woman's been here two days and I've felt emotions I thought I'd got rid of by the time I graduated from high school. Believe what I say next, Mario. If that woman is found murdered, you won't have far to look for a suspect."

"Who is she? What happened to Mrs. Regoli?"

"Oh the poor woman had a stroke. What do they call them now—a cardiovascular accident, a CVA. A stroke's a stroke as far as I'm concerned. Yes. I'm coming back from a novena, and she's waiting to tell me she's made tea and toast and it's here in the office, and she gets the last word out and down she goes. Dropped like a rock. Like all the bones in her legs turned to overdone pasta. I called nine-one-one as fast as I could get to the phone and they were here in minutes. Really. Very quickly. And we got to the emergency room in just a few minutes more. And from there, of course, she's taken to the intensive care unit for cardiac patients, and there she is. And she hasn't regained consciousness." The priest dropped into a chair finally and took two more gulps of wine. He looked at the glass, which was almost empty, stood abruptly and refilled his glass. He went behind the desk and sat down. "So the Bishop, in his infinite wisdom, majesty, and mercy, delivers unto me, his faithful schmuck, the widow of Genghis Khan, Mrs. Dombrisky." The priest closed his eyes, settled back in his chair, and sipped his wine.

"Surely you're not stuck with her," Balzic said. "Surely there's a limit or a loophole or something somewhere."

"Mario," the priest said, opening his eyes and leaning forward slightly, "the Church is many things, but democratic She is not. If the Bishop believes that the bride of Idi Amin is who I should have for a housekeeper, then Mrs. Dombrisky is who I shall have—until death do us part. Which by the way is the best argument I could ever muster for celibacy. Mario, I feel awful. I mean, just hideous. I feel sorrier for myself than I do for Mrs. Regoli. And when I feel the worst is when I say, hey, at least she's in a coma. I'm awake! Mario, what am I going to do? This woman is absolutely loathsome. And she is going to be in this house twenty-four hours a day to infinity—or my death whichever comes first. Mrs. Regoli is not going to recover. She'll be dead in a matter of days. I've seen that look before—many times. They may as well disconnect all those devices right now."

The priest closed his eyes again and sagged backward. "Mario, I don't know what to do. All I know is, I cannot stand to be around this person! And I have no choice. All I can do is request a transfer. And even if that is approved it won't be for months. Months! What in the hell am I going to do until then? Tonight . . . tonight at supper she hovered over me while I ate. She kept asking me if this was okay and that was okay, were the beans all right and was the meat all right. Mario, I don't consider myself a gourmet, but the food was truly horrible. It was all boiled. Everything. If you closed your eyes, it all smelled the same, and if you bit into it, you couldn't tell potatoes from beans. Everything was on the point of mush. And she stood there ask-ing me if every-thing was all-right. Mario, may God forgive me, I wanted to hit her. No. What I wanted to do was say, 'Woman, why are you here and why is Mrs. Regoli in the hospital?' That's what I wanted to do. Oh hell, listen to me. You've come for a reason, I know you have. What is it? Tell me."

"Well," Balzic said, laughing softly, "I've got a problem almost as tough as yours."

"Oh please let it be tougher. Please, Mary, let it take my mind off mayhem. Mario, please, give me something else to think about."

Balzic laughed again. "Lady's got you, uh, itchin' in places you can't scratch, huh?"

"Oh! She's got me scratchin' on the wrong side of my skin. I've got hives on the side next to the muscles."

"I've felt a little of that myself lately," Balzic said.

"Then for God's sake, tell me."

Balzic said what his problem was with Joey Case and his father and with John Itri and his mother and asked at the end, "So if John Itri was to come to you and ask for guidance, what would you tell him?"

"Well, if that's really what you want to know, Mario, the answer is very short. I'd tell him to follow his conscience."

"Follow his conscience, huh? No more guidance than that?"

"Certainly not. I mean, of course, some priests might tell him what to say and what color socks to wear while he was saying it, but those would be from another time, another era."

"So, uh, what is it you think I really want to know?"

The priest closed his eyes and laughed from the diaphragm. "Well, of course, what else? You want to know how far you can squeeze him—in good conscience."

"Well," Balzic said, raising his brows slightly, "how far?"

"Are you asking me whether you could go to his mother? Or are you asking whether you could tell him you were going to his mother?"

"Maybe I am. To both."

"I'd say to you what I'd say to him: follow your conscience."

"Oh come on," Balzic said, snorting. "A little while ago you were practically begging for something to take your mind off the housekeeper and, now, when I give you something, you cop out."

"I'm not copping out. I'm giving you the toughest answer there is. I could tell you what to do, but so what? If it worked, I wouldn't get the credit, and if it didn't work, I'd sure as hell get the blame. That's the trouble with advice. So I'm not going to give advice."

Balzic stood. "My friend, I got some advice for you. Get another housekeeper. This one's got you thinkin' in circles."

"Mario, sit down, sit down. Have some wine."

Balzic started for the door, shaking his head. "G'night, Father."

The priest jumped up and hurried to catch him. Balzic refused to slow down until they reached the front door. Balzic tried to open it, but couldn't figure out the lock and the priest was in no hurry to help him out.

"Whatta you gonna do, Father? Keep me locked in here till I get your point?"

"Something like that, yes."

"Look, I came to you because I got one of these funny little problems that doesn't have any real quick, real easy answer. And the last thing I wanna hear is to follow my conscience."

"And why's that?"

"Because followin' my conscience is how I got here. I mean, I know what my choices are legally. I'm probably over the line with Itri already. No probably. I'm over it. So I need some guidance."

"I have given you the best guidance I can give you. And if you'll give yourself a chance to think about it, you'll see that what you came here for is for me to absolve you of the responsibility—"

"Open the door, Father, huh?"

"You want me to make your decision for you? You want me to take the heat? If you didn't want that you could have prayed to God to know what to do. But God wouldn't have given you an answer, would He? Not one you could hear. So that's why you didn't ask Him. That's why you asked me. But you don't like my answer. You think it's *no* answer. You think I'm trying to run and hide, but, my friend, you're the one who's trying to do that and you're getting very angry with me for pointing it out to you. Well, that's okay. You go right ahead and get angry. Be my guest." The priest fiddled with the lock and opened it, pulling open the door and standing out of the way. "There are several priests in the diocese who would be delighted to tell you exactly what to do, Mario. You want their names?"

"That's okay, Father. I think I can live without that. G'night."

"Good night, Mario, good night."

Balzic walked out to his car and just as he reached the door he heard behind him: "For God's sake, Mrs. Dombrisky, don't sneak up on me like that!"

Balzic shook his head and sighed. He drove off quickly, heading for Muscotti's, hoping it would still be open. Every night for the past week, every time he'd driven by after leaving the station, the lights had been out in Muscotti's windows. This night was no different, the lights were out, but Balzic could see a yellowish glow coming from the tiny kitchen. He parked and went to the side door and banged on it with the side of his fist.

"Closed!" came Muscotti's cheerless voice.

"C'mon. It's me. Balzic. I wanna talk to you."

"For crissake," Muscotti growled, coming toward the door, undoing several locks and bolts, and opening the door. "You don't go home no more or what?"

"How do you know where I go?" Balzic said, slipping past Muscotti and taking a seat on the last stool at the bar near the kitchen.

"I know you're spending sixteen hours a day in your shop, and I know you ain't had a drink in a week," Muscotti said, going behind the bar and pouring two fingers of whiskey into a water glass. He added four fingers of water and sloshed it around. "You still not drinkin'?"

"Yeah. I don't want anything."

Muscotti put his glass down and leaned forward, peering intently at Balzic. "What the hell is your problem?"

"Well, my immediate problem is Joey Case's old man."

"Nah nah nah, I know all about that. I mean what the hell's the rest? Why the hell ain't you goin' home? How's come you're down the friggin' station all day?"

"Whatta you mean? Hey, people get sick, you know? Somebody gets sick, somebody else has to fill in."

"Okay, so, uh, okay. So it's none of my business."

"That's right. It isn't."

"Then tell your mother to quit callin' my mother about it, if it ain't none of my business, okay? 'Cause somethin' goes wrong with your mother, sooner or later she calls my mother, and what gets in her ear winds up in my ear."

"I'm not responsible for who my mother talks to."

"I'm not responsible," Muscotti mimicked him. "I ain't responsible for who my mother talks to either, but when she talks to me about it, that makes me responsible. And my mother thinks I'm the smartest guy around, so she can't understand why I say I don't know somethin'. It makes her nervous and that makes me nervous."

"Jesus Christ, can we please change the subject, huh? Is that all right with you?"

"You wanna talk about Joey Case, I guess, huh? Piss on Joey Case. He's dead. His old man's nuts. And nothin' you're gonna do is gonna change either one of those things."

"Joey's old man is nuts? That's a switch. Everybody's tellin' me how crazy Joey was—as if I didn't know. But I never heard this thing about his father. That's new."

"What're you talkin' about? The whole family's nuts. Always been."

"We talkin' about the same people or what? I've known that family all my life. I never had any trouble with his parents. The only one ever gave me trouble was Joey. So who you talkin' about?"

Dom took a long swallow of his drink and set the glass down disgustedly. "Mario, I cannot believe that in all the times you busted Joey, and all the crap you had with him, it never once occurred to you to ask yourself how come he got like that. That, I don't believe."

"I honestly never had any problem with his parents. They always seemed like reasonable, sensible people who got stuck with a nutty kid. It happens, you know? The brain-strainers can't explain everything in terms of fucked-up parents ruinin' kids. Sometimes bad kids happen to good people, just like retarded kids get born to smart people."

"That's different," Dom grumbled, "and you know I know it is. That ain't what I'm talkin' about."

"Well, what *are* you talkin' about?"

"I'm tellin' you, if you think Joey got like that all by himself, you don't know his family as good as you think you do."

"Well, shit, clue me in. Tell me."

"Nah nah. You find out for yourself. I tell you—the way you're lookin' at me now—you ain't gonna believe nothin'. I'll just tell you one thing about Joey I know you don't know."

"Hey, please do."

"Okay, so you knew Joey got thrown out of the Navy. Unfit for service, or some shit like that. So he was in Great Lakes, when he got kicked out. I got a call from a guy in Chicago, he does a little of this, little of that. So he calls me up and asks me if I can vouch for this guy says he knows me. It's Joey. So I told him, yeah, I know the kid, what's the problem? Guy says there ain't no problem, the kid's busted out, he's lookin' for work. He asks me what kinda work should he let him do. I tell him, hey, he's just a kid, he ain't nobody, don't give him nothin' serious. He says okay, we hang up, and I don't think nothin' more about it until Joey comes back here, oh, maybe six, seven months later.

"So," Dom interrupted himself to freshen his drink, "I ask him about Chicago, you know, he's sharp, I wanna see what he picked up, you never know. So he don't wanna talk about it. I approach him about it five, six times. Every time, soon as I bring it up about Chicago, all of a sudden Joey got someplace he's supposed to be, like five minutes ago. Hey, pretty soon it's a game. I mention Chicago just to see what kind of excuse he's gonna give me for why he gotta go.

"So one day I get a call from the guy in Chicago. It's about somethin' else, but before I let him get away, I ask him about Joey, whether the kid worked out all right for him or not. And he says, oh he didn't work for me, he worked for a cousin of his wife's. I said, oh yeah, what's he do? He goes, 'He runs a freak show.' I said, you mean with the funny guys? He said, yeah, yeah, like that. I said, well, you know, what'd Joey do? 'Cause I had no idea what I'm gonna hear. But you know what he says? Huh? The kid's a freak, he says. He dresses up like a broad and he does a strip. I said, oh, uh-huh.

"So now I say to myself, hey, here's a guy gets booted out of the Navy. He's young, he's strong, he's smart, he's in the second biggest city in the whole friggin' country, and of all the ways there are to make money, he picks the one where you gotta dress up like a broad and do a striptease in front of a club full of people who think shit like that is entertainin'."

"You sayin' Joey was queer?"

"I'm not sayin' anything more than what I said. Nothin' more, nothin' less. All I will say is this: Joey did not get that way by himself. He had lots of help."

"From his parents, right?"

"Of course from his parents. Who the hell am I talkin' about?"

"Maybe he got a physical problem from his parents."

"A what?"

"A physical problem. Maybe his chemicals were screwed up. Maybe his hormones were screwed up. It's possible."

Dom's glass was poised midway between the bar and his mouth. He set the glass down and leaned forward. "Chemicals my ass."

"Hey. What makes you an expert on this? This is complicated. You could put a urologist in a room with a psychiatrist and they wouldn't know all there was to know about it. It's a bunch of different things, you know?"

"Yeah?" Muscotti said. "Maybe so. Maybe I don't know everything there is. But I know the way people raise their kids. And you raise a boy to be like a girl, that's the way it's gonna grow up. And vice versa. And I don't give a crapola about the chemicals."

"You know what? It's a good thing you're a wise guy."

"D'you come in here to tell me that? Huh? You come in here to insult me? Is that what you come in here for?"

"Oh Christ, give me some wine, will ya?"

"What for? Your friggin' chemicals out of whack? You need a little alcohol in your formula there?"

Balzic pursed his lips and bounced his head from side to side as though to say, "That's cute," but he said nothing.

Muscotti snorted and grumbled under his breath and sidled off to get a glass and some jug Chablis. He returned and filled the glass in front of Balzic. "I ain't gonna give you a sermon about this. All I'm gonna say is this: go have yourself a talk with Joey's mother. Okay? And when you finish talkin' to her, then you come back here and talk to me about chemicals and hormones and all that other crap. Okay?"

"Okay. I'll do that." Balzic raised his glass and clinked it against Muscotti's. "Salud."

"Salud, salud." Muscotti sipped his drink. "Now you gonna tell me, or what?"

"Tell you what?"

"Whatta you think? What you quit drinkin' for for a whole friggin' week! You sick or what?"

"Yeah I'm sick. I got your problem. And I never had it before—not to this extent anyway—and it scared the hell outta me. And I'm still scared."

"So that's why you quit drinkin'." Muscotti threw back his head and laughed.

"Very funny. I'm glad I bring a little humor into your life."

"Mario, you kiddin' yourself or what? You been drinkin' since you come home from World War Two. So now what—you think 'cause you lay off for a week that's gonna reverse everything? Get serious."

"I am serious. I told you I'm scared."

"Hey, that's all right. Be scared. Ain't no shame in that. But you think you're gonna turn it around in one week, now that ain't a shame, but it ain't smart. You ain't gonna reverse in one week what took you since 1945 to do."

"Maybe not. But on the other hand, I don't know if that's what caused it. It might be somethin' else."

"Hormones I guess," Dom said, snorting.

Balzic put his hands on the bar and stiffened his arms. "Hey, you wanna talk to me about this or you just wanna jack me off about it? I mean, I just come from gettin' my ass chewed by

Father Marrazo, I really didn't look—never mind." Balzic stood and tossed a dollar on the bar and headed for the door.

"Hey, you're half-a-buck short," Muscotti called after him.

"That's all I have. I'm good for it. Or did I lose my credit too?"

"For crissake, Mario, you ain't the only guy this ever happened to. This been happenin' to guys as long as there been guys. What's so special about you?"

Balzic came back to the bar and stood there a moment, thinking about what he wanted to say. "What's special about me is that I always saw myself as bein' hard, bein' as hard as I had to be, but I never saw myself as bein' mean. I deal with mean people all the time and I always told myself, hey, I ain't one of them. No matter what, I ain't one of them. But in the last month or so, I found out where meanness comes from. It comes from feelin' weak, it comes from feelin' you got no power. It's adolescent bullshit is what it is. And I always pride myself on not fallin' for that crap. And now I find out it isn't something you fall for. It's somethin' that falls on you. And once it falls, everything you do from then on is a struggle to keep everything else up. And Christ, in the last week I've been mean to people, chicken-shit mean. I can't stop it. It just pours outta me. . . . I'll see ya, Dom, g'night."

Balzic let himself out and drove to city hall. He went inside and down to the lockup and slept in one of the cells. Sometime in the middle of the night, he jolted awake. He'd been dreaming. He was back in the Marine Corps and he was on the second floor of a frame building that was built in the same style as a barracks except that it was no larger than a house. He was standing at attention in a room with just a small desk and a plain chair and a sergeant kept walking around the chair and desk and asking Balzic over and over, "Where's Herky?" And Balzic kept saying over and over, "He's dead. He walked up to the bar in the Rocksburg Hotel and ordered a beer and when the bartender brought it to him he dropped over dead." To which the sergeant said, "Don't give me that shit, where's Herky?" "He's dead, I'm tellin' you. He's not here. He ordered a beer and when the bartender brought it, he just keeled over."

Balzic tried to focus in the tar black of the cell and couldn't even see his hands. He felt his face and it was clammy and damp. The dream woke him up twice more during the night and both times he kept trying to see his hands even though he knew it was ridiculous to try.

* * *

Balzic sat on the examining table, swinging his feet, drumming his fingers against the vinyl. Then he stood, thought about weighing himself, decided against it, and after a moment of rocking on his heels and toes dropped into the straight-backed chair where the nurse had minutes before taken his blood pressure. He closed his eyes and took long, deep breaths and tried to imagine a calm, quiet place. What he sensed instead was the too rapid hammering of the pulses in his neck and what flashed on the insides of his eyelids was one calamity after another. It looked like the six o'clock news from Channel Six: fires, car wrecks, and ambulances. He opened his eyes wide just as Dr. Bradford James opened the door and came in carrying Balzic's folder.

Bradford James, Balzic thought. How in hell did somebody named Bradford James wind up practicing medicine in Rocksburg? James had been Balzic's doctor for as long as he could remember. James had presided over the delivery of Balzic's daughters, he cared for Balzic's wife and mother—his mother was vehement in her admiration for him—and he had been giving Balzic physicals for years, but Balzic not only didn't know much about James, he also never felt really comfortable around him. How could that be? You trust a man to care for your whole family and yet the mere thought of having to talk to him makes you so nervous you can't be still.

For one thing, Balzic had never seen him anywhere except in his office or in Conemaugh General Hospital. Balzic had never seen him in any club or saloon or restaurant, not in church, not in any market or garage or shop. Balzic had heard that James played tennis and well, but there were no tennis courts in Rocksburg. Maybe, Balzic thought, maybe it was that goddamn toupee James wore. It had been an excellent fit and color long ago, but no man's hair stayed as thick as when he was twenty—or the same color—and surely James had to know that.

"Mario, how are you feeling today?" James said, pulling a small stool with wheels from under the table and sitting on it. He put Balzic's folder on the table and studied it.

"The same I guess."

"Well, we got the results of your tests back and that's why I asked you to drop by. It was very surprising to me, quite frankly. I mean, your problem is very common. Very common. So I always order this test just to eliminate the possibilities because—well, it just isn't the usual result."

"Uh, what result is that?"

James smiled quizzically. "Your testosterone is way down. It's clear down at the bottom edge of the scale. See for yourself." James turned the folder around and pointed at some numbers.

"What do these numbers mean?"

"Well, by themselves, they don't mean anything. They just represent a range of what the normal level of testosterone would be, and yours, as you can see, well, it's just way, way down."

Balzic frowned and rubbed his chin. "What's that mean?"

"Well it means that—first of all, it's very surprising. The problem as I said before is very, very common, and usually we can attribute it to some medication, for high blood pressure for example, or to undiagnosed diabetes, or to chronic overconsumption of alcohol, or to emotional problems, depression, for example, or chronic anxiety, but it's very rare that somebody actually has a deficiency of hormone."

Balzic thrust up his thumbs. "Is that good or bad?"

"Well, it's good in the sense that you're hormonally deficient and there are pills you can take that will correct that deficiency." James drew a prescription pad out of the pocket of his smock and wrote out a prescription. "We'll start you out with ten milligrams a day, and, uh, call me in a couple of weeks, let me know how you are."

"You mean I take this pill and, uh, the problem goes away? Just like that?"

"Just like that."

"Uh, how soon do I, will I notice a difference?"

"Well I would surely think in four or five days you'd notice some activity, some change."

Balzic thought for a moment. "So, uh, how's this happen?"

"Mario, take my word for it. It's not something you want to spend a great deal of time analyzing. Besides which, it's extremely complicated. Many glands, many organs are involved, circulation, and there's a great interconnectedness among all of them that I don't pretend to understand. If you want me to make an appointment for you with a urologist, I will, but I can tell you right now that even he won't have all the answers. My advice to you is that if your impotence can be alleviated by artificial testosterone, then you should take the pills and you should stop worrying about why your natural hormone quit producing itself."

"Okay. I'll try."

"Don't try. Do it. There are some things it's better not to think about."

"Maybe so, Doc, but it so happens I've got a problem with somebody else that sort of involves this. It's gonna be hard to stop thinkin' about it just because I can take a pill."

James tore the prescription sheet off the pad and handed it to Balzic. "Do what you have to do. Just one more thing. Are you still drinking as much as you used to?"

Balzic shrugged sheepishly. "I don't know how much I used to."

"That's not true and you know it. I think now's a good time to quit. I'm sure it contributed to your problem. It's probably the primary cause of your problem. No probably. It *is* the leading cause."

"Uh, wait a second. You're confusin' me here. A second ago you said my problem is my testosterone is way down. And then you give me a prescription for a pill. Now you tell me drinkin' is *the* cause of *my* problem. Which is it?"

"No, no, you're mistaking me. I didn't say it was the cause of *your* problem. I'm saying it is usually the cause of impotence among men your age—when all other considerations are eliminated. That's what I meant. I probably didn't make myself clear." James paused and folded his arms. "What I *am* saying is it's probably a good time for you to quit drinking."

"You mean—quit, that's it? Just quit?"

"Sure. Why not? It's a wise move. What's alcohol? Empty calories, a depressant, sexual inhibitor. The incidence of liver cancer, all sorts of cancer, is higher among people who drink excessively. Then there's high blood pressure—and yours is creeping up—"

"It is?"

"Sure. It's one-forty-six over eighty-eight. You quit alcohol, you come back here in a month I'll guarantee your pressure will be one-thirty-six over seventy-eight."

"I had enough trouble givin' up cigarettes."

"Yes, but you did it."

"Hey, cigarettes, that was a stinky, smelly habit that I quit as much for my family as for me. I found out my wife and my girls and my mother, they were gettin' smoke in their lungs, that's why I quit. It wasn't just my lungs. But no wine? No. Nah, I can't do that. I wouldn't want to get up in the morning thinkin' I couldn't drink wine."

"Sometimes the things we think we love are the things that kill us."

"Hey, I'm sure that's true," Balzic said, nodding his head vigorously. "But I'm also sure that, well, some of the best times in my life I associate with wine. Besides, I been drinking it all my life—since I was a kid. The only time I didn't have wine—the worst time of my life—was when I was in the Marines, in the war. . . . Some of the most peaceful times I know are when I'm just sittin' with my wife and she's havin' some wine with me. We're sittin' on the deck, watchin' the birds and the squirrels, hey, that's peace for me—or as near as I'm ever gonna get to it."

"As I said before, sometimes the things we think we love—"

"Yeah yeah, I heard what you said. There's somethin' else you gotta understand. I spend a lotta time in saloons. Doc, you can't spend time in saloons and not drink. The only people who can do that are bartenders, and most of them can't get through a shift without drinkin' something. Can you imagine bein' in a saloon and not drinkin'? Hell, Doc, there's no—you talk about alcohol bein' a depressant—hell, there's no more depressing place on earth than a saloon when you're not drinkin'. Sittin' around, sober, watchin' other people drink? Jesus, a guy told me once—and I believed him—he said the only place more depressing than a saloon when you're not drinkin' is a church when you got nothin' to pray for, when everybody you love is healthy and when all your enemies are either dead or paralyzed from the neck down."

Dr. James stood abruptly. "I see. Well. Come back in a month and we'll see how you're doing. Remember, one pill a day, and, uh, see the receptionist on the way out. Say hello to your mother." He was gone before Balzic could say good-bye.

Balzic put on his shirt, tie, and coats, and went out to the receptionist. He told her to bill him and then made an appointment for his return in four weeks. Then he went outside into a stinging wind and sleet like needles. He buried his chin against his chest and walked around the block to the pharmacy. Inside, he handed over the prescription and decided to wait for it.

All this fretting, all this fuming, he thought, all for what? To find out your chemicals have gone haywire. No reason. Things just get out of line. And now you stand in a pharmacy waiting for your potency to be given back to you in a pill. Despite Balzic's best intentions, he found himself studying the pharmacist to see how he was taking it. Was he smiling? Was that a smirk? Or was he just being his professionally pleasant best? And so what if he was? It wasn't as though you went out and purposely screwed up your own chemicals, Balzic thought, as though you got up one morning and said, "Well, lemme see, what can I fuck up today? I got it. Today I'll cause my testosterone level to drop off the shelf where I keep all my hormones. Yeah. Great. That's what I'll do today. I'll send my marriage into a swamp, put my self-respect into the toilet, and drop my masculinity right on the tops of my shoes. Boy, this'll be fun. Yessir." Right, Balzic thought, so what kind of look's he giving me? The sonofabitch. . . .

"Sir? Sir? Chief? Your prescription's ready."

"Huh? Oh. Yeah. Guess I was daydreamin'."

"Will that be cash or charge?"

"Wanna charge it please?"

"Certainly, Chief. Will there be anything else?"

"Uh, no. Say, uh, you sell a lotta these?"

"A lot of what, sir?"

"Uh, these pills you just gave me."

"Ummm, no sir. They're prescribed rather infrequently."

"Oh." Balzic put the prescription in his pocket and turned up his collar to step outside. "Uh, you're not from around here, are you?"

"No, sir. I'm from Philadelphia originally. I met my wife in pharmacy school and she was from Pittsburgh and, well, one thing led to another and here I am. Why do you ask?"

"I don't know. I was just wonderin' when was the last time I heard anybody say 'rather infrequently.'"

* * *

Balzic went to his cruiser and dropped into the seat. He closed the door and took out the bottle of artificial testosterone. He snapped off the lid and then held up the bottle to read the instructions. "Dissolve one under tongue each day." He pulled out the wad of cotton and dumped some pills into his hand. They were oblong, yellow caplets. "This is bizarre," he said. "The goddamn things are yellow." This is crazy, he thought. Artificial balls turn out to be yellow. Balls have nothin' to do with erections. Courage has nothin' to do with an ability to have erections. Courage has nothin' to do with an ability to screw. Screwin' has nothin' to do with being able to love somebody. Being able to love somebody has nothin' to do with feelin' as though you're worth loving, with bein' lovable. Bein' lovable has nothin' to do with strength. How much strength does it take to pull a trigger? Do you have the balls to kill somebody? Do you have the integrity to testify? All this crap about manhood, and what does it mean? All those things we say are manhood, and none of them has a goddamn thing to do with the hormones and chemicals or electrical impulses that flow across and through brain and glands and blood. All these things that cause a limp penis to become erect and what the hell do they have to do with refusing to take another man's crap? If you don't stand up for your rights, are you limp? Are you yellow? If you take enough of these oblong, yellow caplets will you be able to assert yourself? Will you be able to tell officious sales clerks to go fuck themselves? If you're cut off in traffic will you be able to thrust your middle finger erect and upwards at the offending driver? In movie theaters will you be able to tell talky people to shut up, they're not home watching TV? What in God's name does all this have to do with a dick that won't get stiff? You can kill people and someone will say you've got balls. You can beat people unconscious and people will say you've got balls. You can stare down a crowd and people will say you've got balls. And they're talking about courage and nerve and control over your nerves and no matter what they're talking about, it has nothing to do with blood and brain, hormones and chemicals, impulses and desires that cause a limp organ to hear the National Anthem and prepare to march.

Good God, Balzic thought, how many young men have died or been disfigured because old men told them that in order to become men they had to demonstrate their willingness to murder or be murdered in the name of a flag waving atop a stiff pole. "Put a flag over her face and fuck for Old Glory" was a bad joke he'd heard about homely women and virile men for as long as he could remember. And what good was an erect dick with most women anyway? Were you a man because you could hump yourself to orgasm? Was a woman nothing but a mass of warm, wet tissue into which a man humped himself till he was what—limp again? What in the hell were all these bizarre characteristics—masculinity, manhood, virility, integrity, potency, power, courage, strength, nerve, guts, balls—what in hell did they have to do with oblong, yellow caplets of artificial hormone? What in hell did they have to do with cunning or guile or intelligence or earning money? What in the hell did they have to do with three-piece suits and neckties? What in hell did they have to do with pistols and shotguns and rifles and intercontinental ballistic missiles? What the hell did they have to do with muscles and motorcycles? What the hell did they have to do with tattoos? Why could an Orthodox priest have a wife and a Catholic priest not and why could a Moslem have four wives? Did they all have a different prescription of oblong, yellow caplets?

My God, Balzic thought, I wear suits and ties, I've killed people in the name of a flag atop a stiff pole, I've beaten people unconscious, I've fathered children, I've seen people at their stomach-turning worst, and nothing humbles me like the sensation of my own saggy flesh. How unfucking pathetic can you get? No matter what else I've done or not done, nothing tears at my self-respect like uncooperative tissue. And never, never have I been so goddamn mean. Petty, stinking, small-minded, chicken-shit mean. And yet, when I find out that a chemical is out of balance, that all I have to do to put things right is dissolve a pill under my tongue once a day, why am I so suspicious? Why do I think this involved something more than chemicals? Why was I hoping it would involve something I could think about? And what would I think about? Oh shit, Balzic, for once in your life, quit thinkin'! Take the goddamn pill, put it under your tongue, and get on with your life.

He put one of the oblong yellow caplets under his tongue and frowned at the medicinal bitterness, a taste unlike anything he'd tasted before. He kept wanting to put the caplet on top of his tongue and suck on it as though it were a throat lozenge and to hurry its dissolution, but its taste kept reminding him to keep it where it was supposed to be.

After a few moments when it occurred to him that the caplet was going to take more than a few minutes to dissolve, he shrugged, shook his head, and started the car and drove off toward city hall trying to convince himself that he was not part of a study by the pharmaceutical company and that he had not been part of the group to get the placebo.

* * *

In the station, Desk Sergeant Vic Stramsky was on the phone and held up two phone messages as Balzic walked by on his way to his office. One was from his wife; the other was from Harold Coblentz.

He looked at the paper Stramsky handed him and went into his office and shut the door. He sat down and looked at the phone for what seemed an hour. It wasn't even a minute. Then coughing, snorting, sighing, tugging at his nose, rolling his head from side to side, he picked up the phone and punched the buttons for his home number.

His wife answered at the end of the first ring.

"Yes?"

"It's me. What's wrong? Something wrong there?"

"No. But that would depend on what we were talking about, wouldn't it?"

"Yeah, but what I mean is, you're okay, Ma's okay, nobody's got an emergency, right?"

"If that's what you mean, you're right. Nobody's got any emergencies. Course we would like to know if you're all right. Nobody here has seen you since the day before yesterday. Or heard from you either."

"I've been busy as hell."

"Mario, busy I'm used to. No word, no message, that I'm not used to."

"I was—hey, I got no excuses. But I really didn't have anything to tell you, so, uh . . ."

"Mario, all anybody expected was for you to check in. You know. It's the way we've done it for almost thirty years now. It's a little late to start changin' the rules."

"You're right. I should've called."

"Yes you should've."

"Well I'm callin' now."

"Okay. I'm listening now. So tell me what's going on. What did Bradford say?"

"Bradford? I didn't know you called him Bradford."

"That's just one more thing you don't know about me. I call

him Bradford cause it makes me feel like I'm in a soap opera. That's what they name men on soap operas. Bradford and Desmond and Elliott and Royce. I don't call him that to his face. Mario, he's the guy who gives me internal examinations, you know? And I do not call the guy who does that by his first name. I mean, first names and rubber gloves up your bottom do not go together—not with me they don't. You still there?"

"I'm still here."

"Well?"

"Well what?"

"Well what the hell did he say?"

"About what?"

"A-bout you, Mario. Jesus."

"He said—he said my testosterone was way down. He prescribed these pills I gotta dissolve under my tongue. I got one in now."

"Oh."

"That's all? Oh?"

"Well, what does that mean?"

"Well it means that I got this deficiency—don't ask me how—and I take these pills and that corrects it. And I should see a difference in four, five days. That's—that's what he said."

"Well, Mario, that sounds good—don't you think? I mean, it sounds great to me."

Balzic shrugged. "Hey, I guess it sounds good to me too. We'll just have to see if these pills work."

"Okay. I guess we will."

"Okay. So I'll see you later then."

"You coming home?"

"Yeah. I'll be home for supper probably."

"Well. Good. Good. I'll see you then."

"Me too. See you."

Balzic hung up and stared at the phone for some moments.

No problem there, he thought. Nooooo. Just try to remember not to apologize for being a jerk and everything will work out just swell. Yeah. You bet. Oh boy. . . .

He forced himself to focus on the other message Stramsky had given him, the one from Harold Coblentz, Collier's attorney. He also had to force himself to poke the buttons of Coblentz's number.

When a receptionist answered, Balzic said simply, "Mario Balzic, chief of Rocksburg PD, returning Mr. Coblentz's call."

Almost immediately, Coblentz was on the other end, his voice a full, rich baritone. "Chief Balzic. At last we connect. You've been calling me for days, as I understand it, and now, finally, I'm free and at your disposal. What can I do for you?"

"Well, it's about a client of yours. Francis Collier."

"I see, I see. What about him?"

"Well, the father of the victim asked me to conduct a sort of unofficial investigation. The father is convinced that the state police have botched it, and, after a few days of nosing around and poking around, I'm inclined to agree with him."

"Chief Balzic, let me put your mind at rest. No matter how badly the state police have botched their investigation—and to put those two ideas in conjunction with one another is to overstate the obvious, i.e., the state police *always* botch their investigations; it is why they are police, number one, and why they are employed by the state, number two. Were it otherwise, they would not be state police; they'd be engaged in reputable, honorable work." Coblentz paused to breathe noisily. "Now, to put your mind at ease, ergo the mind of the father of one Joseph Castelucci, this unfortunate sequence of events matches all the criteria for justifiable homicide. Mr. Collier was attacked. The attack was unprovoked. Mr. Collier made every effort to escape. The attack not only continued but gave every appearance of escalating to the point that Mr. Collier feared for the safety of his very life. Mr. Collier then used every means at his disposal to protect his life. Sad to say, this required that he end the life of Mr. Castelucci. I'm certain that Mr. Castelucci's father would have it be otherwise. So, in fact, would we all. None of us, least of all Mr. Collier, wished to see Mr. Castelucci's life ended in that way. But end in that way it did."

"Yeah, well, that's the way it was supposed to look, I guess," Balzic said, "but there are a few things that don't fit the sequence."

"Indeed. Such as?"

"Well, there's a pattern of shots fired. Three witnesses say that one shot was fired, then there was a long period, from thirty to sixty seconds before the next shot was fired. Then there was a rapid sequence of shots. That doesn't fit too good with the attempt to escape the attack. It also doesn't fit too good with Mr. Collier's statement that he got the piece from the glove compartment in his car. One other witness says he always carried a piece in a holster in the small of his back and she was with him that night and she never saw him put the piece in the glove compartment. And he was never out of her sight. In other words, he had the piece on him the whole time, from the first time he saw Castelucci."

"Interesting," Coblentz said evenly. "Mr. Collier, of course, will dispute those allegations under oath in a trial that should not be happening because the charges will be dismissed. The state does not have a case, Chief. You know that and I know it, and why the state is going to waste all of our money trying to prove the contrary is beyond my understanding."

"Well, when I first started looking at this, I think I would have been inclined to agree with you. But the more I talk to people, the more fuzzy some things get."

"Chief Balzic, things, as you put it, can get as fuzzy as cheap wool, but some facts are indisputable. And the law speaks to those facts, incontrovertibly, no matter how much one might wish it otherwise."

"Yeah? Such as? Which facts?"

"Oh," Coblentz said, chuckling softly, "I think you know which facts I mean. Now, it has been interesting chatting with you, Chief, but my schedule really is very rigidly structured these days, so, I must say good-bye, unless of course, there's something else you wish to say?"

"There's a witness," Balzic said.

"A witness? If you're referring to Mr. Itri, I'm strongly convinced he is not going to be much use to the state. And if you're referring to Miss Cooper, I'm absolutely convinced she is of no use to the state."

"You know about Itri, huh?"

"Oh my yes. We found Mr. Itri within a matter of days. It wasn't very difficult. All we had to do was look at the right time. Yes, yes. We looked, we looked. We found him. Mr. Itri is not going to be speaking about anything. Even if he did see something, which I strongly doubt, he is conscience-bound not to speak about it. Anything else, sir? Anything at all?"

"Conscience-bound?"

"Yessir, that's what I said."

"Look, he may be conscience-bound, but he's got no protection for that conscience of his. If he's subpoenaed, he'll have to testify."

"And what is the state supposed to do when he says that he saw nothing—which is what he will do I will wager sizable money on it—what then? Chief, he can be subpoenaed, he can be sworn, he can be asked what you think are the most pertinent questions in what I will surely think is a most impertinent manner, but he cannot be made to testify about an event he has not observed. I mean, really, Chief Balzic, short of some medieval test for truth, how do you expect the fellow to violate his principles, his conscience?"

"He saw it, didn't he?"

"Oh come now, Chief, how do you expect me to reply to that?"

"Tell the truth. How 'bout that? That's simple enough."

"Chief Balzic, I hardly need to remind you that this is not Great Britain. We're not a merry club of truth-seekers here, all devoted to the carriage of justice. My allegiance is not to the truth. My allegiance is to my client's defense. The state and I are not cooperating partners. The state, sir, and you know this as well as I do, is my adversary. I live in Pennsylvania, I pay taxes in Pennsylvania, I am a proud citizen of this commonwealth, but when I walk into that courtroom on behalf of Mr. Collier, well, sir, Pennsylvania is my client's mortal enemy, and I am his champion. Corny as it sounds, *that* is my truth.

"And should that enemy choose to put Mr. Itri on the stand—and one may never really know how a witness is going to proceed—why then, sir, I would be doing less than my duty to my client if I did not see to it that Mr. Itri's mother was seated among the spectators."

"You would, huh?"

"I would indeed, sir. Oh yes." There came the sound of Coblentz drinking, followed by a satisfied sigh. "Will there be anything else, Chief?"

"I guess not."

"Oh, Chief, there's no reason for that tone of dejection. Look at it this way: it's not your case, nobody's going to fault you. I'm quite certain that if you had been the investigating officer I would have had to work much more diligently than I have."

"Well, then maybe you could tell me what I'm supposed to say to old man Castelucci."

There was a long silence. Then Coblentz said, "I'm sure I cannot advise you about that. And I do not envy you your task. Uh, I really must go, Chief."

"Oh. Yeah, sure. Listen, thanks for, uh . . . Thanks."

"You're welcome. Good-bye."

Balzic hung up and folded his arms on his desk and rested his chin on them. God, he thought. If *I* had been the investigating officer, *he* would've had to work "much more diligently." Yeah, sure. I've been so goddamn diligent I haven't talked to the goddamn paramedics and I haven't talked to the goddamn lab people, I haven't laid eyes on the gun, I don't know what the blood reports look like, if the lights went out I couldn't find my ass with either hand because all that's on my goddamn mind—what I think is left of my goddamn mind—is that bunch of shriveled potential I never used to worry about or wonder about or think about, it was just there, and then it was but it wasn't and god what crap I laid off on Ruth and of all the things that scare me nothing scares me like the thought of never ever again in this life doing what is nothing but natural stuff, and just thinkin' about it and thinkin' about it until you can't do anything but look for a place to hide because all you can do is think about why you can't do something and now there's a pill, Jesus Christ Almighty, there's a pill and all you have to remember to do is to take the goddamn thing every day and hope it works hope it works hope it works . . . marriage is work, everybody says that and what the hell does that mean, how come work gets into it, it's broken, you asshole, and when a thing gets broken, somebody has to repair it, and repair means work, and that's how work gets into it . . . what *is* this, I'm losin' it, I got no control, the thing is out of my control, I'm sittin' around waitin' for artificial balls to work, artificial balls manufactured by strangers in a factory, half of them are probably women, and God knows where the factory is, probably in Japan, they make every other goddamn thing, no reason why they don't make that, no matter where it is it's strangers, for crissake, I have to rely on strangers to reclaim my potential . . . I gotta get outta here, I'm thinkin' nonsense . . . Jesus Christ, I never even asked Coblentz if it was all right with him if I talked to Collier. Oh God. . . .

* * *

Balzic started out through the duty room, heading for where he had no idea. The odor of excrement stopped him. Patrolman Harry Lynch was being pushed away from the radio console by Sgt. Joe Royer who was pinching his nostrils.

"C'mon, Joe, goddammit."

"Go stand over there by the door. I can hear ya. Just get the hell away from me."

"What's goin' on?" Balzic said.

"We got a problem, Mario," Lynch said. "I got this woman out in the cruiser. You ain't gonna like this but it's the only way I could do it. I got her handcuffed to the cage."

"Yeah. So?"

"So I was cruisin' up on Norwood and a guy run out and practically threw himself on the hood, he's all outta joint, he says I gotta do somethin' about the stink or the animals or somethin', I forget exactly what he said. Anyway he takes me out to the end of the street, out where the old hospital used to be, the last house." Lynch hung his head and took several long, deep breaths.

"Anybody got a cigar? I gotta smoke somethin'. If I don't I'm gonna be sick."

Royer reached in the bottom drawer of the console desk and fished around until he found a cigar. He tossed it to Lynch who quickly unwrapped it and got it lit and going. "So anyway this guy never stops yakkin' at me, the woman's nuts, she's got dogs, she's crazy, the dogs are killin' each other, they're all starvin', the stink's so bad when the wind is wrong he's gonna kill her himself and all her dogs too, and the health department's a joke and on and on. So I'm thinkin' maybe he's looney tunes, right? Wrong. We get to the house and it's everything he said only it's twice as bad." Lynch puffed hard on the cigar and sent up billows of smoke. He closed his eyes and rubbed his brow.

"I swear to you, I have seen a lot of stuff in my time, but I never—I mean I abso-fucking-lutely never saw anything like this. You could smell that—I mean I parked at least thirty yards from the front door and I was gaggin' every step I took." Lynch took time out to send more smoke into the air.

"Mario, as God is my witness, the shit on the floor in the first room I started into—well, it came up over my shoes. And I'm talkin' about dry *and* wet. And then here she comes, screechin' at me and honest to God she's makin' noise like a fuckin' dog, she ain't talkin', she's whimperin' and cryin'. And then—and then! The goddamn dogs started. And then I *saw* the dogs. The live ones *and* the dead ones. I don't know how many there are, I mean, I wasn't gonna stand there and count 'em, but I saw three heads on the floor and there were at least eight live ones and—Jesus Christ, she was in her bare feet—and I'm not goin' out and get in that car with her again. Here's the keys for my cuffs and here's the keys for the cruiser." Lynch tossed both to Joe Royer.

"I got sick days, I got personal days, I got vacation time and if you think I'm gonna get in that car with that woman again, I'm gonna take all the time I got comin' startin' right now. You understand me, Mario?"

"I understand you, Harry. Just take it easy and tell me who you called."

"Who I called, who I called, I'll tell you who I called, lemme think. I called the health department first. They're gonna send somebody up there. When, I don't know. Then I called the dog officer. I don't know where the fuck he is, he don't answer. This was after I jerked that woman outta there, carried her to the cruiser, and cuffed her to the cage. And I only threw up once gettin' her there and only once gettin' her here. But I'll be fucked by little gorillas first before I touch that woman again, you hear me, Mario?"

"Nobody's askin' you to touch her again—"

Lynch slapped his thigh and threw up his hand. "Oh oh oh I didn't tell you the best part. Before I brought her here, I took her up the Mental Health, right? That's sensible, right? You don't have to be a head doctor to see the woman's a nut case, right? They got no rooooom! They don't wanna know nothin'. The boss is in Bermuda somewhere, the other shrinks are in a budget meeting over in the main hospital, and every bed's full anyway, so here I am with this woman she don't talk, all she does is make dog noises, her feet are black from dog crap, she's got drool runnin' all over her face—she got dog shit in her hair! Mario, in her hair, Jesus . . . Christ," Lynch said, gagging and retching. "Mario, I gotta go home and take these clothes off, these shoes. I'm gonna burn 'em. And I may not come back for a couple days. I'm goin', I'm goin', right now. I'm goin'." Lynch put his head down and started for the door, stripping off his tie before he barged through the inner door and then the storm door.

Balzic sighed and pushed his glasses up his nose. He turned to Royer and said, "Call Mutual Aid, tell 'em to get down here with a strait jacket and get that woman into the hospital one way or another. Then call the hospital and tell 'em what they got to look forward to. And tell 'em that if that woman is not in a hospital bed until somebody can figure out what to do with her,

I'm gonna call every newspaper and TV station within fifty miles and tell them about her. And find that goddamn dog officer and get those dogs outta there.

"Oh shit, did you get the address from Lynch?"

"Yeah, he was puttin' it on the desk when I was pushin' him away from me."

"Good." Balzic went toward the door to the parking lot. "And after they get that woman out, get that cruiser cleaned."

"Where you goin'?"

"Damned if I know. Someplace else."

* * *

Balzic drove around Rocksburg, just keeping up with traffic, forcing himself to observe things, pedestrians, vehicles, drivers, buildings, signs, guys hanging out, so he wouldn't have to think. It was something he'd discovered years ago—he couldn't remember exactly where or when—when he was practicing observing details about people or vehicles or places. When he was studying, say, the shape of the front end on a model of car he hadn't seen before, he found that he couldn't think of anything else. When he'd first become a cop, he did it to sharpen himself, to tune his mind to observe and remember details about people and numbers and places, but ever since he'd made the discovery that he could not think while he was doing that, he also found he did it because sometimes doing it was very pleasant and relaxing and because in order to do it well he could not think about anything else. Focusing on a thing, the stones above a window or a person's face or the cornice on a building he'd passed a hundred times before forced him to forget time, because if he was really trying to see what was different about that person's nose or that taillight assembly, what set it apart, then he found that he would lose track of time.

In the last week or so, he'd come to another conclusion. He'd had almost nothing alcoholic to drink and he found himself turning more and more to this habit of observation, and as he was driving along now, he got the idea that this habit was as much a way out of himself as alcohol was. When he found himself staring hard at the folds and shadows and colors in some person's coat, focusing on something that would have been extremely difficult for him to describe to another person, that's when he knew he was doing it to get out of his thoughts, to get out of thinking. Sometimes he thought that the cause of all addiction—drugs, alcohol, religion, politics, work, play, sex, money, power, food, noise, sleep—was the fear of being alone with no way to shut off your mind. You'd do damn near anything to avoid that. Nothing was scarier than being free and sober, because you had to figure out what to do next and you knew that no matter which way it went you couldn't blame anybody else for how it turned out. You'd say anything, tell any lie—I was tired, I was drunk, I was high, I was low, I was pissed off, I was pissed on—to cop a plea to avoid doing time with yourself. Ask any con, ask any political prisoner, what was the worst time they had to do and they would all tell you the same thing: solitary. It didn't matter what it was called—administrative segregation, protective isolation, individual discipline, personal re-education—the terror of being left alone with their thoughts had socialized more people than the Ten Commandments, the Apostles Creed, and the Magna Carta combined. It seemed to Balzic that it took a special gift, almost a talent, like musical or athletic ability, for a person to be alone with no means of altering his sobriety. Balzic figured that, given those terms—no sound, no company, and nothing to consume to distort reality or change sobriety, most people would be screaming in fifteen minutes. . . . God, Balzic thought, ain't theories wonderful? Where am I going with this? Where am I going, period? Wonder if I could go to Muscotti's and drink water in the middle of the day and not explain why I was doing it? The hell with that. I'd sooner sit through a city council meeting when they were listening to appeals about zoning decisions. Talk about fun . . . Dom said go see Mrs. Castelucci. Well, hell, why not? Trial starts tomorrow. May as well talk to her. I'm out of luck as far as Collier's concerned.

* * *

Balzic set off for Rocksburg Manor, the newest high-rise for the elderly. It had been built on the site of a former supermarket about six blocks south of city hall. Balzic hated going near the Manor, as it was called, because it had been built with two things in mind: ease and speed of construction. There was nothing to distinguish it. It was a seven-story rectangle, curtain walls made of unpainted concrete, windows framed in unpainted aluminum, the architectural equal of fast food. But if the outside was dismaying, the inside was positively depressing. After the first time Balzic had reason to see an apartment there, he went home and told Ruth that he hoped she understood, but that no matter what happened to them, no matter what screwy things life might drop on them, they would never, ever spend the last year of their lives in Rocksburg Manor.

He thought of that while he searched names on the mailboxes in the lobby. The last time he'd visited the Casteluccis they were living in one of the coal patches in Westfield Township. He found their name and pressed their bell.

"Yeah. Who is it?" came Castelucci's wheezy voice.

"Balzic. I'd like to talk to you."

"Yeah. Go 'head. But whoa, wait a minute. You gotta use the steps. The elevator's on the fritz again."

The inner door popped open and Balzic hustled through it and went up the stairs. By the time he got to the fourth floor, he was breathing through his mouth.

Castelucci was standing in the hall by his apartment and motioning for Balzic to come on.

"How long's the elevator been out?" Balzic said as he was steered into the apartment.

"Aw that goddamn thing, it's been kaflooey three times since we been here. C'mon in, sit down, sit down."

Balzic looked around for a place to sit and decided that he'd rather be at the kitchen table, which was in the middle of the room that was supposed to serve as a dining–living room combination. The kitchen was too small to have a table. It was too small to have two persons in it. Two persons could stand in it, Balzic supposed, but not if one of them wanted to open the stove or the refrigerator.

"You want a coffee or somethin'?"

"No. Nothing, thank you," Balzic said, taking off his raincoat and draping it over the back of his chair.

"So, uh, is this when I get my report?"

"Uh, where's your wife?"

"She's in the bedroom." Castelucci poked his thumb in the air two or three times.

Balzic took those thumb pokings to mean the bedroom was behind him.

"Maybe you ought to ask her if she wants to hear any of this."

"Huh? No. Nah. I thought I told ya. My wife don't wanna

hear nothin'. Nah, she's in there rockin'. Rockin' and rollin' I used to tell her when she'd be in our place we had in the patch. She used to think that was funny, she used to laugh. Now, she don't even look at me."

Castelucci was overcome by coughing. After it passed, he wiped his eyes, mouth, and nose with the hankies he had in both hands.

After a moment, he said, "So don't hold back. Let's hear it." He folded downward into a chair across the table from Balzic.

Balzic pursed his lips and licked them and said, "Mr. Castelucci, I'm gonna be brief and blunt. The state police made a very sloppy investigation. The trooper who was assigned to the case was the one who responded to the first call. And he is not what you would call a good police officer. He made several mistakes in, uh, in how he handled the whole thing. But no matter—"

"See, that's what I told you. Didn't I tell you that?"

"Yes, yes, I know, you told me that, but, Mr. Castelucci, there are certain facts in the case that have nothing to do with his competence."

"Yeah? Such as what?"

"Well, the biggest one is that without apparent provocation—and notice I said *apparent*—without apparent provocation Joey attacked this man with his fists and his feet, and right before he was shot, he threw a cinder block, a regular building block through the man's car window at him.

"Now, no matter who is investigating this, whether it's Trooper Helfrick or me or Sherlock Holmes, you know, those things are not gonna change. Those facts are facts, verified by witnesses at the scene, and by the coroner, and by the emergency room physician. The coroner's gonna say that Joey had what are called aggressive wounds on his hands, scrapes, bumps, bruises, cuts, that came from punchin' somebody else. The ER doctor will say that he spent a long time sewin' up this other guy. The other guy's lawyer is gonna produce photographs of what he looked like as a result of the beating he took from Joey. The lawyer took those pictures himself. And the doctor saw him takin' 'em—"

"Aw so what? That ain't the important thing. The important thing is they set him up. They suckered him into comin' up there, they suckered him into a fight, and then that shiney-ass shot him."

"Mr. Castelucci, that's, uh, that's what we call highly speculative."

"Well that's what I wanted you to check out! That's what I got you into this for!"

"Mr. Castelucci, how? How did you expect me to check this out? I'm not a mind reader. Let me explain something—"

"Aw baloney."

"Just listen a minute, please. You listenin'?"

"Yeah yeah I'm listenin'."

"You're talkin' about premeditation. You're talkin' about the willful thought that one human being has that leads him to do something and—and that can be proved according to the rules of evidence. Mr. Castelucci, you're talkin' about something that is very difficult, very, very difficult to prove. See, what the prosecutor's thinkin' about is voluntary manslaughter—"

"What?"

Balzic squirmed on his chair. "Mr. Castelucci, that can't come as a surprise to you."

"Whatta ya mean surprise? Jesus, that's what I got you into this for." The old man threw up his hands in disgust. "I knew they screwed it up. That's what I wanted you to do. Unscrew it. What the hell—you gonna tell me it's screwed up and that's all there is to it?"

Balzic looked at the folds and shadows in his pants and told himself that if he wasn't careful he was going to just drift away. He forced himself to look at the old man.

"Mr. Castelucci, the rules of judicial procedure do not give prosecutors a whole lot of room to play around with speculation about why somebody did something. Judges want to know facts. They want to hear that A happened and then B happened because A happened and so on. Are you listenin' to me?"

"You're just—yeah I'm listenin', whatta ya think I'm doin' here? I'll tell ya what you're doin' though. You're givin' me the same old crap I been gettin' all along."

"Mr. Castelucci, whatta you want to happen? Tell me exactly what you think ought to happen here."

"They set him up. She was always tryin' to hurt him. I don't know why, what the hell do I know. But she been tryin' to hurt Joey almost—hell, before they was married she started—"

"What do you want to happen? Exactly."

"First degree murder. That's what I want. Both of 'em. Him

and her. She drove Joey there and he was waitin'. And he done somethin'. Don't ask me what 'cause I don't know. But you say Joey just attacked him. That's what everybody says. And that's the part I know is bull. My kid was a lotta things. Some of 'em not too good. But he didn't just go around beatin' hell outta people for no reason. *That* I know."

"Okay," Balzic said, rubbing his throat with his fingernails. "Okay. So why? Why'd they do that? There sure as hell wasn't any profit in it for 'em. Sure wasn't any insurance money, and the nearest anybody can come to a reason is that Rose was on Joey's back to pay for a divorce. But that makes no sense 'cause she could've got a no-fault divorce for, hell, a hundred and seventy-five bucks the most. So why? What the hell'd they have to gain by settin' him up to kill him?"

Castelucci shook his head and snorted and laughed. "Jesus, Balzic, I don't believe you. D'you ever hear of meanness? Plain goddamn meanness? Huh? You mean to tell me in all the time you been a cop you ain't never heard of somebody just killin' somethin' or hurtin' somethin' just for the pure mean hell of it?"

"But Mr. Castelucci, no matter what I've heard of, what I'm tellin' you—what I'm trying to tell you—is that a judge is not going to allow that kind of speculation to enter into it. You might be right. You might be *absolutely* right, but being right in this case doesn't matter because it can't be proved, do you understand what I'm tryin' to say?"

The old man hung his head in his hands. "If you can't prove that, they ain't gonna prove nothin'. The sons of bitches are gonna get away with it. And that's wrong. They planned it, and they set him up, and they killed him, goddammit, her just as much as him and they're just gonna walk away free as goddamn birds. You disappoint the hell outta me, Balzic. I thought you'd do better'n this."

Balzic lurched upward suddenly and said, "I'd like to talk to your wife."

"Hey. Go right ahead. Just go on and talk yourself outta breath. She's in there. And you lemme know if she says anythin', 'cause if she does it'll be the first time she talked in about four months. I don't even remember what her voice sounds like. But you wanna talk to her, hell, why not? Right through that door, go 'head," Castelucci said, gesturing wildly, angrily at a door behind him.

Balzic stepped around the table and went to the door and opened it and slipped inside. He was struck immediately by a strong odor of urine, rising from the carpet. Then he was struck by the sight of a woman in a creaky wooden rocker, going back and forth, a woman he knew but would not have recognized if he had seen her in the street. She was nothing but bones and mottled skin. Her yellowish hair was brushed and her flannel robe looked decently clean, but her eyes were glazed and her mouth was working as though she was talking, but she made no sound. She gave no sign that she was aware of Balzic's presence. She just kept rocking, her head moving no more than four inches in either direction, and her hands were splayed palms up in her lap, her thumbs moving in rhythm with her rocking.

Balzic spoke her name, but if she heard she didn't respond. He went nearer to her, a step away and bent over and tried to make her eyes connect with his by peering into them. If she saw him, she didn't show that she did. She just kept rocking.

"Mrs. Castelucci, do you know me?"

She did not answer.

"I'm here about Joey. I'd like to talk to you about Joey."

Her rocking continued without the slightest change in rhythm.

Balzic straightened up and rubbed his lips. He looked around the room. Besides the rocker, there was a double bed, made but rumpled slightly, two chests of drawers along the wall at the foot of the bed, a small square table near the head of the bed, and a card table and folding chair against the wall. There was an oval-shaped mirror on that table and several bottles of prescription medicines. There was a worn Bible next to the medicines and next to that a photo album. Balzic leaned over and picked up the album.

"May I look at this?"

She did not respond.

He sat on the edge of the bed and started to thumb through the album. There were wedding pictures and pictures taken at picnics and at gatherings in church basements and outside the portals of deep mines and the bath houses and in the union halls. There were pictures of families, stiff, smiling artificially, pressed against each other like mushrooms after a rain, page after black page filled with rectangles of people looking awkwardly at the camera. Very few were smiling.

After thirty or forty pages, the baby pictures began. They went on for about five pages and Balzic had to look at them three times before he could see what was wrong. The first four pages were of the appearance and growth of a girl child. It was not until the first school picture on the bottom of the fifth page that a boy appeared. From then on, the pictures followed the growth of that boy, as well as the family, through his school years and into the Navy. The boy, of course, was Joey. There were no more pictures of him after one very formal portrait of him as a sailor, taken most likely when he was in recruit training.

Balzic retraced Joey's growth until he got to what was obviously a picture of him taken in the first grade when he was six. Balzic looked at the preceding pictures and even after he recognized what he was seeing, he wondered if his eyes were tricking him. He stood, took another long look into Mrs. Castelucci's dull eyes, and carried the album out to the table where Mr. Castelucci sat with his left cheek in his hand.

Balzic put the album on the table and pointed to the pictures of the baby and the infant growing up. "Is this Joey?"

Mr. Castelucci glanced at the photos and nodded slowly.

Balzic waited for Castelucci to say something, but he didn't. "Uh, you mind tellin' me about this?"

"Tellin' you about what?"

"About what? Are you serious? Your son was raised—I mean if these pictures are any indication—hell, he was, I mean I had to look at 'em three times before it finally hit me. This wasn't your idea, was it?"

Castelucci shook his head no.

"Well, uh, if it wasn't your idea, how'd you let it happen? I mean you were around, right?"

"Yeah. I was around."

"Well couldn't you see what was happening? Or didn't you look?"

"I looked. I looked. I ain't blind. But so what? What the hell's that have to do with that sonofabitch Collier shootin' him? You're lookin' at me like you think it was okay for Collier to shoot him 'cause his mother dressed him up like a girl till he started to go to school."

"Oh c'mon."

"Well that's what you're lookin' like. You're lookin' like you solved everything right here. But you ain't solved nothin'.

'Cause I don't care how my wife dressed up my kid when he was little. That didn't give Collier a right to shoot him thirty years later."

"I didn't say it did, Mr. Castelucci. But didn't it bother you why your kid was always in trouble?"

Castelucci stood up quickly and immediately was consumed by coughing. Fully a minute passed before he regained his composure. He wiped his mouth and nose with the hankies and when he talked he could not raise his voice about a loud whisper.

"Balzic, don't go twistin' things around. The question here ain't how my kid got raised. The question here is how my kid got killed. And that's the only question. And if you ain't gonna help answer that, then I made a mistake askin' ya. And when the trial gets goin'—which it is tomorrow—I guarantee you nobody is gonna give a good goddamn what my kid looked like when he was five years old."

"You're right, you're right. But I'm just really baffled by this. I mean you're a—"

"There ain't no big deal here. I can tell ya in a minute what happened. We got to foolin' around before we should've. She, uh, carried it the whole way and when it was time, it was born dead. And it was a girl. And she never got over it. You know, this sort of thing was not looked on like it is today. My wife's a very good Catholic. And she committed a sin. And it, uh, it . . . it caused her to dwell on it. She just could never get loose from it. . . . You satisfied now? Huh? See, that still didn't give that sonofabitch a license to shoot him. And my wife's in there now, and she's gonna go to her grave thinkin' she paid twice for the same sin. And that ain't right, Balzic. . . . Maybe we did a sin the first time. I don't know. I ain't all—I ain't religious. I don't understand all that stuff. . . . All I know is, no matter what we done, no matter what Joey done, that don't make it right for that prick to do what he did. And I'm tellin' ya it was a set-up job and that's what I wanted you lookin' at and I didn't want ya lookin' at what my kid looked like before he ever got his first haircut."

Balzic slumped into the chair he'd been sitting in before and rubbed his temples. "You know, Mr. Castelucci, there are at least two schools of thought on how we, uh, become what we become. The Catholic theory, that says we don't know too much before the age of seven, the age of reason, and so they put all the emphasis on teaching, school, church, catechism, that sort of thing. And then the other extreme goes that we're formed by the time we've been alive for three years, our character, personality. Who knows? The truth is probably something in between, dependin' on all the other things that all these things depend on."

Castelucci squinted at Balzic and whispered, "If you're gettin' ready to tell me I screwed up my kid's whole life 'cause I didn't say nothin' when my wife dressed him up in dresses, save your breath, huh?"

"Okay, I won't tell you anything. I'll just ask you if you never asked yourself why Joey was always fightin', always gettin' in trouble, always gettin' hurt. This stuff just didn't start with his wife. This was goin' on for years. Jesus, his rap sheet started when he was ten. He didn't know Rose then. He didn't know Rose when the Navy booted him out. He—"

"Oh bullshit. Tell me somethin', Balzic. Whatta you know about Collier? You seen his rap sheet? What's his record in the service? He ever punch Rose out? Huh? He been shacked up with her for at least a year. What'd he look like when he was four years old? How old was he when he got his first haircut? You talked to his father? Huh? You asked his old man about how he raised him? Huh? Whatsamatter, Balzic? Cat got your goddamn tongue or what? . . . Jesus, I never thought you'd treat me this way. I really expected a square deal from you."

Balzic threw up his hands. "You didn't really think I was gonna be allowed to talk to Collier or any member of his family, did you? For crissake, Mr. Castelucci, you're dreamin' if you thought I was gonna be allowed to do that. Look, there's a question you're gonna have to face sooner or later. It's the one everybody in the trial is gonna have to deal with. They're gonna deal with it from a completely different angle, but you're gonna have to deal with it no matter what."

Balzic got up and went to the kitchen and got a glass of water. He came back to the table and confronted the old man's intense gaze.

"The case involves a time element. It's how much time passed between the first shot that Collier fired and the next shot he fired. That's really all the case the state has right now, and if they don't screw it up, they're gonna get Collier for voluntary manslaughter." Balzic rubbed his palms together and locked gazes with the old man. "The question you're gonna have to deal with is this: in that time between when the first shot was fired and when the next shot was fired, how come Joey didn't get the hell outta there? How come he didn't run? How come he didn't try to escape? The witnesses are gonna say he had plenty of time to get away. They're gonna say that about *both* of 'em. They *both* had plenty of time to get away. And they didn't get away. But one of the two guys who didn't try to get away had a gun. And the other one who didn't try to get away *didn't* have a gun. Mr. Castelucci, you can be pissed off at me all you want. Be disappointed, whatever, but you're gonna have to deal with that sooner or later. Sooner or later you're gonna have to ask yourself why Joey, instead of runnin' to save his ass, went and got a cinder block to throw at a guy who had a gun."

Castelucci drummed his fingers on the table. "And this is all 'cause I didn't say nothin' when his mother was puttin' dresses on him."

"No no no, that's not what I'm sayin'."

"I think you better go home, Balzic. I think you're talkin' in circles. And I'm gettin' a headache."

"I'm sorry you're gettin' a headache. And you're probably right. I probably am talkin' in circles. I better get goin'." Balzic let himself out.

He walked down the four flights of stairs thinking that he was a jerk for having let Castelucci pressure him into getting involved in the first place. He should have told the old man at the start that he would never have been allowed to interview Collier and that any investigation which did not include the alleged perpetrator is at bottom a waste of effort. The old man had hit it right when he complained that Balzic knew nothing about Collier. But Balzic had known going in that he was never going to be permitted to speak to Collier and he was kicking himself for not making sure that Castelucci had understood as much back then, too.

* * *

The trial was scheduled to be heard by President Judge Milan Vrbanic. As president judge, Vrbanic counted among his perquisites the largest, brightest, most recently refurbished courtroom in the Conemaugh County Courthouse. Five minutes before the bailiff instructed all to rise, something went wrong with the thermostat; and when Judge Vrbanic strode from his chambers to take his seat, his usually pale face was flushed and beginning to bead with sweat. His first act was to send his tipstaff in search of somebody from the maintenance department.

He rapped his gavel once and said, "Ladies and gentlemen, something is obviously wrong with the heating unit. I ask your patience with the circumstances and I ask that you do not try mine. Bailiff, call the case."

Balzic happened to catch the eye of Assistant DA Horace Machlin, and he mouthed the words, "Good luck."

Machlin nodded many times as though to say, "I'm going to need it."

"Mr. Machlin, are you ready?"

"Ready, Your Honor," Machlin said, jumping up.

"Mr. Coblentz, are you ready?"

"I am, Your Honor." Coblentz had been standing ever since Vrbanic walked in.

"Then to save time you will alternate interrogating jurors. Mr. Machlin will begin. Bailiff, get us a live one in here and let's get on with it."

Balzic had come this morning, this first day, only to see Francis Collier. Jury selection would take all of this day, probably most of tomorrow, depending on Vrbanic's patience, and Balzic was only mildly interested in who the jurors might be.

What he wanted to see was something in Francis Collier, something that might point a way to the answer to the question that had been in the back of his mind ever since he had first listened to Joey Castelucci's father ranting on about his idea that his son had been set up. That question was: What possible reason could Collier have had? The court wouldn't care. The trial would never address the question. All the court wanted to know, all Vrbanic would allow, were the facts of the case as the law applied to them, nothing more, nothing less.

But Balzic wasn't involved in the case. He was here as a spectator only, and as a spectator he could speculate to his mind's content. So he sat in the front row behind the prosecution, and he studied Francis Collier, not even trying to cover his curiosity.

After a few moments, Collier turned and glanced at Balzic. "What's your problem?" he said, none too quietly.

"Seems to me you're the one with the problem here, sport," Balzic said.

The gavel banged sharply. "What's going on there, Mario?" Vrbanic said.

"Uh, I'm sorry, Your Honor."

"I didn't ask for your apology. I asked what was going on."

"Uh, I got carried away, Your Honor. I was outta line."

"That man's harassin' me, Your Honor," Collier said, pointing at Balzic. "He's been harassin' me for weeks."

"Mr. Coblentz," Vrbanic said, "do you want to explain the facts of life to your client or do you want me to do it?"

"I will be happy to, Your Honor," Coblentz said, rising to a half-crouch and then quickly dropping into his seat and huddling with Collier.

So, Balzic thought, he's quick to take offense, quick to accuse, quick to appeal to others about what he believed was injustice.

Collier was a trim, smallish man, in his middle fifties. His silvery hair was combed straight back off his forehead with no part. He wore a three-piece suit and didn't seem the least uncomfortable because of the rising heat in the room. But the suit was wrong. It was dark gray, almost charcoal, with a very fine pinstripe. Collier wore a large gold watch with a wide expansion band on his left wrist and he had pinkie rings on both hands. He also wore half-inch-square, gold cufflinks. Balzic would've paid money to have heard the conversation between Collier and Coblentz when they first saw each other this day. Collier's a stubborn bastard, Balzic thought, because obviously Coblentz hadn't succeeded in getting him to park that jewelry or get out of that vest. Now there's a man who thinks what he does is right and is willing to bet three to seven years of his life on it.

Then, when the first prospective juror walked in and was pointed toward the clerk's desk, Collier stood suddenly, shrugged out of his coat, undid his vest buttons and pulled it off, and put his coat back on. He folded the vest and pushed it into Coblentz's briefcase and then slipped off the watch and the pinkie rings and put them in his coat pocket. The first juror, a hefty woman in a coffee brown polyester pantsuit, saw none of this; but Coblentz saw that Judge Vrbanic saw it and Coblentz suddenly thought that was a good time to inquire loudly to no one in particular about progress on the heating problem.

Judge Vrbanic dropped his gaze and attention to a legal

tablet and made some note on it. "Shed your coat, Mr. Coblentz. Jewelry too, if that'll make you cooler."

Balzic had to turn his face away to keep from laughing out loud and thought that would be a good time for him to get back to work. It would take at least one day, maybe a day and a half to pick the jury, and he had many things to do for the city and for his department, every one of them tedious.

* * *

When Balzic got back to Vrbanic's courtroom two days later, the jury and alternates had been picked and sworn and Machlin had made his opening outlining the case and what the state hoped to prove. Coblentz had chosen to make no opening. Balzic learned that from the regulars in the spectator section.

"I like this Machlin," said one. "He's smooth."

"All flash, no cash," said another.

"Strictly a beginner," said a third. "Coblentz gonna chew him a new ass."

"Call Trooper Walter Helfrick please," Machlin said.

Balzic felt a tap on his shoulder. He leaned back without turning around. Somebody whispered in his ear, "Hey, Balzic, I hear this bozo never even Mirandized the guy. What are they, just goin' through the motions here or what?"

Balzic shrugged and put his finger to his lips.

Machlin took Trooper Helfrick through the facts of the case from the moment Helfrick first got the call that shots had been fired to his depositing the tagged and bagged pistol in the crime lab. Machlin did not ask about ballistics tests or about empty cartridges or bullet holes in the car. And he never mentioned the word "rights" in any context.

As soon as Machlin said, "No more questions, Your Honor," one of the regulars turned to another and said in a phlegmy whisper, "Boy, they ain't got nothin'."

Another said, "I don't know if I can watch this. Coblentz gonna put this guy in intensive care."

"Trooper Helfrick, how are you today?" said Coblentz, hitching up his pants and moving to the end of the jury box farthest away from the witness chair.

"I'm fine, sir, thank you."

"Good, good. I just have a few questions."

The voice over Balzic's shoulder whispered, "You oughta go bust Coblentz right now, Balzic. Homicide by interrogation."

"Trooper Helfrick," Coblentz began, "when you first came on the scene, when you first saw Mr. Collier, you said that he said, 'I surrender.' Is that correct?"

"Yes, sir."

"Do you recall what he said he was surrendering for?"

"Objection, Your Honor," Machlin said. "We never covered that in direct, Your Honor."

"Sustained."

"Let me put it this way, Trooper Helfrick. Did you, in all the time you saw Mr. Collier, both at the scene and later on in the emergency room of Conemaugh General Hospital, did you ever advise him of his right to remain silent or his right to counsel or his right to have counsel provided for him if he could not afford counsel?"

"Objection, Your Honor. Not covered in direct."

"May we approach the bench, Your Honor?" Coblentz said.

"Here go the stipulations," whispered one of the spectators.

"Stipulations hell. He's gonna move to throw it out."

"They gotta stipulate it, ya dummy. Vrbanic wouldn'ta let 'em go through the razzmatazz of pickin' a jury. He wouldn't let 'em waste his time like 'at."

Balzic watched the sidebar conference, as first Coblentz and then Machlin went back and forth to Vrbanic, who sat with his index finger over his upper lip and his thumb extended up his jaw, moving only his eyes in the direction of each lawyer as he spoke. After two exchanges, he sat up and said, "All right, gentlemen, let's get it said so everybody can hear it. You first, Mr. Machlin."

"Your Honor, at no time in this case have we ever introduced any evidence about any statement the accused made except the one where he said, 'I surrender.' I did not question Mr. Collier about what he said and I'm not going to question him about it. I fail to see the point of throwing out all our work just because Mr. Collier wasn't Mirandized when Mr. Coblentz thinks he should've been. Because the crucial point here is this: when Mr. Collier was arrested by Trooper Helfrick, that happened in Mr. Coblentz's presence. Why should we throw out a case about not Mirandizing a man when his counsel was standing right there? Is Mr. Coblentz gonna try to tell us that he didn't advise Mr. Collier that he didn't have to say a word? What I'm trying to say,

Your Honor, is Mr. Collier has had the benefit of Mr. Coblentz's counsel from before he was arrested, and I think it just gets in the face of good sense to throw out a case when we're not going to use anything the man said except what we already said we were gonna use, which is nothing. Thank you, Your Honor."

"Mr. Coblentz?"

"Your Honor, the rules are clear. They've been in force for many years now and they've survived the most rigorous scrutiny."

"Make your motion, Mr. Coblentz," Vrbanic said.

"I move to dismiss all charges on the grounds that my client, Mr. Collier, was not informed of his rights—"

"Denied."

"I wasn't finished, Your Honor."

"Yes, you were. Witness is still yours."

Coblentz cleared his throat and stretched his neck. He took his time going back to the end of the jury box farthest from the witness chair. Then he leaned on the railing and said, "Trooper Helfrick, I don't want to bore you or to try the patience of the jurors by asking you a lot of technical questions about the firearm, the pistol, you took, the one you say you took—"

"Objection, Your Honor. He didn't say a word when we submitted the weapon as evidence and now he's talkin' about 'the one you say you took.'"

"Mr. Coblentz, it's getting hotter by the minute in here. Bailiff, for God's sake, see if you can find some fans. And if you can't find any, then go buy some. And find out what happened to my tipstaff, will you? Mr. Coblentz, we're all here under trying conditions, and you know how the trial is to proceed as well as anyone here, so let's do it, shall we?"

"All right, Your Honor." Coblentz cleared his throat again. "Trooper Helfrick, did you recover any bullets—and just so the jury knows what we're talking about, bullets are the things that come out of the barrel after the trigger is pulled, is that correct?"

"That's correct, yes, sir."

"Did you get any bullets? Anywhere? From the body of the victim, from the ground, from Mr. Collier's automobile, anywhere at all, bullets that you can say with one hundred percent certainty came from the pistol that was submitted into evidence earlier?"

"Uh, no sir."

"So you have no bullets, is that right?"

"He already answered that, Your Honor."

"So he did, so he did. I withdraw it. Now, Trooper Helfrick, do you have any empty shell casings that you can connect to this pistol we've been talking about—and just so the jury understands, the shell casing is what holds the powder and the primer and the bullet and once the hammer falls on the primer, the shell casing is what is ejected from a semi-automatic pistol like the one submitted earlier as evidence. Do you have any shell casings to connect that pistol with what happened on the night we're talking about? The night Mr. Castelucci died, the night you arrested Mr. Collier. You have any shell casings?"

"Uh, no, sir. But I did have. I had seven of 'em."

"Just answer the question, Trooper. Don't embellish. Just answer what you're asked, nothing more, nothing less."

"Thank you, Your Honor. Just to clarify, Trooper Helfrick, you did say no, you do not have them, is that correct?"

"Yes, sir, that's correct. I don't have 'em."

"All right. Now, let's turn your attention to this cinder block that was submitted earlier as evidence. You did say, I believe, that you had the blood tested to find whether it matched the blood of Mr. Castelucci, is that right?"

"Yes, Your Honor."

"No. He's 'Your Honor,'" Coblentz said, pointing to the judge.

"Oh. Sorry."

"No apology is necessary," Coblentz said, waiting for the laughter to subside. "Now, Trooper Helfrick, did you ever ask that a blood sample be taken from Mr. Collier?"

"No, sir."

"I see. Now, Trooper Helfrick, you requested that many photographs be taken of the scene of the shooting, did you not?"

"Yes, sir."

"Did you ask that any photographs be taken of Mr. Collier?"

"No, sir."

"Trooper Helfrick, when you first saw Mr. Collier, what was his condition? Was he bleeding?"

"Yes, sir."

"Was he bleeding a lot? Would you say he was covered with blood?"

"Uh, yes. I guess I would."

"You guess?"

"No, I don't guess. He was covered with blood."

"In your opinion as a police officer, as one trained to observe such things, would you say that was Mr. Collier's blood?"

"Uh, yes. I would, yes."

"Would you say that that blood was definitely Mr. Collier's and was not Mr. Castelucci's? Would you say that?"

"Huh?"

"Let me back up here. In your opinion, as a trained observer, had Mr. Collier been injured?"

"Yeah. That's the way it looked to me. Yes."

"And later on, when Mrs. Castelucci approached you and asked if it was all right with you if she took Mr. Collier to the hospital, you didn't object to that, did you?"

"Uh, no, sir."

"In fact, you arrested Mr. Collier in the emergency room of Conemaugh General Hospital, is that correct?"

"Yes, sir."

"In fact, you placed Mr. Collier under arrest while he was still being attended to by a physician and a nurse, is that correct?"

"Yes, sir."

"Trooper Helfrick, I ask you, as a trained observer, is there any doubt in your mind that Mr. Collier had been pretty badly injured that night?"

"Uh, no, sir."

"Trooper Helfrick, what do you think caused all these cuts and abrasions to Mr. Collier?"

"Objection, Your Honor."

"Your Honor, he's a police officer. As such, he's got some expertise. All I'm asking him now is for him to give us his expert opinion about how those injuries might have happened."

"Your Honor," Machlin said, "he's trying to get around to what was said—"

"I am not! Your Honor, what I'm trying to get on the record early on is Trooper Helfrick's observation of Mr. Collier's physical condition and I want to know about the blood on that cinder block."

"Then, Mr. Coblentz, why don't you just ask about that?"

"All right, Your Honor, I will. Trooper Helfrick, did you ask anybody on that night or since that night to draw blood from Mr. Collier and to have it analyzed?"

"No, sir."

"Trooper Helfrick, when you ordered that blood be taken from the corpse of Mr. Castelucci, what purpose did you have in mind? Why did you do that?"

"Uh, I wanted to see if it was his blood on the block there, the cinder block."

"And was it? Was it Mr. Castelucci's blood on the block?"

"Uh, we're not real sure. But I can't explain it. You're gonna have to ask the lab guy—technician."

"Uh-huh. Well. I want to be very specific about this, Trooper Helfrick. You cannot say with certainty whose blood that is on the cinder block, now can you?"

"Uh, no, sir."

"Thank you, Trooper Helfrick, for your patience and cooperation. I have no more questions, Your Honor."

At that, Vrbanic's tipstaff and bailiff both came through the double doors of the courtroom and approached the bench. Vrbanic put his hand over the microphone and leaned forward, listening intently. After a moment, he rapped his gavel once and said, "We've got some fans en route, so until they get here and get set up, we're going to take a fifteen-minute recess."

Balzic stood and looked around the spectator section, trying to spot Mr. Castelucci. He'd heard the old man's coughing throughout Helfrick's testimony, so Balzic knew the old man was there; but everybody was in a rush to get to the doors and out in the cool corridor, and Balzic couldn't spot him.

Balzic inched forward along with everyone else until he was out in the corridor, where it was like a cool fall day, and went to the marble balustrade and put his rump against it. He took off his glasses and wiped his face and neck with a hanky and felt somebody beside him.

"So you're Balzic?"

Balzic put his glasses back on. It was Collier. He had his arms folded and was rocking on his heels and toes, looking confrontational. Hovering to Collier's immediate right was Harold Coblentz. "Francis, you don't want to do this, there's no need to do this, so why don't we go get some fresh air?"

"This guy been buggin' me for weeks."

"Francis, that is beside the point. Which is, you don't need to do this, it would be very unwise, and if I have to tell you again, you're going to have to get someone else to represent you because I will not, am I making myself clear to you?"

"Hey, okay, all right, I get your message. I just want this, uh, this mushroom to get the message—"

"Francis, this is my last warning. Let's go."

"All right, Christ Almighty. You act like it's a fuckin' sin to let people know where you stand."

"Chief Balzic, we meet at last," Coblentz said, extending his hand and pushing in front of Collier.

"How do you do," Balzic said, shaking Coblentz's hand.

"As well as can be expected, given the circumstances. How about yourself?"

"Doin' all right, I guess. Not as good as you."

"Me? Really? You think so?"

"Aw c'mon. You're gonna beat the hell outta everybody on the appeal."

"I wish I shared your confidence."

"What the fuck you talkin' to this creep for?"

"Uh, Chief, my pleasure. You'll have to excuse us. We've really got to get some air. Come along, Francis."

"What the fuck you bein' nice to him for? He's been makin' me miserable for weeks."

"Francis, for God's sake, there are women everywhere."

"Fuck 'em, let's go, you wanna get some air? Let's go. And before I forget, my vest is in your briefcase, okay? Don't lemme forget and leave it in there, okay?"

Coblentz led the way through the people with Collier following, saying, "Look out, comin' through, comin' through. . . ."

* * *

Balzic found an alcove by the water fountain and backed into it. As soon as he got comfortable, he could see Mr. Castelucci coming at him from his left and Assistant District Attorney Leo Gaudiosi coming from his right. They arrived at the same time; Balzic said hello to both of them at once. They looked at each other quizzically, so Balzic introduced them.

"This'll only take a minute, Mario," Gaudiosi said, looking at Castelucci.

"Hey, go 'head."

"Oh, thank you. Mario, you're not gonna have to testify against that bastard Sapinsky. He copped out, kicked down to voluntary manslaughter, three to five."

"That's not enough."

"C'mon. He gets to do it in the Wall. He's gonna get the hell beat out of him once a week for twenty-five months guaranteed, which doesn't make up for what he did, but it's a taste of it, you know? Don't look so glum. I thought you'd be happy to know you didn't have to testify."

"To tell you the truth, I was kind of lookin' forward to it."

"Well, that's the way it goes. Hey, I gotta tell you this one. You'll love it. I get this mugger about a week ago. He's gonna be his own lawyer, right? So it's one, two, three. Victim is walkin' along, tra-la, tra-la, this chooch comes by, tries to grab her purse, she struggles, he clips her one on the chops, she stops strugglin', he cops the purse, and runs into a building about three doors away. Here comes a cop in a black and white, the lady hollers, the cop goes into the building, starts knockin' on doors with the victim right behind him. Ta-da! The chooch opens the door, and the lady says, 'That's him!'

"So that's the way I run it by the judge—who's Vrbanic, by the way. What could be simpler, right? I call the victim first, I'm gonna call the cop second, the whole thing's just one more pimple on the law's ass. Except, see, the chooch, he's got his best polyester on, right? Hey, it's his day in his court, he's all cleaned and pressed. So I finish with the victim, and the chooch stands up and he starts pacin', back and forth, like three times in each direction in front of the victim. All of a sudden, he turns on her, he sticks his finger in her face, and he says—so help me Christ—he says, 'Just how good a look did you get at me when I stole your purse?' "

"Aw, no!" Balzic howled, throwing back his head and shaking with laughter.

"Oh yeah! Vrbanic was laughin' so hard he had to call a recess. First time in my life I ever saw Stoneface laugh. I've seen him smile, you know, that smart-assey smile he gets? But I never saw him laugh. Trial ain't fifteen minutes old and we got a recess 'cause Stoneface can't stop laughin'. Hey, I gotta go. I knew you'd love it. Say hello to your mother. And Ruthie. Don't forget Ruthie. Nice to meet you, Mister, uh . . ."

"Castelucci."

"Yeah, right. Mr. Castelucci. Take care of yourself. You too, Mario."

Balzic, still laughing hard, nodded and waved.

"What was that guy—a DA?"

"Yeah. An assistant, yeah. A part-timer."

"What was that he was talkin' about? A guy defendin' himself and everybody laughin', the judge, everybody? The way you laughed it was like it was a pretty big joke."

"Well, it wasn't a joke, Mr. Castelucci. It was a true story. But it was very funny."

"He was talkin' about a trial?"

"Yeah, right."

"How could that be funny? A trial is serious. I don't see how a guy's supposed to be a DA could be tellin' jokes in the first place. That ain't right."

"Mr. Castelucci, it's just another day in the mines for him. If he doesn't tell jokes on his breaks or doesn't listen to jokes, somethin' that's gonna make him laugh, he'd've been apeshit in about six weeks on this job."

"Yeah, still, he's dealin' with people's lives here."

"He has to deal with his own life first. If he doesn't get things right in the right order, he's on his way to the laughin' academy. You know why they call it that?"

"What?"

"The nut house. You know why they call it the laughin' academy?"

"No."

"'Cause the only people who ever get outta there are the people who learn how to laugh again. The ones who don't learn how to laugh all over, brand-new, again? They don't get out. That's all Gaudiosi was doin' here. Just tryin' to protect himself, that's all. He's lucky. At least he can tell jokes. I can't tell jokes for shit. Never could. So I have to wait until somebody tells me one. But no matter how gross it is, man, I listen."

"I don't think it's right."

"Aw shit, Mr. Castelucci. You ain't the only one with problems. That Sapinsky I was supposed to testify about? He had a little girl. Fourteen months old. It wasn't some stranger. It was his. Both her legs were broken. Twice. Both her arms. Twice. She had cigarette burns on her tongue. It was his daughter. You understand me? His! You know what he didn't like? He didn't like her cryin'. And the more she cried, the more pain he gave her, and the more pain she got, the more she cried. And—"

"That's a reason to tell jokes? Jesus."

"No, that ain't the reason. You know what the reason is? He beats his own daughter to death and all the law can do to him is lock him up for three to five. You know who's gonna punish him? Other cons. You know why? 'Cause in a con's scheme of things, the lowest thing you can be on this earth is a guy who beats kids. You know why? 'Cause you scratch a con deep enough, you'll find a guy who was beat up by his old man or his grandfather or his mother's boyfriend or an older brother, and they can't wait for one of these guys to show up inside."

Balzic screwed up his face. "But the real reason I have to laugh is, the only satisfaction I get is knowing that this child beater is gonna get beat up by cons who are all screwed up because *they* got beat up. And I laugh—I have to laugh—because I can't answer myself when I ask, how in the fuck did we wind up with a system of justice like this? See, 'cause I get pissed 'cause I don't get the opportunity to testify against this scumball, so I call the prison where he's gonna go, and I tell somebody that he's comin'. Now tell me the truth, Mr. Castelucci, don't you think that's pretty funny? Don't you think that's somethin' worth laughin' about?"

"Boy oh boy, Balzic. You're a mess." Castelucci turned away and shuffled off toward Judge Vrbanic's courtroom.

You don't know the half of it, old man, Balzic said to himself.

* * *

The fifteen-minute recess dragged into twenty and then thirty as an electrician gave up trying to repair the thermostat and had to go to the basement to get a replacement. Even after he replaced it, it would be hours before the radiators cooled off, so Judge Vrbanic called everyone to order and said they'd all just have to grin and sweat it out.

"Call Henry Pospisil, please."

"Who's this guy, Balzic?" came the whisper over Balzic's shoulder.

"Mutual Aid EMT," Balzic whispered back.

After Pospisil had been sworn, he testified to establish more facts in the sequence of events for the jury. Machlin led him through a series of questions to reinforce details of the scene and the times involved for the jury, how Castelucci's body was situated, where Collier's car was in relation to the tree, where Collier was, and so on.

Coblentz, on cross-examination, asked, "Mr. Pospisil, did you give aid or assistance to anyone else at the scene?"

"Just my partner."

"Your partner?" Coblentz cleared his throat. "I don't know that this is relevant, but what are you talking about?"

Pospisil shrugged. "Well, see, it was that girl's first time. She had all the training and everything, but she'd never been out before. And, uh, well, when she saw that body there, I don't know, she just sorta flipped out or something. She just kept sayin', 'We gotta save him, we gotta save him.' And she wouldn't pay any attention to me."

"What did she do?" Coblentz said.

"Your Honor, this isn't really relevant, is it?"

"Not really, Mr. Machlin, but I'm a member of the Mutual Aid Board and I'd like to hear this. Please go on, Mr. Pospisil."

"Well, next thing I know she was trying to give this body CPR and I tried to tell her the man was dead. I knew he was dead before I turned him over, but when I turned him over I was sure of it. There was no breathing, his eyes were open and he had voided, so he was dead and at that point, I mean because a police officer was there, I mean I've been to enough crime scenes to know you don't go messin' around with the evidence, and at that point the body was a piece of evidence. I'd already messed with it by turning it over but there she was beatin' on the guy's chest and tryin' to do CPR, so I went over to the state trooper to get him to tell her to let things alone, but he either didn't understand me or he was too busy, but anyway he didn't come over, and then, when I got back to her, heck, she had got the gurney out and had him strapped in and was pullin' it into the back of the vehicle and I was sayin', you know, what the heck you tryin' to do here, and she was really nuts. She kept sayin', 'We gotta get him to surgery, we gotta get him to surgery,' and don't ask me how she got him into the vehicle, I don't know, 'cause she was just a tiny, little girl and he was a fair-sized guy, and—bang! Darned if she didn't shut the back doors and jump into the driver's seat and start the engine. I just did make it inside, and I want to tell you, that was the wildest ride I've ever had in a Mutual Aid vehicle."

"What happened when you got to the hospital?" Vrbanic said.

"Oh it was just—real bad. No control at all, she was just nuts. She was disruptin' everybody and finally I just told the head nurse, 'Hey, you know, load up a syringe and give us a break!' And that's what we had to do finally. I had to tackle her and hold her down while the nurse hit her with the syringe. And while I was sittin' on her, waitin' for the stuff to kick in, I said to her, 'Girlie, I don't know what you want outta life, but you're gonna have to find another hobby, 'cause you ain't never, ever, gonna get in the front end of an ambulance in this town again.' "

By the time Pospisil finished talking, both Coblentz and Machlin were exchanging sidelong glances and trying not to laugh. They weren't the only ones. Most of the jurors were squirming and covering their mouths or pretending to yawn to keep from laughing.

"What the hell was that all about, Balzic?" came the whisper from behind.

"All I can figure is Vrbanic needed to hear somethin' about Mutual Aid—hell, I don't know."

"Your Honor," Coblentz said, "there is nothing further I wish to know from this witness, I assure you."

"Mr. Machlin, let's proceed."

"Your Honor, I was going to call as my next two witnesses, Coroner Grimes and Dr. Rolando Cercone, the emergency room physician on the night of this incident, but I've been told that neither one is in the building and I really don't know where they are, Your Honor. I apologize. It's going to make it tough to present a logical sequence of events if I have to go back to them, but I don't have any choice, Your Honor."

"Well call somebody, Mr. Machlin."

"Yes, sir. Call Mr. Ralph Gioia, please."

Okay, Balzic thought, now we find out how good this Machlin is.

Ralph Gioia wasn't in the witness room. The deputy sheriff assigned to the courtroom had to be sent to find him, and when Gioia appeared about five minutes later, everybody—Judge Vrbanic, Machlin, Gioia, and most of the jury—was looking impatient and disgusted, but none as much as Gioia.

Immediately after he was sworn and seated in the witness chair, Gioia began to complain about having had to take—"to waste" were his words—not one but two vacation days to testify. "I absolutely wasted a whole day sittin' around here yesterday—"

Vrbanic didn't bother to use his gavel. He brought his fist down with such force that the gavel bounced.

"Mr. Gioia," he said, his eyes almost shut and his shoulders hunched up to his ears, "in this courtroom only one person complains about wasting time and that person is me and that's because I'm the only one who's allowed to complain. What you're allowed to do is answer questions that are asked of you. And that's all you're allowed to do. Mr. Machlin, begin please."

Gioia's eyes had popped wide at the sound of the judge's fist on the bench, and while the judge was talking Gioia drew farther and farther away so that by the time Vrbanic stopped talking Gioia was almost out of his chair.

Jury's going to love this, Balzic thought. Justice in action. First the ambulance driver, now this. They never saw anything like this on TV.

"Mr. Gioia, would you state your full name, address, and occupation, please?" Machlin was standing at the far end of the jury box.

"Huh? Oh. Gioia. Ralph. I live at fourteen Westfield Drive, Westfield Township, Rocksburg, RD 2. What else d'you wanna know?"

"Your occupation?"

"Oh. Yeah. I sell cars. Previously owned cars."

"Mr. Gioia, exactly where do you live at fourteen Westfield Drive?"

"On the second floor."

"You live in an apartment?"

"Yeah. Yes."

"You have outside windows in your apartment?"

"Yes."

"Who lives directly below you?"

"Rose Castelucci."

"She's the wife of the man who was shot and killed, is that right?"

"Yeah."

"Now, your windows, do they look out on the parking lot at the rear of that house?"

"Sure. Of course."

"Since you're on the second floor of that house, it would stand to reason that if you had your windows open you'd be able to hear pretty well, wouldn't you, any unusual noise that came from the parking lot? Or from the apartment below, is that right?"

"Yeah, I guess. I wouldn't hear people talkin' real low, real quiet."

"We'll get to that in a moment, Mr. Gioia, but first I want to know if you had your windows open that night, June first?"

"Yeah."

"You sound very sure of that. How can you be sure?"

"I'm sure 'cause my air conditioner was broke. It went south the night before. I had it outta the window, I was gonna take it to a guy I know the next day, it was sittin' on the floor by the door."

"Okay. Mr. Gioia, before you tell us what you heard, will you tell us what you were doing when you heard it?"

"I was in bed."

"Were you asleep?"

"No, I was tryin' to go to sleep, but I was up. Awake, I mean. I was listenin' to a record."

"A record of music?"

"Yes."

"Loud music, soft music, what kind of music?"

"Soft. It was my goin'-to-sleep music."

"I see. Well, tell us then, what did you hear?"

"Well, I heard a car pull in. Two doors open and close and then, maybe two minutes later, I heard this scufflin' and bangin'."

"Now, Mr. Gioia, was this unusual noise? Was this out of the ordinary?"

"No."

"You've heard this kind of noise before?"

"Yeah. Many times. A lot."

"Did you get up and get out of bed to try to see who or what was causing the noise?"

"Nah. I knew what it was. It was somebody fightin' in Rose's apartment."

"So this was so commonplace, this kind of thing had happened so many times before, you were not even curious enough to get up to see what it was, is that right?"

"Right."

"Did you *do* anything?"

"I turned up the stereo a little bit."

"And then what happened?"

"Then I heard somebody running, and then I heard a shot. Pow! That got me up, like real fast. Then I heard somebody get in a car and I heard the car start and the wheels spinnin', you know, throwin' gravel. And then I heard a big bang. And by then I'm hangin' out the window. I took the screen out and I'm tryin' to see what's goin' on, but I can't see anything because there's this huge branch from this tree right outside my window."

"Then what did you hear?"

"Then I hear somebody walkin' around, and then, a little while later, I hear this grunt, and a window breakin' and then a whole bunch of shots, one right after another. Six or seven. You know. Bam bam bam bam bam, like that, real fast."

"Then what? What did you hear next?"

"Well, for a long time—well I don't know how long it was. It seemed long. But it probably wasn't. Then the next thing I heard was Vic Marcelli, he's the landlord, Vic's talkin' to somebody, but I didn't hear what he was sayin'."

"All right, Mr. Gioia," Machlin said, "I want to make some things clear. First, you couldn't see anything that was happening in the apartment below you—that's obvious—but, because of the tree outside your window, you didn't see anything in the parking lot, is that right?"

"Right. Yes."

"All right, Mr. Gioia, would you recall as specifically as you can, how much time passed between the first shot you heard and the next shot you heard?"

"Oh, that was at least twenty seconds. Maybe thirty."

"But no less than twenty?"

"No. It was at least that long."

"Thank you, Mr. Gioia. Your witness."

Coblentz hitched up his trousers, buttoned his coat, and smoothed his collar as he walked to the far end of the jury box.

"Mr. Gioia, are you a weapons expert?"

Gioia laughed. "A what?"

"Did you serve in the military?"

"No."

"Do you hunt?"

"No."

"Are you a target shooter?"

"No."

"Are you a weapons expert? Or let me ask it this way: are you familiar with firearms at all?"

"I guess not."

"Have you ever fired a handgun of any kind?"

"No."

"Mr. Gioia, you say you sell cars for a living. Have you ever earned your living by identifying sounds?"

"No."

"Have you ever worked with sound in any way, with, uh, say, ever selling hearing aids?"

"No."

"I see. And a little while ago you said you couldn't see anything in the parking lot, is that right?"

"That's right."

"Well then, would you please explain to this court exactly how you knew that the sounds you say you heard were the sounds of a gun being fired?"

"Hey, later on when I went down I saw the guy with a bunch of holes in him—"

"Mr. Gioia, I'm not asking you about later on. I'm asking you about what you *heard*. And Mr. Machlin was very specific about that, the sounds you heard. He didn't ask you what you saw later on. He asked you what you heard. Which is what I'm asking you about now. So please explain your certainty about those sounds, especially the first one. That's the only one I'm really interested in now. How do you know that one was a pistol shot and not, say, a firecracker? How do you know that?"

Gioia shrugged and looked miffed. "I guess I don't."

"Thank you, Mr. Gioia, I have no more questions."

"One question, Your Honor," Machlin said, jumping to his feet.

"Go ahead, Mr. Machlin."

"Mr. Gioia, the first sound you heard, the one you say you thought was a shot, no matter what it was, did it sound exactly like the sounds you heard later on, twenty, thirty seconds later on?"

"Yes."

"Exactly?"

"Exactly."

"I'm done, Your Honor."

"Good. Then let's go to lunch. Ladies and gentlemen of the jury, I caution you not to discuss what you have heard so far with each other or with anyone else. I caution you not to discuss any aspect of this case, is that clear? We'll resume at two o'clock."

"All rise," said the bailiff, but everyone was already scurrying for the doors.

* * *

Balzic eased onto a stool near the front door in Muscotti's and rubbed his hands together, thinking about what he'd just seen and heard in Judge Vrbanic's courtroom.

"What's it gonna be?" Vinnie the bartender said.

"Water."

"What?" Vinnie's mouth and eyes were wide open.

"Water. You heard me."

"Get the hell outta here. I can't make no money sellin' water."

"Don't sell it. Give it to me." Balzic continued to rub his palms.

Vinnie hustled away, shaking his head and cursing. He returned in a moment with a beer glass two-thirds full of water.

"Jesus, can you spare it?"

"Hey, don't gimme no shit. I don't make money on guys drink water."

Balzic breathed noisily and deeply. Just as he picked up the glass, he felt a nudge on his arm. It was Iron City Steve, shoulders jumping, hand sawing the air, his eyes rheumy and focused on some distant reality only he could see.

"Consider," Steve said, pausing, his head swinging from side to side, "consider the weeds of the field. They weave not, nor do they spin . . . and everybody hates 'em anyway. They're always pullin' 'em out. Now, they don't even pull 'em out. They put garbage bags down so the weeds don't even get a fightin' chance."

Vinnie was back, flicking the back of his hands at Steve. "Go sit down. You're drivin' me nuts with this weeds shit. That's all you been talkin' about since you came in this mornin'. This is winter comin', you understand? Nobody's growin' anything now."

"Until you find out it's good to eat," Steve said, "it's a weed. Four hundred years ago, nobody in Italy ever heard of a tomato, now you guys can't live without 'em."

"Hey, that reminds me, Mario, I got a joke for you. Even though you're not a thoroughbred wop, you'll like this one."

"A minute ago you're hasslin' me 'cause I'm drinkin' water, now you're the floor show? Just for me?"

"Hey, it's to show you I don't hold a grudge."

Balzic looked at Steve, who was twitching so much his clothes should've been smoking from the friction.

"He's a weed," Steve said under his breath.

"I heard that, I heard that. Just keep quiet while I tell this. You hear me?"

"I'm not stopping you. I'm not able to stop you."

"I know you can't stop me. Just shut up."

"Tell the joke for crissake."

"Okay. Okay. Listen. So there's this vampire over in Italy. And every night he comes down and grabs another wop and bites him in the neck and sucks all his blood out, you know, drains his blood, and then he takes the dead wop and throws him over this hill. And as soon as he does that, he hears music. Somebody singin', get it?"

"So far I get it."

"So every night the vampire does this and every night, as soon as he drains the blood and throws the wop over the hill, he hears this singin'. So after about a week, this singin' gets to the vampire, and he says to himself, 'This is drivin' me nuts, this singin'. I gotta find out what this music's all about.' So that night, right after he grabs another wop and drains his blood, when he throws the guy over the hill, he runs down real fast to see what's goin' on. You with me so far?"

Balzic looked at Iron City Steve. "You still with him?"

"Absolutely," Steve said, drawing the back of his hand across his nose back and forth.

"So whatta you think he finds? There's this alligator down there singin', 'Drained wops keep fallin' on my head.'"

"Oh for crissake," Balzic said, laughing in spite of himself.

"Pretty good, huh?" Vinnie said, beaming.

"Pretty stupid," Steve said.

"Stupid! What're you talkin' about, stupid, Jesus."

"There's no alligators in Italy," Steve said.

"What? Who cares. That ain't the point. The point is the song, drained wops, you know like the song, 'Rain drops keep fallin' on my head'—d'you ever hear that song?"

"It don't matter what the song is," Steve said. "There ain't no alligators in Italy."

"That ain't the point, I'm tellin' ya. Whatta you know anyway? Go sit the fuck down."

"I know the only place they got alligators is in Florida and Louisiana and places like that—and none of them's in Italy."

"No alligators in Italy—go sit down! Try to tell a joke and you gotta listen to bozos like you."

"Yeah? I might be a bozo," Steve said solemnly, "but a joke's more'n just the punch line. All the rest gotta be good too."

"Okay," Vinnie said hotly, "this vampire was killin' wops in Naples, Florida! How you like that? I guess you're gonna tell me they don't have a Naples in Florida now, huh?"

"It's too late," Steve said, and shuffled off toward a table near the wall.

"Look at him," Vinnie said, staring at Steve until he dropped into a chair. "Guy got an eighty-proof brain and he's tellin' me how to tell jokes."

* * *

Back in Vrbanic's courtroom, the temperature had come down ten degrees, mostly because no human radiators had been in it for two hours. Fifteen minutes later, when everybody who was supposed to be there finally got there, the temperature rose again, but fortunately, it was nowhere near as hot as it had been in the morning.

Machlin called Vic Marcelli first and his wife, Angie, second, to establish the timing of the shots, as well as to corroborate the sounds of the fight that Gioia had testified to. Machlin also had them reconfirm the physical aspects of the house, the way it had been divided into apartments, who lived where, what the parking lot looked like, where the tree was, and so forth, while he sketched it out on a portable chalkboard.

Every so often, there would come a wheezy acknowledgment from the back of the spectator section, a reminder to Balzic that Mr. Castelucci was paying careful attention. When it seemed that Machlin was going to stop questioning Vic Marcelli, there came this raspy outburst: "Ask him who he worked for!"

Nobody's antenna went up more quickly than Judge Vrbanic's. "We'll have no more of that. This isn't audience participation."

"Just ask him," Castelucci growled back.

"That's enough, whoever you are. Once more and the bailiff will remove you." Vrbanic's eyes skimmed over the spectators trying to identify the irritant.

While Vrbanic and the jury were scanning the crowd,

Machlin shrugged and said, "Mr. Marcelli, who were you working for at the time of this incident?"

"Franny. Mr. Collier."

"Right, yeah, now we're getting somewhere," came the growl from the back of the room.

"As soon as I find out who you are," Vrbanic said, "you're gone."

"Hey, Balzic," came the whisper over his shoulder, "you get the feelin' you're back in junior high school?"

"Now that you mention it, yeah."

"Jesus, look at Vrbanic. He's so red he's startin' to turn purple. Any second now he's gonna make us all stay after school."

"Lord I hope not."

"Hey, Balzic, I been meanin' to ask you somethin'. You gonna testify here?"

"No."

"You just a spectator?"

Balzic nodded.

"Well when you're spectatin', who's doin' your job?"

Balzic turned to see the face behind the voice. He didn't recognize it, could not recall ever having seen it. "I'll tell you. I've done it so long, when I'm not there to do it, it does it by itself."

". . . Your Honor, I apologize for the delay, but we still can't seem to locate the coroner or the emergency room physician."

"Are you going to call somebody, Mr. Machlin?"

"Yes, sir, I am. Call Mrs. Rose Castelucci."

Rose had been to court so many times, she could've dressed blindfolded. She wore no makeup, no jewelry, her white blouse was buttoned up to her neck and down to her wrists, and her gray skirt with many pleats came down to the middle of her calves. She wore plain black pumps with a one-inch heel. Balzic felt like jumping up and shouting to the jury: "This is all false advertising, folks. This woman could give a pit bull two bites headstart and whip its ass."

After Rose was sworn, she sat in the witness chair with her feet together on the floor and her hands folded in her lap. Her head was level and her gaze steady. She never took her eyes off Machlin.

After Machlin asked her to state her address and occupation and the name of her employer, he led her through the sequence of the events of the night, beginning with her ride home with Collier to her ride with him to the emergency room. Rose related for the jury for the first time the confrontation and fight between Collier and Castelucci.

"Mrs. Castelucci, I want to clarify some things," Machlin said. "You were married to the deceased Joseph Castelucci twice, married, divorced, married again, and on the verge of divorce again, is that correct?"

"You might say so, yes."

"Uh, Mrs. Castelucci, how would you describe your marriages with Mr. Castelucci?"

"Objection, Your Honor. I don't see the relevance."

"Where you going, Mr. Machlin?"

"I'm just trying to establish the kind of relationship they had, Your Honor."

"What's *their* relationship got to do with anything, Your Honor?"

"Your Honor, these two people did not have what most people would call your everyday marriage. And I would like to establish that for the jury."

"Go ahead, Mr. Machlin, but don't get carried away."

"I won't, Your Honor. Mrs. Castelucci, were you or your husband ever arrested because of something you did to each other?"

"She's not on trial, Your Honor. Where's he going?" Coblentz said gently.

Vrbanic shrugged. "Just get to your point, Mr. Machlin. Don't beat around the bush."

"Sorry, Your Honor. Mrs. Castelucci, I know you've been arrested many times. Would you tell this court, please, why you were arrested?"

"People didn't like us fightin', I guess."

"When you say fighting, exactly what do you mean?"

"Fighting. What's that mean? We fought."

"Did you ever strike your husband?"

"You mean hit him?"

"Yes."

"Sure. Lotsa times."

"You ever kick him?"

"Yeah."

"You ever strike him with a club or a bottle?"

"Yeah."

"How many times were you arrested for these incidents?"

"Five or six times, I forget."

"Did any of these arrests lead to misdemeanor or felony convictions?"

"Just one."

"Which one was that?"

"That was the one I chased him with the car and his legs broke."

"Don't you mean you chased him with your car and pinned him against the side of a building with enough force to break both his legs—isn't that what you mean?"

"I guess. If you say so."

"I say so, Mrs. Castelucci, because the record of your trial says so. Now. Your husband can't speak about what he did to you, so I'm going to ask you. Did your husband strike you with his hand or fist or kick you or strike you with some instrument?"

"Yeah. To all of 'em."

"Did your husband ever throw you out of a moving vehicle?"

"Yes."

"And when you divorced your husband the first time—the only time I mean—what prompted you to do that? What caused you to finally go to a lawyer to begin the process of a divorce?"

"He locked me in my car. In the trunk. And then he drove me clear to Pittsburgh and back. It was right at the end of the winter. He hit every pothole between here and there and back."

"Why did he do that? Why did he say he did it? Did he tell you?"

"Your Honor, this is getting pretty far afield."

"I agree, Mr. Coblentz. Where to, Mr. Machlin?"

"I was just trying to establish for the jury the kind of relationship they had—"

"I think they get the picture. Let's move on."

"Yes, sir, Your Honor. Mrs. Castelucci, just to get some facts clear. Number one, you left work with your boss, Mr. Collier, and you drove with him while he deposited money in the bank and then you returned to your apartment, is that correct?"

"Yes."

"And then you borrowed Mr. Collier's car and drove around town trying to find your husband, is that correct?"

"Yes."

"And you finally did find him, right?"

"Yes."

"And you persuaded him to go with you to your apartment, correct?"

"Yes."

"Why did you do that?"

"Your Honor," Mr. Coblentz said, shaking his head. "What is the relevance of this?"

"Mr. Machlin?"

"I'm just trying to find out why she did this, Your Honor. It's something that just baffled me from the beginning and I—"

"Don't be baffled, Mr. Machlin. Just stick close to the trail like a good scout and we won't get lost, okay?"

"You're lost as hell right now," came the wheezy growl from the back of the room.

"Bailiff, find him and remove him!"

The bailiff shrugged and looked awkwardly and sheepishly at Judge Vrbanic. "I'm sorry, Your Honor, but I don't know who it is."

"Then go stand in the back and keep your eyes open. It's somebody back there," Vrbanic said, waving his right hand in the general direction of the rear of the courtroom. The bailiff did as he was told, amidst much whispering, coughing, and suppressed laughter. "Mr. Machlin, continue!"

"Yes, sir. Uh, Mrs. Castelucci, you've already told us that you were employed by Mr. Collier—Your Honor, would you please direct the jury to pay attention to what's going on up here? Most of them are looking back there." Machlin flung his left arm toward the rear of the room.

"Ladies and gentlemen, I know that we've all been faced with a lot of distractions. I ask you to please direct your attention to counsel and the witness. Continue, Mr. Machlin."

Machlin sighed heavily. "Mrs. Castelucci, in the course of your employment with Mr. Collier, did you know him to carry a gun?"

"Yeah. Yes."

"Where did he carry it, do you know? Can you tell us?"

"He had one of those little hickeys—"

"A holster?"

"Yeah, right. He had one of those."

"And did he wear it all the time?"

"The holster you mean?"

"Yes."

"No. He just put it on when he was goin' to the bank."

"Did he have it on the night your husband was killed."

"Yeah. Yes."

"You saw him put it on?"

"Yeah. Right before he put his coat on."

"Where did he put it exactly?"

"In the middle of his back. Or his pants. It had a little thingey that fit on his belt."

"I see. Mrs. Castelucci, during your ride with Mr. Collier, from the time you left his club and went to the bank and then went to your apartment, did you ever see Mr. Collier remove that gun?"

"No."

"In all that ride, did you ever see him remove either the gun from the holster or the gun and the holster from where you saw him put it on in the club?"

"No."

"I have no more questions at this time, Your Honor."

"Mr. Coblentz?"

"Thank you. Mrs. Castelucci, when you brought your husband to your apartment, did Mr. Collier open the door? Or did you open the door?"

"Franny did. Mr. Collier."

"I know you said this before, but I want to clarify it. Was Mr. Castelucci in front of you or behind you when the door opened, when Mr. Collier opened the door?"

"He was in front of me."

"I see. Now I want you to think carefully about this. When that door opened, did anybody—Mr. Collier, Mr. Castelucci, or you—did anybody say anything?"

"No."

"And within seconds, as you testified earlier, within seconds of Mr. Collier opening that door, Mr. Castelucci attacked him, is that correct?"

"Yes. Right."

"Okay, Mrs. Castelucci, let's get back to the matter of the gun."

Rose shrugged ever so slightly.

"Did you know—did Mr. Collier tell you that he had a permit to carry a handgun?"

"Yes."

"Did Mr. Collier ever show you that permit?"

"Yes."

"On the night your husband was shot, you said—and correct me if I'm wrong—that Mr. Collier put on the gun and holster in his club and that you never saw him take them off, is that what you said?"

"Yes. That's what I said."

"Did Mr. Collier—to your knowledge—ever carry a handgun in his automobile, either under the seat or in the glove compartment?"

"He told me he did."

"Did he tell you that on the night your husband was killed?"

"I don't remember that."

"What I'm getting at, Mrs. Castelucci, is that Mr. Collier—as far as you know—could very well have had a pistol in the glove compartment of his car that night, could he not?"

"Your Honor," Machlin said, standing and raising his hand, "he's asking the witness to—"

"I know what he's doing, Mr. Machlin. Are you objecting?"

"Yes, sir."

"Sustained. Jury will disregard that question. Mr. Coblentz, shame on you."

"I apologize, Your Honor." Coblentz leaned forward and canted his head to his right. "Mrs. Castelucci, from the time you saw Mr. Collier put the gun on his belt until you left him in your apartment, as far as you know, Mr. Collier did not take the gun off, is that right?"

"Right. Yes."

"How long did you say you were gone from Mr. Collier, from the time you took his car to go find your husband, until you saw Mr. Collier again, how long were you gone?"

"I don't know. Forty-five minutes."

"Three-quarters of an hour. I see. So in that time, he could have done any number of things with that gun while you were gone and you wouldn't have known anything about it, would you?"

"I guess not."

"Of course you guess not. There's no other way to guess. You have no idea what Mr. Collier did or did not do with a gun that you saw him put on, in the three-quarters of an hour you were not with him—is that true or not?"

"I don't know what he did, yeah. I guess."

"That's all, Your Honor."

"Mr. Machlin?"

Machlin went to the clerk's table and picked up the pistol that had been submitted as evidence earlier. He held it high over his head with just his index finger and thumb on the barrel. "Mrs. Castelucci, this is a pretty distinctive looking pistol. All shiny chrome-plated, pearl grips. Is this the gun you saw Mr. Collier put on in the club?"

"Yeah. I think so."

"You think so? Or you know so?"

"That's the one."

"That's all, Your Honor."

"Mr. Coblentz?"

Coblentz walked deliberately to the table where Machlin was returning the gun and picked it up as soon as Machlin put it down. He held it over his head as Machlin had done.

"Mrs. Castelucci, do you know what caliber gun this is? Is it twenty-five, thirty-two, thirty-eight, or forty-five caliber? Can you tell that just from looking at it from where you are?"

Rose rolled her eyes. "Whatta I look like, Sherlock Holmes?"

"Is that a no or a yes?"

"It's a no. I can't tell."

"Because you don't know one from another?"

"Right, yes."

"No more questions."

"Step down, please." Judge Vrbanic picked up his gavel and brought it done once, sharply. "We'll adjourn until tomorrow at ten o'clock. Ladies and gentlemen of the jury, remember what I said about not discussing this case."

Balzic was up and moving as soon as the gavel sounded. He didn't want to spend any time discussing the testimony with old man Castelucci, so he was hustling to get out and away.

He made it to the third floor before a deputy sheriff stopped him on the landing between floors.

"The mayor wants you to come to city hall right away, Chief."

Balzic waved a thank you and tromped down the stairs and through the lobby, moving no faster or slower than he had been before he got the message. He grabbed his raincoat, scarf, gloves, and cap out of the room where the charladies hung their clothes and stored their lunches and ducked out the side door. He buried his chin in his scarf and pulled his cap down so he wouldn't lose it to the wind and set off toward city hall with his hands deep in his pockets, thinking that if it got any colder he'd have to drag his wool overcoat out of the attic. That damn coat was getting heavier every year. Maybe it was time he went shopping for one of those nylon coats filled with polyester fibers. Balzic hated shopping for clothes, but every four or five years he finally conceded that it had to be done. He occupied himself with sour shopping thoughts until he covered the short distance from the courthouse to city hall.

Once inside, Balzic found Mayor Kenny Strohn trying to look calm behind the counter in the duty room. Next to him stood a man in a three-piece suit, the coat of which was at least one size too small for him. He was studying some papers while rubbing his earlobe with his thumb. Balzic pegged him for a bureaucrat.

On the outside of the counter a young man with pale eyes and a ghostly complexion and large pink lips seemed close to eruption. He was so thin he looked cancerously ill. Every part of him was moving, but Balzic knew that wasn't true. It just seemed that way. He was either drumming his fingers on the counter or rubbing his palms together or bouncing on the balls of his feet or snapping his fingers—and he'd done all of those things in the time it took Balzic to walk into the room and through the lift-door in the counter.

Strohn had started talking the instant he'd spotted Balzic, something about the county Health Department and somebody's mother and trying to find somebody for more than an hour.

Balzic stripped off his outer clothes and tossed them on a desk next to the dispatcher, who was a woman civilian who substituted when one of the desk sergeants called off sick.

"Who you workin' for?" Balzic said to her.

"Joe Royer." She squirmed around trying to move her chair closer to the desk on which the console was placed. "He called me at ten o'clock, said he was sick, and could I come in. I said sure."

"Mario, we have a problem here," the mayor said.

"In a second, Mister Mayor, I want to find out—"

"He said we have a problem here, jerk. Can't you understand English?" The voice had come from the pale stick figure with the large pink lips, and Balzic thought he was having auditory hallucinations. The voice sounded like it came from a funeral director on amphetamine.

Balzic turned his back on the stick figure. "I know I've met you at least once before," Balzic said to the dispatcher, "but I can't think of your name."

"Melody. Derzapelski."

"Yeah. Sure. I remember now."

"Hey, jerk!"

"Melody, would you slide back, huh, please? I wanna get into that middle drawer there."

"Oh sure." Melody pushed away from the desk.

Balzic opened the drawer and found the 9mm Browning semi-automatic pistol that belonged to Desk Sergeant Vic Stramsky. It was under a mess of papers, rubber bands, pencils, pens, and paper clips. It was what Stramsky called his "just-in-case piece," just in case of nuclear war or attack by a bunch of bikers or, like now, just in case a skinny smart-mouth showed up and you didn't want to hunt for the keys to the shotgun rack. Balzic wasn't even sure it was loaded. He slipped it out of the drawer and put it down by his left leg, closed the drawer, and sidled up to the counter.

He made eye contact with the stick figure and tried to listen as Mayor Strohn advised him that the stick figure was the son of the dog lady and he had come all the way from Cleveland, a trip of almost two hours by car, at great inconvenience to himself and to his employer, to find out what in the name of all holiness had happened to his blessed mother, who was practically a second cousin to the Virgin Mary.

Balzic never took his eyes off the stick figure. "What is your name, sir?"

"My name, you jerk, if you knew what you were doing, if you gave a damn about people instead of pretending to be a Nazi, you would know from what you've done to my mother!"

Balzic brought the Browning up and laid it gently on the counter. Then, as though as an afterthought, he picked it up again and made a deliberate show of pulling the slide back and putting a round in the chamber, even though he had no idea whether there was even one live cartridge in it. No matter. The show seemed to serve its purpose: stick figure stopped moving all his parts.

"I ask you again, sir, what is your name?"

Stick figure came to life as suddenly as he'd stopped. He snapped his middle finger and thumb on his right hand, rocked from side to side while bouncing on his toes, dug in his ear with his left index finger, and stammered, "I'm—I'm—my name's Mister Robert Bauk."

"Your mother's name the same?"

"Uh—no. No. Her name is Baukauskous. B-A-U-K-A-U-S-K-O-U-S. Mary."

"Ah!" Balzic said. "A Lithuanian lady. So. So what is your problem, Mr. Bauk?" Balzic intertwined his fingers and leaned on his forearms on the counter. "Your problem, Mister Robert Bauk?"

Balzic was not prepared for what happened next. He had thought that Bauk's reaction to the pageant with the Browning had been fear, and that was what caused this bundle of metabolic excesses to stop moving and to stammer. Balzic could not have been more wrong.

Bauk snatched the Browning in a blur and whirled and heaved it through the window in the door coming from the parking lot.

"Listen, jerk," Bauk snarled, "right now the biggest problem I have is you and your stupid fascist macho mind. I want to know where my mother is!"

Balzic turned and gawked stupidly at the mayor. "The goddamn thing was empty. He threw it through a window into the goddamn parking lot and the goddamn thing didn't go off."

"Hello!" Bauk said. "Anybody home over there?"

Balzic ignored Bauk and asked the mayor: "Who is this guy here?" He pointed to the man in the three-piece suit.

"He's from the county Health Department, that's what I've been trying to tell you. He wants me to institute condemnation proceedings—"

"No no," three-piece suit said. "I—the Department, that is—has already condemned the house. I want you to institute proceedings to raze it."

"Yes. Right. And I told him that that has to go through the Traffic and Safety Committee and then through the full Council before I can sign any order to raze the property."

"Where the hell is my mother?" shrieked Bauk.

"Excuse me a minute," Balzic said, sliding between the mayor and the bureaucrat from the Health Department and going through the lift door in the counter.

Bauk began to jump up and down and hammer his stick-like thighs with his fists. "Where the hell are you going? Where the hell is my mother?"

"I'm going outside to get that pistol you threw out there, and your mother, as far as I know, is in the Mental Health Clinic of Conemaugh Hospital. Which you could've found out for yourself, if you really wanted to, which you didn't, 'cause you wanted to come down here and hassle people instead, now isn't that right?" Balzic didn't wait for Bauk's answer, hurrying instead to the parking lot where he found the pistol against the chain-link fence separating the city hall parking lot from the parking lot of the adjacent shopping center.

Balzic found that the hammer had fallen, so he reasoned that the pistol had to be empty. He worked the slide, whistling as a cartridge went arcing through the air and clattered to the ground. He picked it up and found it to be complete, bullet and shell, with the unmistakable depression of a strike from the hammer. He held the cartridge up to his ear and shook it and heard the powder rattling. "Now how the fuck do you figure this," he said aloud to himself. "A goddamn misfire. An honest-to-god goddamn misfire. Fuckin' dead primer."

Balzic extracted the magazine and saw that it was full. He started back toward the duty room door, thinking about the many possibilities that could have been created by that dead primer and decided to have a talk with Stramsky about how long it had been since he'd fired the Browning. At the top of the steps, he was confronted by the ever-moving Mr. Bauk.

"Where—jerk—is Conemaugh Hospital?"

Balzic slipped around him and through the door.

"I'm talking to you!" Bauk screamed.

"You ain't talkin' to anybody," Balzic said, going through the lift-door in the counter. "What you're doin' is havin' a tantrum."

"Mario," the mayor said. "I've never done this before. What do we do?"

Balzic found a phone book and put it on the counter near Bauk. "You know how to use a phone book? Conemaugh Hospital, Mental Health Clinic."

"Can't you just tell me?"

Balzic shook his head no. He turned to Mayor Strohn. "First thing you gotta do is run a title search on the property. House and land. Probably it's the same person. Hey, you know about titles. Then you gotta go through your committees and then you gotta hope nobody has any objections."

"Such as what?"

"Such as the motion machine over there. You never know.

And then I think, to be on the safe side, you gotta get a judge's name on the papers."

"Why?"

"Just because you're gettin' ready to tear down somebody's house, somebody's property, and, uh, I'd want all the due process on paper I could get before I did that."

"And that's it?" Strohn said.

"Hey, don't make it sound like I'm makin' it sound simple. Nothin' like this ever is. Christ only knows who owns that house."

"*I* own the house!" Bauk said.

"See," Balzic said, throwing up his hands, "there's your first problem right there." He walked back to the radio console, asked Melody Derzapelski to move back, and put Stramsky's pistol back where he'd found it.

* * *

Balzic never got back to Francis Collier's trial. It ended two days later and Balzic spent nearly all of his waking hours in those two days dealing with Mr. Bauk and his mother the dog lady, and with Mayor Strohn and the county Health Department.

The first problem came when Bauk finally quit screeching at everybody and called the Mental Health Clinic. Before the phone was hung up that time, everybody Bauk, Strohn, three-piece suit from the Health Department, and Balzic—tried to make sense with the receptionist at the Mental Health Clinic, but they all wasted so much air because the woman didn't know who they were talking about. She was not the regular receptionist—they were both sick—she worked in the main hospital and she couldn't find any name that even sounded like Baukauskous. She put each of them on hold at least twice.

The second problem came when Balzic called Conemaugh General Hospital which was across the street from the Mental Health Clinic, and learned that no woman named Baukauskous was registered as a patient there either. By this time, Robert Bauk was moving so many parts so fast that Balzic asked him if he was on medication.

"Just skip the smart stuff, jerk, and find my mother. A couple of phone calls ago I was down here having a tantrum and harassing people. Now none of you authoritarian geniuses knows where she is. Isn't that amusing?"

Next, Balzic called Patrolman Harry Lynch, only to learn he'd made good on his threat to take sick leave. He was off hunting or fishing or getting drunk in Canada somewhere, his sister said, and he wasn't coming back until they ran out of beer or until somebody proved to him that the dog lady was either dead or in New Jersey, and he really didn't care which of those two it was.

Balzic then looked through the phone logs to see when Lynch had brought the woman in, to get a line on which crew of EMTs from Mutual Aid Ambulance Service came to the station and took her to the Mental Health Clinic. He found the entry and then called Mutual Aid to have their dispatcher look for a corresponding entry in their logs. That was easy enough. The dispatcher found the names and home and work phones for all three EMTs who had responded to the call. What wasn't easy was that one was vacationing in Georgia, another was looking for work in Tennessee, and the third one was visiting his mother who was in a hospital in Maryland.

"Look," Balzic said, "she's gotta be in one of those two places. We're just not talkin' to the right people. Here's what we do: I'll go up there and find her, Mr. Mayor, and you and the Health Department there do what you have to do with the property, and then—"

"Not so fast, jerk. Nobody's doing anything to that property. I own that house and the lot and there are no liens and nobody—and I mean nobody like the likes of you fascist bureaucrats is going to lay one finger on that house until I get my mother's silver and jewelry out of there, is that clear? Not to mention the dogs."

"Nobody's saying anything to the contrary," Mayor Strohn said.

At about that moment, Balzic saw the three-piece suit check his wristwatch against the clock on the wall. He zipped up his briefcase, put his ballpoint pen in his shirt pocket, and with a slight hint of a nod and a barely perceptible wave, ambled on out.

"Where in the hell is he going?" Mayor Strohn said.

"It's quittin' time, Mr. Mayor," Balzic said. "We don't need him anyway. Listen, you take Mr. Bauk here to get whatever he wants from his house. I'm goin' to the hospital and the Mental

Health Clinic to find out what happened to his mother. Uh, Mr. Bauk, did you just say something about dogs?"

"You bet your ass, jerk. Some of the most valuable dogs you've ever heard of."

Balzic turned slowly and went and stood by Melody Derzapelski and whispered in her ear, "Get me the dog officer. And put it through to my office, okay?"

Then he turned back to Bauk. "Uh, these dogs, the ones you say are so valuable? How valuable are these dogs?"

"That would have to be determined by reps from the American Kennel Club—if you mean future earnings. If you're talking about earnings, I would have to look it up. But one of them, Bobo, the border collie, well, he's already earned five thousand in stud."

"Uh, Mr. Bauk, how long did your mother take care of these dogs?"

"How long? A year, maybe thirteen months."

"You gave your mother custody of these dogs?"

"I did."

"Uh, where were you in this year, or thirteen months?"

"I don't think I'm obliged to tell you that."

"Oh no, you're not obliged. I just wanna know."

"Well, you're going to find out anyway," Bauk said, moving so rapidly he made Balzic tired just watching him. "I was in Western Psychiatric in Oakland. I'm sure you've heard of it."

"Oh yes, sure have. It's well known." Balzic scratched his chin. "Uh, your mother. She ever been in any place like that?"

"Haven't we all?"

"Well, I haven't—and I'm not sayin' that I shouldn't be there, and the longer I'm in this job the more I think I'm eventually gonna wind up there—but I haven't yet. And I don't think the mayor has either—"

"Not yet, knock wood," the mayor said, rapping himself lightly on the forehead with his knuckles.

Bauk came to a sudden stop. He looked almost normal, metabolically speaking. "I don't know why I didn't think of this before," he said, glowering at Balzic, "but exactly where *are* the dogs?"

Balzic headed for the door. "Mr. Mayor, I've got a call in to the dog officer, and when he calls back, you can straighten Mr. Bauk out on that, okay?"

"Not so fast, jerk-o. Where are you going?"

"I told you before," Balzic said, moving faster the closer he got to the door, "I'm goin' to the hospital and then to Mental Health to get a line on your mother. In the meantime you can give a description of your mother to the dispatcher there and she'll pass it to people in the mobile units and everybody will be keepin' an eye out for her, just in case."

"Just a god-damned minute, jerk-o. . . ."

Too late. Balzic had slipped around him and through the door and down the steps and into his cruiser. He started it, put it in gear, and burned tires getting out of the city hall lot into traffic.

His first thought was about the dogs. He called his station and when Melody Derzapelski answered he begged her to find the dog officer. "Every free minute you get, Melody, call him. Find out what he did with those dogs. I'd hate to think what kind of problems we're gonna have if he put those dogs to sleep, Jesus."

Balzic's second thought as he made his way in traffic was Bauk and the Browning. The little weasel started calling me names, and I go for a gun. I could've picked that skinny sonofabitch up with one hand and I went for a gun! He calls me a name and I give him a goddamn movie move and nobody even says, hey, wait a second. It's like it's the most natural thing in the world. Call the cop names and the cop goes for a gun. The cop gets the gun, puts on a pageant, and what's the cop hear? Nothing. Not a discouraging word. Nobody says, hey, man, what the hell you think you're doin'? Not the mayor, not the dispatcher, not the three-piece suit from the Health Department. They don't say a word. No. It's up to the skinny little prick to bring me back to earth. The irresponsible little shit couldn't care less what happens when that piece comes to earth. Fuck no, he just throws it. And I just go waltzin' on out after it and when I come waltzin' back in, does anybody say, hey, where you been? Hell no. Run across any guns while you were gone? Hell no. Stumble on a Browning while you were out there? Hell no. How come it didn't go off? Hell no. Anybody say anything? Hell no. Happens all the time. Cop produces a gun to impress some skinny little snot, he throws it through a window, and everybody stands around like, hey, you wanna pass the potatoes? Jesus H. Christ, Balzic said to himself, if I don't get laid soon, somebody's gonna cart me off in a jacket and teach me how to stuff envelopes or string beads. . . .

Balzic parked on the street in front of the Mental Health Clinic. He hustled inside and talked to the receptionist, the woman who was substituting for the two regulars, and naturally enough, she didn't know any more in person about the Baukauskous woman than she had when she'd been pestered on the phone.

Balzic persuaded her to let him look through the admissions log on the day Mrs. Baukauskous was brought in. He was looking for a Jane Doe entry but there wasn't any, and there certainly wasn't one under the Baukauskous name. Balzic pushed the log across the counter, thanked the woman, and hurried to his cruiser. He drove it around the block until he came to the doctors' parking lot and parked there.

He trotted across the street to the main lobby and admissions office of Conemaugh General. Ten minutes of conversation there produced the same results. That left only the emergency room, the "Trauma Unit" they were calling it these says. No matter what name it went by, it had its own admissions desk, and Balzic trudged along the painted stripes on the floors until he came to it. Neither name—Baukauskous nor Jane Doe—produced anything from the logs or the memories of the clerks.

"Anybody remember a lady stinkin', naked?"

"Oh, her! Sure, why didn't you say so in the first place?" one clerk said. "You remember me tellin' you about her, Mary. The one that stunk? God I felt so sorry for the people had to clean her up."

"Uh-ha. Well, now that we're both talkin' about the same person, you know where she is?"

"No."

"Well can't you find out?"

"How? I don't know what her name is in that data base."

"You didn't process her, then?"

"Nobody did."

"Somebody had to."

"How? The woman didn't have any identification, and every time somebody asked her a question, all she did was make noise like a dog. She barked, she whimpered."

"Who, uh, who was in charge here at that time?"

"Cercone."

"The one they call 'Beans'?"

"Sure. He's back there now."

Balzic nodded and said thanks. He pushed through double

fire doors into the treatment room area and wandered around until he found a nurse who seemed not to be busy and asked her for Doctor Cercone's whereabouts.

"Who calls?" came the cheerful gravel of Cercone's voice, followed by the squeaking of his runner's shoes on the tile floor.

"I call, Beansie, I call."

"Hey. Chief. What's happening?" Cercone appeared from around a corner, his hand extended in greeting.

Balzic shook it. "What's happening is I wanna know about a woman who was brought in here the other day, stinkin', covered with dog crap, naked."

"Oh Jesus, say no more."

"You remember her?"

"*Remember* her? Christ, I have olfactory flashbacks about her. You wanna smell somethin' ferocious, as in stink? Man, there is nothing in the world smells as bad as rehydrated excrement. And when we put that woman in the shower, that's exactly what we got, rehydrated excrement. Old dried up ka-ka turned into brand new wet ka-ka. You should've seen that. Two nurses and me, we're scrubbin' down this woman in a shower, and we *all* smokin' cigars. I don't know who I felt sorrier for, that woman or us. It took us forty minutes, man. For-ty minutes. Three of us, with scrub brushes. I wanted to cut the woman's hair off, she was screamin', it was so tangled up with, uh, you know. But the nurses wouldn't let me." Cercone shook his head and looked at the floor.

"Where is she now?"

"Second floor."

"You seen her recently?"

"Oh hell, everybody on staff has seen her recently. I didn't know how else to try and identify her except to send everybody in to take a look at her. So far, nothin'. And I think everybody's seen her. Course, there's no tellin' how much her appearance has changed since who knows when."

"Well, you can forget about tryin' to ID her. We know who she is."

"You do?"

"Yeah. Her name's Baukauskous, somethin' like that. She's got a son. He's not wrapped much tighter'n she is. Uh, what kind of shape's she in?"

"Not very good. Tell you the truth, I don't know why she's alive. There's no tellin' how long she was in that condition, and when we finally got her cleaned up enough to check her out, we found any number of open sores, on top of which, she was extremely dehydrated and malnourished."

"How long was she like that?"

Beans shrugged and shook his head. "Two weeks, three maybe. I doubt more than that."

"God, Lynch said the shit was up over his shoes."

"What?"

"Nothin'. I was just thinkin' out loud. Just wonderin' when she lost it."

"Oh hell, you'll never know that. She could've started talkin' to the animals years ago."

"Lotsa people talk to animals."

"No no, I mean in *their* language. Hey, Chief, you close your eyes around her when she starts makin' noise, you know, I thought I got lost in veterinary school. The woman does not make anything we would call a human sound. She's a two-legged dog."

"Aren't you curious about that?"

"Hey, Chief," Cercone said, laughing, "I'm a trauma guy. I operate on heads, I don't operate on minds, and when I operate on heads it's 'cause we can't find a real head cutter."

"Jesus, that's so fucking sad. I don't know why it is, but it is."

"It's sad 'cause people are supposed to make people noises. That's why we say we're people. And when we don't make that kind of noise, well . . ." Cercone peered at Balzic. "You sure you're okay?"

"Huh? What?"

"Man, you're askin' a lot of, uh, vague questions. You like vague today, right?"

"No, I don't like vague, ever. But lately, all I see is vague. I mean, nothin' seems solider than vague. I feel like I'm tryin' to walk on fog. I feel like I'm tryin' to swim through rolled oats."

Cercone leaned back in his chair and patted the arms of the chair with his palms. "Man, what brought this on?"

"Shit, I don't know. Every once in a while, everything starts to blur. It'd be okay if I was drinkin', but I'm not. So I got no excuse. Things just start to blur all by themselves. And no matter how many times I say to myself, 'Hey, man, get hold of yourself, you've got to hold things together,' it doesn't work. I just see things gettin' blurry wherever I go. . . . My mother looked really old last time I saw her. And the thing that bothers me is, I can't remember when that was. Now ain't that some shit?"

* * *

For the rest of the next two days, Balzic was filled with vague, if such was possible. And it got vaguer and vaguer. Nobody could find the humane officer. The city pound, at the far end of the parking lot behind city hall, was locked. Dogs were yapping and howling inside, but there was no sign of the humane officer and nobody had a key. Every time Balzic turned around, there was Bauk yapping at him to find the dogs and threatening endless lawsuits if he didn't.

The mayor, being a prudent man, prudently requested the help of the city's solicitor, since nobody knew where the city stood, legally speaking, vis-a-vis Bauk and his dogs. The only problem with this was that Balzic and the solicitor, Pete Renaldo, couldn't stand each other, so that now, every time the subject of Bauk and his dog came up—which was every time Bauk appeared, which was just about all the time—Balzic had to deal with two people he disliked: Renaldo, whom he had disliked intensely for many years, and Bauk, whom he was growing to dislike even more intensely than Renaldo.

Renaldo was the son of a coal miner, an immigrant who had sweated in the deep mines to send his son to college and law school so he wouldn't have to go into the mines. Renaldo's discourtesy to his father was well-known. He was notorious for belittling his father in markets. It was always over simple things: the old man, slowed to a shuffle by respiratory disease, simply took too long choosing eggplants or peppers or olive oil. As for Renaldo's social aspirations, his father held him back just by being alive. Renaldo was doing his duty by caring for his aged and sickly father, but his resentment for having to do so was something he could not endure quietly. He was always guiding the old man, his tone and manner like a teacher who couldn't wait for the children to go home, except that, in Renaldo's case, he would go home when his father did and not a minute sooner.

As for Bauk, all he had to do to set Balzic's teeth on edge was to open the door to the duty room and walk in. Just the sight of him, whispy hair, bulging eyes, pink protuberant lips, livid complexion, and constant movement, coupled with his tirades about "Balzic's Bureaucrats" and the "Rocksburgian Rodents of Red Tape" made Balzic lose his composure.

And it seemed that every time Balzic looked up over the next two days Bauk was practically sprinting through the door, the window of which he had shattered when he'd tossed the pistol now replaced by plywood. Bauk never glanced at the wood, even though Balzic never failed to remind him that he was going to pay for the new window and the labor it would take to install it.

Bauk couldn't be bothered to think about that. All he wanted to know about was the dogs. The broken window had as much interest for him as his mother did.

"You ever goin' to ask about your mother?" Balzic said to him on one of his forays into the duty room.

Bauk froze for a second. Then his body shifted into its other speed. "My mother? My moth-er. Chief-o, have you ever asked yourself why the grossest word in our language is moth-er-fuck-er? Have you ever asked yourself why it isn't fath-er-fuck-er? Or broth-er-fuck-er? Or sis-ter-fuck-er? Or dog-gie-fuck-er? Huh? Have you ever asked yourself that?"

"Uh, no. I guess I haven't."

"Well it's time you did, jerk-o. Moth-er-fuck-er is not the grossest word in our language for nothing. It serves a purpose."

"It does? A purpose?"

"Yes, jerk-o. A pur-pose. Which purpose is to sound the alarm for all you sleepwalkers to wake up."

"Wake up to what?"

"Wake up to all your rocket-cock macho mentality, that's what. Comes from eating all that white bread and watching all those super bowls. Let me put it this way, Chief-o. Very few people who voted for Rocket-cock Ronnie ever say moth-er-fuck-er. All they know is they don't like it. It never even occurs to them to wonder why the profanity of choice is not baby-fucker, even with all this la-de-dah about child abuse."

Balzic knew he was in trouble when he turned to Renaldo after one of Bauk's tirades and asked if Renaldo knew what Bauk was talking about. Balzic knew how serious his trouble when he found himself actually waiting to hear Renaldo's reply.

"I think Mr. Bauk is under a lot of stress," Renaldo said somberly.

"No shit," Balzic said, snorting. "For fifty bucks an hour, that's your best thought?"

"With all this hoop-de-doo about child abuse and kiddie porn," Bauk said, "you have to wonder why somebody hasn't started a campaign to take a child to dinner. Course, I suppose, that wouldn't look too good."

Balzic glared at Bauk. "Hey, without the editorial this time, you, uh, you ever gonna ask about your mother again?"

"Oh Christ," Bauk said, "the word moth-er itself is an editorial, Chief-o. A one-word editorial. Don't you think it's interesting that it was the descendants of slaves who gave us our foulest, vilest profanity? Imagine that we all love God, the flag, apple pie, and motherhood, and that we hate niggers because they call us fuckers of mothers. We think they're talking about *our* mothers, but what they're talking about is *their* mothers."

"Yeah, yeah," Balzic said. "Just tell me one thing. You been to see your mother yet?"

"I've been to see my house," Bauk said. "I tramped through all the shit I could tramp through. And you know what I found? I found Bobo's head. I found his head! And before you ask me again, you fascist bastard, I don't care where my mother is. You pick your friends, you don't pick your family and all that, but she promised she'd look out for my dogs when I was gone. . . . I hope you won't be offended when I say fuck moth-er, I mean, I hope your goddamn stinky white bread macho sensibilities won't be too, too offended."

"If you'll excuse me," Balzic said, "I have to go now."

"Of course you do, white bread. Go ahead. Run! That's what white bread does best."

Balzic stopped at the door and said, "Whatta you want from me?"

"Well, you could start by telling me where my mother's jewelry is."

"Her what?"

"Her jewelry, jerk-o. It's gone. It's not in the house."

"Oh. So what're you sayin'? Somebody from my department copped it? Is that what you're sayin'?"

"Maybe *you* did."

"Wait just a goddamn minute here," Balzic said, advancing on Bauk. "You accusing me of something?"

"If the shoe fits, you know. . . ."

"The shoe's gonna fit right up your ass, you scrawny little

shit. I haven't set foot in your house, I don't even know where it is."

"Yeah. Sure. Right. You don't know where it is but you want to knock it down and plow it under or whatever you do when you raze property, but that is my property. My property you're getting ready to raze, and unless I've gotten lost in a time machine and fell asleep and waked up in Nazi Germany, I just don't understand how you can destroy something that belongs to me without paying me a fair market value just because my mother decided she was going to turn into Lassie."

"Oh Jesus," Balzic said.

"Oh fuck him too. *And* his mother. *And* the donkey he rode in on. Where's my mother's jewelry? And her silver? And where the hell are the rest of my dogs? Bobo's dead. Are the rest of them dead too? Do you know? Would you tell me if you did?"

"Right now, you little prick, I wouldn't tell you what time it was if we were both lookin' at a clock."

Balzic turned around and headed for the door again, but stopped. "Hey, Renaldo. Solicitor! You explain to him, will ya? Tell him what's gonna happen to his house."

"Tell me about what's happened to the stuff *in* the *house*! Tell me how much you're going to pay me for the house! Tell me where I can find a goddamn pharmacist to give me a prescription on credit!"

"What pharmacist? What prescription, what the hell're you talkin' about?"

"I believe," Renaldo said, "that he's trying to tell you that he's a pauper and that he needs medication."

Balzic rolled his head from shoulder to shoulder trying to loosen some muscles in his neck that had started to go into spasm the moment he saw Bauk this time.

"Renaldo, he's all yours. You and the mayor and the briefcasers from the Health Department, he's all yours. Wrap him up and take him down the welfare office, maybe they'll buy him his medicine. I don't care where you take him, just get him the fuck outta here."

"Where are my dogs? What about my dogs?"

"Hey, you hear that, Renaldo? Find him his dogs, buy his house, get him his medicine, and then put him on a fuckin' bus to Cleveland."

Bauk bobbed over to Balzic and thrust his index finger under Balzic's nose. "You're not getting rid of me that easy. There's thousands of dollars' worth of jewelry and silver in that house and it's not there!"

Balzic tried to turn away but Bauk grabbed him by the arm.

Balzic spun around swinging his left arm to swat Bauk's hand away and in the same motion grabbed Bauk by the neck with both hands and jerked him off the floor and slammed him into the wall.

The next thing Balzic knew somebody was slapping his forearms and shouting his name.

"Let go, Balzic, let him down!" It was Renaldo and when Balzic turned to see who it was, Renaldo was shouting and saliva was flying everywhere and he was the color of an overripe peach.

Balzic turned away from Renaldo and saw Bauk, as though suspended in space against the wall, except that his throat was in Balzic's hands and Bauk's face was crimson and his eyes were bulging nearly out of their sockets and he was drooling all over Balzic's wrists.

Balzic let go and Bauk slumped against the wall, hacking and coughing.

"For God's sake," Renaldo blustered, "have you lost your mind? Are you crazy? You could've killed him!"

Balzic stepped back and looked at both of them. He took another step back and then pointed at Renaldo. "You get him the hell outta here. Take him upstairs, take him to your office, take him to the mayor's house, I don't care where you take him, just get him outta here, I'm sick of that geek screamin' at me."

"You are not fit to be a police officer," Renaldo said. "I've been telling everybody for years you're unfit and nobody pays any attention. You're unfit! You are psychologically unsuited to do what this city pays you to do!"

"Yeah, yeah," Balzic said, licking his lips and loosening his tie.

"Do you know what you've done now?"

"I'm sure you're gonna tell me."

"In addition to everything else this man has going for him against this city, now you've added aggravated assault! Jesus, Balzic, the older you get the dumber, I swear! Why don't you do the city a favor and resign? Huh? Why don't you?"

"Yeah. Sure," Balzic said, squinting and glaring at Bauk who was struggling to regain his normal breathing. "Hey, Bauk, can you hear me? Don't ever put your shoes in this room again. Don't even think about it."

"Oh my god," Renaldo said, covering his face with his hands. "Official oppression, terroristic threats, malfeasance. What else, Balzic? What else are you going to do that's indictable?"

"I'm gonna tell you once more: get this goddamn geek outta here." Balzic pushed past Renaldo and hurried through the door into the city hall parking lot.

It was snowing, tiny flakes swirling this way and that. Balzic found himself without his raincoat, hat, or gloves, but he refused to go back into the station to get them. If he had to look at Bauk again—or Renaldo—he didn't know what he'd do. He stood there, hands jammed deep into his coat pockets, imagining what he would do to Bauk if he ever saw him in the duty room again. Every fantasy ended in Bauk's painful death.

He shook himself out of his fantastic reverie and went to his cruiser and got in. Before he turned the key in the ignition, he said aloud, "I'll bet that's why that sonofabitch did it. I'll bet he just got sick of lookin' at him. I'll bet he was just as pissed off at her as he was at him. . . ."

* * *

Balzic was driving through town, trying to breathe deeply from his diaphragm, deeply and slowly to slow his heart and to cool himself down and having a terrible time doing it, when he saw somebody waving both hands at him.

He pulled through the first intersection past the courthouse and up to the curb and twisted around to see who it was. It was a black man wearing well-tailored clothes who approached Balzic's cruiser on a trot.

Balzic wound down the window and waited, but the black man came around to the passenger window and rapped on it with the back of his hand. Balzic reached over and popped the lock.

"Machlin! Hell, I didn't recognize you. Get in, get in."

Machlin dropped onto the seat and left the door open. "It's probably the hat, right? This a baaaaad hat. Bought it last night. I knew we were goin' beat his ass today. Told my girl, I gotta get me a hat celebrate beatin' his ass."

"Uh, who you talkin' about?"

"Collier, man! We got him. Voluntary manslaughter."

"No shit?"

"I'm tellin' ya. Sentencin' in thirty days. I'm lookin' for a solid one to three."

"How long were they out?"

"Hell, they were out less than an hour. Oh man, Vrbanic was beautiful, man. Beautiful. He laid out the justifiable homicide defense so clear a third-grader could've understood it. They had no choice but to convict. I love it, Chief, I love it. Hey, let me buy you something. Really. Coffee, cake, wine, cheese, whatever. Any good places close by?"

"Right there, dead ahead, on the right."

"Oh yeah? Is that that Muscotti's I been hearin' about? You sure I should be seen in there?"

"I'm not sure I should be seen in there," Balzic said.

"That sounds to me like the kind of place you and me oughta be practicin' not bein' seen in, whatta you think?"

"My feelings exactly."

* * *

Balzic sat across the table from Ruth in Vallozzi's. It was the middle of the afternoon, three o'clock or so, and except for them, the restaurant was empty.

Ruth pointed hesitantly with her left hand toward the painting beside them, then brought her finger back to her lips. "I love this table," she said, "because of that painting. I never saw a painting that had so much action in it. I never thought it was possible."

"Action?"

"Sure. Look at it. The musicians are right in the middle of a song, the people are listening, the waitress is waiting tables—it's full of action. And it's so dark and it looks like it's frozen. Like all the people are frozen. But, God, Mario, look how much action there is in it."

"You sound like you've looked at it a lot."

"Sure. Every time I'm with your mother, this is where we sit. She loves it here. She's the one who made me look at the painting. She's who made me see the action."

"Have you been here a lot? Really?"

"Mario, God, we have to go someplace. We have to do something. And where is there better to go than a good restaurant? Look around. It's beautiful. Look at the paintings, look at the flowers, look at the windows, look at the sun coming through the stained-glass windows. And Mario, oh God, wait'll you taste the food! These women—and they're all women, Mario. There's not a man in the kitchen! They're great! Oh! They do things to food here that . . . you'll see. Believe me."

"Hey, Ruth," a waitress said, appearing suddenly from behind Balzic's back. "How are you today? You want the white zinfandel?"

Balzic leaned forward and peered at his wife. "The waitress knows your name? And she knows what kind of wine you drink?"

"Hello, Patty. Yes. I want the white zinfandel. And bring him a burgundy."

"All rightee, I'll be back," the waitress said, hurrying off.

"The waitress knows your name?"

"We come here once a week, Mario."

"Once a week?"

"Mario, we love you. Both of us do. Nobody loves you more than I do. Not even your mother. But, Mario, we can't wait for you for us to live. My God, you're never home."

Balzic took off his glasses and toyed with them. He felt his eyes filling up.

Ruth put her hand on his. "Mario, I didn't say that to make you feel bad."

"I know, I know."

"Then, listen. Talk to me. Tell me what's going on."

"Oh, Christ, where do I start?"

"Well, start with Collier. Yesterday when you came home, you were white. You looked like hell. Start with that. C'mon. We're gonna eat, we're gonna drink, we're gonna talk."

"Collier," Balzic said, rubbing his knuckle across his lips. "That sonofabitch. He really foxed us. Bastard foxed everybody."

"How? Tell me how."

"I don't know if I can. It's complicated. I'm not tryin' to avoid givin' you an answer, it's just complicated. I mean, from the start, when old man Castelucci started buggin' me, I thought it was strictly a heat-of-the-moment thing. I thought Joey ran into a guy as goofy as he was, only the guy had a gun and he didn't. I never thought for a minute it was anything else. I thought the old man was just whacked out with grief and guilt.

"I thought, you know, when Collier was convicted and he got

one to three, I said, yeah, that's right. That's exactly what it was worth."

The waitress interrupted him to put the napkins on the table and set the wine on them and was gone. Just as Balzic leaned forward to speak again, the waitress came back with a pitcher of ice water and filled their goblets. Then she asked if they were ready to order.

"Hell, I haven't even seen a menu yet," Balzic said, taking a sip of his burgundy.

"Oh. I'm sorry. Ruth always says she has the menu memorized, so I just thought, you know—I'll be right back."

"God, Ruth, you got it memorized?"

"I have a lot of free time, Mario. Remember?"

"Look, you wanna go to work part-time, that's up to you."

"I was joking, Mario. Look at me. It was a joke."

"Yeah I know it was a joke. *Now* it was a joke. I also know you were serious the other night."

"Let's not start that again, okay?"

"Hey, Ruth, it ain't gonna go away. But, uh, what the hell, we've been through this a hundred times."

"And I'd like to remind you we're still together. So maybe it's not perfect, but it's the best we've got. It's the best *I've* got." She put her hand on his. "I love you, Mario. You're a low-life son of a bitch sometimes. But I love you. Now shut up about the other night and tell me about Collier."

"The other night's not gonna go away—"

"Ready to order yet?" chirped the waitress who seemed to materialize out of nowhere.

"You were goin' for a menu, darlin', remember?"

"Oh!" the waitress smacked herself in the forehead with the heel of her hand and trotted off.

"She always that spacey?"

"No. She's usually very sharp. Your mother really likes her. She always wants to sit at her table."

Balzic shook his head. "This is a whole new thing for me. I feel like a PT in your life."

"A what?"

"A PT. Peepin' Tom."

"Oh, Mario, for God's sake."

"Well, I do sometimes. Hey, we're talkin' about damn near twenty-five years here. And I missed the best part of it."

"You did not miss the best part. Honest to God, Mario. The best part is *now*!"

"Yeah, I know."

"Oh, Mario," Ruth said mock-disgustedly, "I swear, sometimes I think you should have been a priest, no shit, I do." She held up her glass of white zinfandel. "Here, come on! Put your glass up there."

"What for?"

"When somebody puts their glass up, that's a signal for a toast. It's a little custom we have in our country. You bonk your glasses together and then the person who held her glass up first, she makes a little speech. It's very popular."

"God," he snorted, "sometimes you're a real ball-buster, you know that?"

"It's one of my jobs, yes. And I'm good at it. C'mon, get your glass up there."

Balzic bonked his glass against hers and waited.

"To my husband. The cop. The low-life son of a bitch who sometimes maybe, every once in a while, should have been a priest. To the man who I love, who doesn't understand that there's no bigger waste of time than worrying about time you wasted."

Balzic shook with silent laughter. "Oh God."

"C'mon. It's no good, it's all for nothing unless you drink up. So drink!"

Balzic took a large mouthful and swallowed three times, slowly, savoring it. "Okay," he said, "I promise I'll try not to worry about time wasted."

Ruth leaned forward, smiling and chuckling, and said, "You'll be worrying before your feet hit the floor tomorrow morning."

"Hey. Thanks for your confidence."

"Are you going to tell me about Collier or not?"

"Every time—"

"Are you ready to order now?"

"Jesus," Balzic said, "I still haven't seen a menu."

"Mario," Ruth said, "you don't need a menu. Let me order, okay? Okay?"

Balzic shrugged. "Go right ahead."

"Well, first we want two small spinach salads, with house sweet-and-sour dressing. Then bring me the lemon sole. What's the lunch special, by the way?"

"Oh it was fried cod, but we're out of it."

"Okay. So I want the lemon sole. And bring my husband the fettucini Alfredo with spinach. It's not fettucini, Mario. It's thick spaghetti, but they make it here, so it doesn't matter what they call it, it's great. You're gonna love it."

"That's with cream and butter and parmesan? I can't eat that."

"Mario, once a year is not going to kill you."

"Yeah, but I was really tryin' to stick with that."

"You can stick with it. Only not today. Today you take a break. And if it kills you, think of it this way. Think of everything I'll inherit."

"God, you're awful," said Patty, the waitress, trying not to laugh too hard.

"Oh," Ruth said, "and an order of garlic toast. But don't bring it until you bring the food. Don't bring it with the salads, okay?"

"Sure. All rightee. Will that be all then?"

"What's left?" Balzic said.

"Dessert! Whatta you think?"

Balzic rolled his eyes as the waitress hustled away. "Couldn't she be a little less friendly?"

"Why are you asking me?"

"'Cause you seem to be on such good terms with her, you know?"

"Mario, it's her job to be friendly. That's how she makes her living. You know what your problem is? You spend too much time in Muscotti's. Not everybody who waits on people treats them the way Vinnie does."

"Yeah, yeah."

"So. Finish your story. Tell me about Collier."

"Before I tell you about him, did I ever tell you about a guy named Bauk?"

"Oh Mario. It's a touch of senility I think. My God. Bauk and his mother the dog lady were all you talked about for weeks. I couldn't get you to talk about anything else."

"Yeah. Well, that's 'cause the little bastard made everybody crazy. Especially me. I mean, he absolutely made me lose it twice. First time I saw him I showed him a pistol. In front of *three other people*. I'll never forget that. I mean, I knew how stupid it was the whole time I was doin' it. But I thought I had to do this performance for him, to wise him up. I thought—"

"Mario, I've heard this story at least—over the last year? I heard this story five times the first week after it happened. I'll bet I've heard it at least twice that many times in the last year."

Balzic took another sip of wine and rubbed his chin. "Did I also tell you what I thought I learned from it?"

"Many times. You became really obsessed with it. Honest. I don't know how many times you told me: that's how you knew how Collier killed Joey."

"Yeah. Except it was just a little different angle. With me, the first time I ever encountered Bauk I showed him the gun. With Collier, it was the last thing he did. Joey opened the door and there was Collier, standin' there with the gun in his hand. And Joey flipped out. Just like I flipped out when Bauk kept hasslin' me about the goddamn jewelry and the silver and dogs."

"Mario, don't get mad, okay? But you've told me about this ten times. Really. At least ten times. And it never changes. And it's never going to change anything else. So why don't you tell me about Collier?"

"I *am* tellin' you about Collier. I could've killed Bauk. If Renaldo hadn't been there I would've killed him. I didn't know I had my hands on him until Renaldo got me off him."

"You're not telling me about Collier. You're telling me about you. Believe me, okay?"

"I believe you. You have to believe me. See, Joey's old man kept tellin' me, it doesn't matter what Joey was, that didn't give Collier the right to shoot him. And I could agree with that in my head, but in my gut?" Balzic shook his head no. "In my gut, I was like everybody else: hey, this was Joey Case. It was only a matter of time. Joey was goofy, Joey was an asshole, Joey was this or that or who knew what. Joey Case was headin' for an ugly end. It was what everybody had been predictin' for years. Me too. But Joey's old man, what he was sayin' was, hey, screw your predictions. You guys are satisfied 'cause your predictions came true, so you stopped lookin' to see if there was anything else there."

The waitress came with the salads then and a peppermill almost two feet long and asked if they wanted fresh pepper.

Balzic looked at her quizzically. "What's that next to the salt right there?"

"Pepper."

"Your pepper better than the pepper that's on the table all the time?"

"No. It's fresh!"

"Hey, don't take this wrong, okay? But in my whole life I never knew anybody who complained about stale pepper. Honest."

"Does that mean you don't want any on your salad?"

"It's nothin' personal, but, uh, no."

"You can put some on mine, Patty," Ruth said.

"Gee, thanks for lettin' me." She exchanged winks and pokes in the arm with Ruth and they both laughed. Balzic snorted and laughed and shook his head.

"Mario," Ruth said after the waitress left, "why don't you let people do what they're supposed to do?"

He shrugged. "I'm not sure I know what you mean."

"Why didn't you let the girl do the pepper on your salad? You know she was only doin' it 'cause her boss told her to do it."

"Yeah I know. But I don't care."

"Well why not? That's what I'm asking you. Do you know why you do that?"

"No. The only reason I can guess at is, I can't stand bullshit. And sometimes I can tell people about it, like with this waitress here, and I know nothin's goin' to change, and sometimes I know that there's nothin' I can say or do that's gonna change anything, like with Collier."

Ruth stared at him for some seconds, then shook her head and began to eat her salad. "I don't follow you," she said between bites.

"It's, uh, it's not really hard to follow. Collier murdered him."

"Oh," Ruth said, frowning.

"No. I mean it. I thought it was some . . . I don't know what. A justifiable force thing that wouldn't hold up because of the time element between the first shot and the rest. And then . . . and then Collier sat down next to me yesterday in Muscotti's and he gave me this bunch of bullshit that just . . . it just made my skin crawl."

"What did he say?"

Balzic snorted. "The bastard quoted the Crimes Code at me."

"He quoted what?"

"The Crime Codes. Good ol' Title 18, Crimes and Offenses, Pennsylvania Consolidated Statutes. Threw it right in my face."

"Mario, for God's sake, what did he tell you?"

"He quoted Section 109, Paragraph One. Right off the top of his head. He didn't have to go look it up and read it like I did.

He had it memorized. I had to go look it up and then I had to write it out and read it about five times to realize what it was he was tellin' me. You want to know what it says?"

"Sure. Of course."

Balzic found a piece of paper in his shirt pocket and read, " 'Section 109. When prosecution barred by former prosecution for the same offense. When a prosecution is for a violation of the same provision of the statutes and is based upon the same facts as a former prosecution, it is barred by such former prosecution under the following circumstances:

" '(1) The former prosecution resulted in an acquittal. There is an acquittal if the prosecution resulted in a finding of not guilty by the trier of fact or in a determination that there was insufficient evidence to warrant a conviction. A finding of guilty of a lesser'—this is the key sentence here—'A finding of guilty of a lesser included offense is an acquittal of the greater included offense, although the conviction is subsequently set aside.' "

"What's that mean, exactly?"

"It means that his conviction was overturned, that's what he sat down to tell me, and then, of course, when he started quotin' what I just read, then he was just laughin' in my face, he was just sittin' there tellin' me how he had got away with it and the most anybody could do now was charge him for no more than he'd already been convicted of."

"I'm not sure I understand."

Balzic sniffed and scratched his nose. "What I'm tryin' to say is, he got the conviction overturned on appeal. He got word of that yesterday."

"Okay, I understand that."

"So, he was originally charged with murder."

"Uh-ha."

"But he was only convicted of voluntary manslaughter."

"All right."

"So when that conviction was overturned, the most anybody can charge him with is voluntary manslaughter. No matter if somebody comes up with new facts, new evidence, new witnesses, new facts that say he's guilty of murder one, he can't be charged with anything more serious than the charge he just beat on appeal.

"And there he was, sittin' there and grinnin' at me bigger'n shit, tellin' me that wasn't how it was. He sat there and told me how he'd planned the whole goddamn thing and there wasn't anything, nothin', I could do about it."

"What did you say?"

"Oh I said a really intelligent thing. I said, 'You're lyin'. You're makin' this all up after the fact to make yourself out to be a real shrewd bad-ass.' That's what I said.

"And he looked at me like he was really enjoyin' himself and he leaned real close, and he said, 'All I had to say to him was one word. "Josephine." That's all. One little word. And he was all mine. And he thought he was so tough.'

"And then he looked at me like I was a special kind of shithead, and he said, 'And you think you're so smart. Whatta you gonna do now, smart guy?' "

"Is he right? Can't you do anything?"

Balzic shook his head. "Nope. Not a goddamn thing. Hope he gets hit by a car, that's about it."

"Oh, Mario, that's not right."

"Right or not, that's it."

"Mario," Ruth said, putting her fork down and wiping her mouth with a napkin, "if he's so smart that he planned this all out, why? Why did he go to all that trouble? Why did he put himself in a position where he was going to get all beat up? Joey was crazy, even I know that."

Balzic shook his head for some moments. "I don't know. All I can do is speculate. And you know what that's worth."

"Go ahead and speculate."

"Ruth, it's not gonna matter a damn. I can speculate all day and it won't mean diddly. The point is, the fact is, he singled me out, he sat down beside me, and he ran Section 109 of the Crimes Code on me."

Ruth shook her head many times and said, "What are you getting at? What are you thinking about?"

"I don't know. Every time I think about Joey I think about that little creep Bauk. How easy it was for me to wanna strangle him. And all he was tryin' to do was find out what was gonna happen to his property."

"I thought you said he was lying about the jewelry and the silverware in the house."

"Oh hell yes, he was lyin' about that. But he wasn't lyin' about the house—or the dogs. They were his. He had title to the house and land and he had papers for the dogs. And the city just wiped him out. Killed his dogs and demolished his house.

Took a bulldozer in there and flattened the house down to the foundation and then filled the foundation up with dirt."

"Uh, are you making a connection between those two?"

"Hell yeah, I'm makin' a connection. Collier—don't ask me why, I don't know why—decided he was gonna off Joey and so he did. And if we can believe him, he knew exactly what he was doin' and how to use the law to walk it. 'Cause you know damn well the DA's not gonna try to prosecute him again. I mean, hell, he's walked it! And Bauk, shit, he got into a jackpot and I tried to strangle him and the city just wiped him out and there's not a goddamn thing he can do about it. Who's he gonna sue? His mother? She's still barkin' down at Mamont. He can't recover damages from the city 'cause his property violated city and county health laws, and a zillion people have found out the hard way, you don't get compensated for condemned property."

"Mario, why are you trying to connect them? Why do you think you have to connect them? I don't understand."

"I didn't set out to connect them. Who cares whether they're connected? They're not connected in any way except in my mind. 'Course, Bauk calls me every week to remind me of all this."

"He calls you? You never told me that."

"Yeah. From Cleveland yet. Calls the mayor too. The mayor wants me to bust him for harassment by communication. I tell him, nothin' doin'. I don't ever want to see that skinny prick again. I think the mayor's startin' to believe me, but that's his mistake, 'cause it's a lie."

"Oh Mario, you're making way too much out of this."

"No I'm not. It's good to be reminded of who we are and what we did and what we do. This guy Bauk reminds me every week of what power is and what it isn't."

"I knew it," Ruth said, putting her hand over her mouth and shaking her head. "I knew it was going to have something to do with that. Mario, you have to quit thinking about that. It's over. You're better now. You've been better for months. For months and months. Why do you keep thinking about it?"

Balzic emptied his glass of burgundy. "I keep thinkin' about it because, as you say, I am a low-life sonofabitch at times, but I was never lower than when I . . . I was never meaner or lower than I was then. And I always kind of thought about Collier, that what really goaded him was that Rose was always goin' back to Joey, this goddamn gooney who used to dress up like a woman. And that must've really pissed Collier off. Imagine. He had to seek me out, to tell me that he called him 'Josephine'."

"Here we are," said Patty the waitress, putting their food in front of them. "Would you like another glass of wine?"

"Not for me," Ruth said.

"Please," Balzic said.

The waitress took his glass and hurried away.

Balzic leaned forward and inhaled. "Well, if it tastes as good as it smells and looks, I'll know I shouldn't be eatin' it."

"Mario, put your shoulds away for a little while. Trust me. Pick up your fork and eat it."

Balzic picked up his fork and tried to twirl some of the thick spaghetti around it. It didn't work too well. "This isn't fettucini, why—"

"Forget about what it's called. I told you it wasn't. Just taste it!"

Balzic put the pasta and spinach and Alfredo sauce in his mouth. It was like biting into a spring morning. He closed his eyes and chewed and after a long moment, he swallowed and then opened his eyes. "I don't listen to you enough," he said.

"Then listen to this. Wait'll you taste the garlic bread. Nobody—and I mean nobody—makes garlic bread like this."

Balzic took a piece of garlic bread out of the cloth in the basket. He bit into it and he could feel his eyebrows go up. "Oh my," he said. "Oh my."

"And there's not a man in the kitchen. Not a one."

Balzic chewed and swallowed the garlic bread. "Why are you tellin' me that? Have I been coming on like some sort of male chauvinist asshole lately?"

"No. Not at all. I just, I don't know. I just felt really good the first time I found out there weren't any men in the kitchen here, because the food's so good."

"God, this garlic bread is good."

"Isn't it?" Ruth shook her head. "Really. Nobody's is as good as that."

"Uh, I don't understand. Why're you so happy there's no men in the kitchen here?"

"It's just that here's a thing—I don't know. I'm sick of going to restaurants and everybody brags about the chef. It's that old dumb argument about men are always better. They even cook better. It's like there's nothing women can do better."

"Ruth," Balzic said, squinting at her quizzically, "I never talk to you about that stuff. Do I? Do I ever tell you women aren't as good as men?"

"No. Not in so many words."

"Whatta you mean, not in so many words?"

Ruth put her silverware down and clasped her hands. "You say it—you say it by telling me things and you never ask what I think."

"I do what?"

"Just listen a minute. In all the times you told me about that guy Bauk, you never once—not once—ever asked me what I thought. And you acted like it was only happening to you."

Balzic scowled. "Well it sure wasn't happenin' to you."

"*That's* my point. See. What you don't get is when you tell me something about what's happening to you, you think it's only happening to you. But every time you told *me*, it was also happening to me."

"Now that's, uh, that's really reachin', you know?" Balzic pushed the pasta around on his plate. "All of a sudden I feel like I just been indicted. What's goin' on here, huh?"

Ruth heaved her shoulders up in a deep breath and then exhaled and let them drop. "I'm sure I'm not going to say this right, but here goes."

"I feel like I walked into a trap. Here goes what?"

"It's no trap. It's just something I wanted to say for a while, that's all."

"Well hell, say it."

"Uh, you know how excited you were after you found out the pills worked?"

"Yeah."

"And you know how you told me about Joey Case and his father and that Bauk? Over the last, I don't know—what was it?—year?"

"Yeah."

She leaned forward, shaking her head. "Mario, in all that time you never said you were wrong about the way you blamed me when things first started to go wrong with you—with us. And I can't help it, Mario. Every time I think about that, it hurts me."

Balzic turned up his thumbs and canted his head. "I thought we been through that. Like about a dozen times."

"No, Mario. We've only been half-way through it. 'Cause

every time I bring it up, you listen to me with the same kind of look you've got now and—"

"What kind of look's that?"

"Disgust."

"Aw come on."

"No. I won't come on. You're the one has to come on. You think we've been through this a dozen times. *I've* been through it that many times. *You* haven't been through it once."

"I don't believe this."

"Of course you don't. But you have to. I want you to, please? I need you to. You know what it's like? It's—it's—it's like that guy you said would never agree to come forward, that teacher, the good-looking kid, you remember, the teacher, the one with the blonde wife in the bank, and there he is with this mouse up on the third floor, remember?"

Balzic nodded. "I remember."

"You remember what you used to say about him? He wouldn't face up to his life, remember? You said he was taking all these detours around his life. You told me once how you went to see him and you told him how it didn't matter to you whether he saw where he was going but one day he was going to find himself all alone and there'd be no way he could tell himself that he didn't know what he should've done. You remember that?"

"I remember."

"Well *that's* what *you're* doing, Mario. I'm telling you, so many times I lost count, and I'm telling you again that you and me have a problem because of something you keep wanting to detour around. It's not going to go away, Mario. Your sex life is great. Our sex life is great. But something happened . . . You blamed *me*. When *you* couldn't do it, you blamed *me*. And a year's gone by, and we're better than we were when we were in our forties. And you're still trying to act like you didn't hurt me, and when I mention it, you try to run."

Balzic folded his hands in his lap and started pushing his cuticles back and rubbing his fingernails. Eyes downcast, he said, "What do you want?"

"I want you to stop running. Look at me. Please?"

Balzic looked at her under his brow and over the tops of his glasses.

"Not like that. God. Look at me like I'm not the enemy. Look at me like I'm your friend. I am! I am your best friend."

"I know that," he said, looking at his hands again.

"Well then . . . goddamnit, you did your friend wrong. And your friend's pissed off . . . and hurt. And you need to do something about that."

"Okay. So I need to do something. What?"

Ruth sagged ever so slightly. "I—I don't know what."

"Well shit. That leaves me—where the hell's that leave me?"

Ruth put her hands in her lap and leaned forward. "Well, see . . . there's where—no, that's what I think it is. You're thinking about you. Where's that leave *you*—you know? And—"

"So?"

"Well that's not what I think you should be thinking like—I think."

"Huh?"

She dropped her head, then raised it chin up as she inhaled. "I think what I want is for you to quit thinking about where that leaves *you* and where that leaves *us*. I mean I want you to start thinking about where that leaves us."

Balzic scowled and sighed and rubbed his chin hard with the pad at the base of his thumb.

"I don't know what's goin' on here," he said.

"I know you don't," she said gently. "I'm not sure I do either. But we can't keep on like this, without you even starting to think about what I've said. I can't let it go like that, Mario. Honest. I do—I do things for you that you don't even know I do. Things you never say anything about."

"Huh? Like what?"

"Like—like, like phone change."

"Like what?"

"Phone change. Who do you think always made sure you had change when you left the house? Every day, whenever you left the house, the last thing I do is put change where you can find it. I've been doing it for thirty years. And you don't even know I do it."

"I thought I did that."

"See? I know that's what you think because that's what I let you think. Because I thought I was supposed to let you think you did it. I'm tired of letting you think you do it. You did it. You do it. You know what I mean."

Balzic leaned forward and squinted at his wife. "Ruth, what the hell're you talkin' about?"

"What I'm talking about is you and me and what you've done

to me and what I've done for you and I want some strokes for what I've done for you. I'm not—I'm gettin' mad at you 'cause I've let myself turn into a wall you bounce your life off of. I know that doesn't make sense. I mean I don't want to be anymore somebody you talk to just so you can feel good after you finish talkin'." Her eyes were glistening with tears.

"Jesus, Ruth, what brought this on?"

"I told you. Aren't you listening? You—you really hurt me last year and you still have never said you were sorry. Not once did you ever look like you thought you even needed to. God, Mario, sometimes you're such a stonehead! A real *capo tost*." She was trying hard to laugh. The longer she tried, the easier it became.

"Listen," she said, reaching out and motioning with her fingers for him to extend his hand, "c'mon, give me your hand. I—c'mon. Don't be scared. I'm still me. I still love you."

He put his hand on the table and she covered it with hers.

"You don't have to say anything now, Mario. Honest. I just want you to think about it. Will you? Please?"

He nodded. "Okay. I don't know what I'm supposed to think, but I'll think about it."

"Good. Thank you. That's all I really want." She took her hand away and fiddled through her purse until she found some tissues. She wiped her eyes and blew her nose. "Go 'head and eat before it gets cold."

"That's okay," he said. "I'm stuffed. I've really put on a lot of weight with those pills. . . ."

They made small talk with the waitress when she brought their check. They fussed over how much of a tip to leave, she wanting to leave more, he wanting to leave less. They compromised by leaving what he wanted to leave and she adding to that what she thought was fair after they had walked away from the table.

In the parking lot on the way to the car, he asked her: "What's the point of discussing what we should do, if after we quit discussin' it, you go back and do what you want?"

"It's fun, that's why. First you talk about it, then you do something else, then you talk about why you didn't do what you said you were gonna do. It's almost as much fun as sex." Her eyes were alive with kind mischief.

"Oh Christ, Ruth. I'll never keep up."

"Yes you will," she said. "Yes you will."

* * *

Balzic hurried into the station to avoid a woman who'd been hounding him for days about her son's refusal to return her car, which was really his car because the title was in his name and which he'd let her use since he got married because his wife had a newer car and which he'd taken back because his wife had left him and had taken her newer car with her.

Royer motioned with his thumb that there was somebody waiting for him in his office.

The woman hooked her arm around Balzic's arm and tried to grab her wrist to lock him in. He jerked his arm free and danced away from her.

"Lady, you don't have a police problem. How many times do I have to tell you? It's your son's car. There are no outstanding warrants against him or his car. It's his. Do you understand? *His!* It is not yours and it is not my problem—"

"How'm I supposed to go anywhere?" she howled.

"Lady, that ain't *my* problem. That's your problem. Now go home. Please. For crissake go home." Turning to Royer he said, "Who is it?"

"Some guy. Said he had to talk to you. Itri something. I didn't catch it. He looked harmless, I told him to wait."

"I can't go nowhere anymore! He told me the car was mine. He gave it to me. He can't take it back now!"

"Lady, if you don't get outta here, I swear to you I'm gonna arrest ya for harassment, for being a public nuisance. You know what that'll cost you if I do that, huh? About sixty-seven bucks for the fine and costs. Is that what you want? You got sixty-seven dollars?"

"Go ahead and arrest me. My son'll have to pay to get me out."

"Outta where?"

"Outta jail 'cause I won't pay the fine. Nyaaah!" She put her hands on her hips, thrust her shoulders forward, and stuck out her tongue.

Balzic turned toward his office. He looked over his shoulder at Royer and said, "If she isn't out in one minute, sixty seconds, lock her in. Don't book her. Just lock her in and forget her."

"Hey you can't do that," she growled.

"Be here a minute from now, lady, and watch."

Balzic opened the door to his office and stepped in. A dark, handsome, very nervous man jumped to his feet. He held his right hand out awkwardly. "Chief Balzic, I guess you don't remember me. Maybe you do remember me."

Balzic ignored the hand and went behind his desk and sat down. "I remember you," he said. "You're John Itri. You were in Joellen Cooper's apartment the night Joey Case got shot. You're a teacher. You're married to a real foxy blonde who works in a bank. Your parents wanted you to be a priest, and, uh, that's more or less all the reasons you didn't—wouldn't—testify."

"Well. I guess—I guess you do remember me."

"I never forget witnesses who refuse to testify."

"Well, see, uh, that's why I'm here now. That's what I came here to do. I'm ready."

"You're ready for what?" Balzic scowled and pressed his thumbnail between his upper front teeth. "Oh I get it. *Now* you're ready to testify about the shooting. Hell, Itri, you're too late by a year—shit, a year and a half."

"Too late?"

"Oh sure. Hell that's already been overturned on appeal. He was convicted on voluntary manslaughter, and then that was overturned."

"Well can't I testify in the new trial? Are they going to have another trial?"

"Probably not. I doubt if the county wants to go through the hassle, never mind the cost."

"But—but that's not right. I saw it. I saw the whole thing. From the first shot. I was looking out the window. I was—I was—I was—I couldn't make—I couldn't do—"

"Mr. Itri, I don't care why you were lookin' out the window. It doesn't make any difference. You're too late. In this state, once a person is convicted of a certain crime, and the conviction is overturned on appeal, that's it. He can't be tried for anything more serious than he was convicted of. But, hey, don't let me stop you. Go talk to the DA. They might have some angle I don't know about. They might, but I doubt it."

"But—but that's not right."

Balzic blurted out a laugh. "I'm sorry, Mr. Itri, I'm not laughin' at you. But, uh, *right* doesn't have anything to do with it. You not only gotta be right, you also gotta be on time. And you're not."

"But you don't understand. I'm—I—I—I'm divorced."

"You're divorced. Uh-huh. So?"

"No. I mean yesterday. It was final . . . yesterday."

Balzic peered at Itri and waited. "Mr. Itri, I know you're trying to tell me something, but you're not gettin' through, if you know what I mean. So if you wanna tell me something, why don't you just say it, okay?"

Itri's eyes darted about and his head swung from side to side. He was on the verge of panic. "My God. I left . . . I left my wife over this. And my . . . good God . . . my mother died over this. I know everybody said it was not my fault but my mother died when I told her. I mean the sequence was not, you know, one two, like that, but you don't have to be a psychiatric genius to put one and one together, I mean, if you tear your mother's heart out when you tell her you're leaving your wife, you have to be totally stupid not to see the connection when your mother's heart just bursts. . . . I mean that's what it did." Itri sank back in the chair. He lifted his hands and let them drop into his lap. "Good God, man, I left my wife, I broke my mother's heart. I watched her die. My divorce is final. As of yesterday I'm excommunicated from my church and now you tell me I can't testify." His hands rose limply. "Holy Father of Jesus, that's why I did everything!" His mouth did not close. His hands fell into his lap again. His eyes pinched shut for a brief moment and then opened to stare at Balzic.

Balzic leaned forward and shook Itri's knee. "You okay? Hey, Itri! You all right?"

Itri's eyes focused again. "What do you mean, all right? You! You of all people. What do *you* mean, okay? It was you who told me I had to quit running. You! Holy Father, my mother's dead, I've violated a sacrament, I've been made an orphan from God, I can't do the thing I set out to do to clear my conscience, and you sit there asking me as though you're asking me what time it is if I'm okay, if I'm all right." He was gesturing wildly, his fingers stiff and slashing the air.

"Settle down, Itri. You're gettin' a little outta joint here—"

"Out of joint!" Itri jumped to his feet. "My life is—is destroyed! It's nothing! And you tell me to settle down! That's what I used to tell my students. Settle down! Do I look like a child to you? Do I?"

Balzic casually opened the center drawer of his desk enough so the lock on the side drawers would open. Then he pulled the top right hand drawer open, the drawer where he kept his blackjack. He put his hand on it while he studied Itri.

"Mr. Itri, I think you need to take a walk. Get your blood pumpin'. Get a little oxygen in your lungs. A nice long walk'd do you a lotta good."

"I listened to you, I did what you said, my life's—I've just found out you don't have to die to go to hell. And now you're telling me to take a walk? One of us is insane. One of us is crazy."

"That may be so, Mr. Itri. But it ain't me. So take the walk."

Itri took a step forward.

Balzic quickly got to his feet, bringing the blackjack out of the drawer and holding it up for Itri to see. "Itri, you got some bad problems here, but they're yours, they're not mine, and I'm not gonna just stand here and let you do somethin' dumb."

"I've already done something dumb. Many things dumb. Do you have any idea what it means to be so consumed with guilt you can't make love and while you're standing there trying to explain it to the woman you can't do it with you watch a man shoot another man to death and then—and then you are consumed with guilt about that—"

"Itri, Itri! Whoa! Stop! Itri, I can't do anything about that—"

Itri began to cry, his eyes filling and his shoulders jerking with sobs.

"—I'm sorry, Itri, that you're havin' such a shitty time with life but I'll be damned if I'm gonna stand here and let you dump it all on me 'cause you waited too goddamn long. And all the rest. Whatever bad happened to you, you can't lay that off on me."

"Why not?" Itri howled.

"Because I won't let you, that's why. I won't fuckin' agree to it, that's why. I ain't your wife, I ain't your mother, and I ain't your goddamn church, that's why. Now get the fuck outta here."

"You bastard!"

"Yeah. Right. I'm a bastard. Right. You know what cons say, Itri? Huh? You ever hear this? If you can't do the time, don't do the crime. You ever hear that? You know what it means? It means takin' responsibility for what you are and for what you do. Go blow your nose. Get outta here." Balzic stepped forward, caught Itri's coat and spun him toward the door. He opened it and pushed him out, pulling the door shut.

He sagged against the wall. "Jesus Christ," he said, blowing out a long sigh. "Jesus Christ Almighty, what did I do to deserve that? Is this all for what I did to Ruth?"

There came a knock. "Hey, Mario, you all right?" It was Royer.

"Yeah. Sure. Why?"

"'Cause that lady's still here."

Balzic jerked the door open. "The one with the son who took his car back?"

"Yeah."

"What about the guy who was just here? Where'd he go?"

"Oh he went runnin' outta here. Looked like his ass was on fire."

"Somethin' was on fire all right. I doubt if it was his ass."

Balzic stepped out into the duty room and spied the lady he'd threatened with arrest. "Still here, huh?"

"I ain't leavin' till I get my car back."

"I thought we settled that. It ain't your car. It's your kid's."

"It's mine. He give it to me—"

"Lady, we been all through this. I don't wanna listen to no more about it. Go home."

"You said you was gonna arrest me for bein' a nuisance!"

"I changed my mind."

"You can't change your mind. You're the cops! You're the law! I want justice!"

"What you want is a priest. Or a family counselor. Now get the hell outta here and find one." Balzic started to turn back to his office.

"No priest is gonna get me what I want," she shrieked.

"Then you got a problem, lady, 'cause neither am I."

"You sonofabitch!"

Balzic stepped quickly toward the woman, caught her left wrist with his left hand, slipped his right arm under her left elbow and reached up with his right hand and took hold of the back of her neck. He led her on her toes toward the door to the parking lot and put her out.

"Nobody calls me that, lady, except my wife. Now get the hell outta here, and go find who I told you to find."

Balzic stepped away from the door and walked slowly past Royer.

"D'you hear her, huh? We're the cops? We're the law? She wants justice? D'you hear that?"

Royer nodded somberly.

Balzic shook his head. "Where the hell do people get this crap from? We're the law. Jesus. . . ."